CAST OF C

Eve North. An aging Broadway [...] both fading. She has the lead in the drawing-room comedy, *Green Apples*.

Carol Blanton. The play's ingenue, a plucky little actress whom somebody tries to poison on opening night. Haila's roommate.

Philip Ashley. The leading man, a suave professional Englishman. He hates it when Eve upstages him.

Clinton Bowen. A celebrated producer/director, he's devoted his career to showcasing Eve North in one hit play after another.

Haila Rogers. She has a small part in the play. She loves the theater, and she loves Jeff Troy. They'd marry if they could afford to.

Jeff Troy. An advertising salesman on temporary leave, during which he's hired by Clinton Bowen to solve the crime. He wants to marry Haila.

Steve Brown. An affable young actor, he's the scion of a wealthy Boston Back Bay family, which is a source of great embarrassment to him.

Alice McDonald. From a legendary acting family, she has more ambition than talent. But she believes herself to be a great actress.

Greeley Morris. The insufferable English playwright. He's deigned to drop in on the Broadway production of his play while on a trip to the U.S.

Tommy Neilson. The stage manager.

Amelia. An old gray sea lion of a woman, she's long been Eve North's trusted maid, assistant, and protectress.

Phoebe Thompson. The capable assistant stage manager, who's also Clint Bowen's secretary.

Vincent Parker. The flamboyant theatrical producer who gave Haila her first break. He believes that showmanship is the secret to success.

Lee Gray. A mystery woman whose identity may well be the key to the crime.

Lieutenant Sullavan. A long-suffering NYPD homicide detective.

Plus assorted actors, cops, servants, elevator operators, doormen, cab drivers, and other supporting players.

Books by Kelley Roos

Featuring Jeff & Haila Troy

Made Up To Kill (1940)*
If the Shroud Fits (1941)
The Frightened Stiff (1942)*
Sailor, Take Warning! (1944)
There Was a Crooked Man (1945)
Ghost of a Chance (1947)
Murder in Any Language (1948)
Triple Threat (1949)
One False Move (1966)

* reprinted by Rue Morgue Press
as of May 2005

Other mystery novels

The Blonde Died Laughing (1956)
Requiem for a Blonde (1958)
Scent of Mystery (1959)
Grave Danger (1965)
Necessary Evil (1965)
A Few Days in Madrid (1965
(Above published as by Audrey and William Roos)
Cry in the Night (1966)
Who Saw Maggie Brown? (1967)
To Save His Life (1968)
Suddenly One Night (1970)
What Did Hattie See? (1970)
Bad Trip (1971)
Murder on Martha's Vineyard (1981)

MADE UP TO KILL

A Jeff and Haila Troy
mystery comedy by
Kelley Roos

Rue Morgue Press
Lyons / Boulder

To
CAROL'S GRANDMOTHER

Made Up To Kill
0-915230-79-8
Copyright © 1940, 1968
New material copyright © 2005
The Rue Morgue Press

Reprinted with the permission of the authors' estate.

The Rue Morgue Press
P.O. Box 4119
Boulder, Colorado 80306
800-699-6214
www.ruemorguepress.com

Printed by
Johnson Printing

PRINTED IN THE UNITED STATES OF AMERICA

Meet the Authors

Kelley Roos was the pseudonym used by the husband-and-wife writing team of William and Audrey Kelley Roos who, like their contemporaries, Frances and Richard Lockridge, wrote about a husband-and-wife detective team. Photographer (though he tried his hand at other careers) Jeff Troy and his future wife, actress Haila Rogers, were introduced to the reading public in 1940's *Made Up To Kill*, the same year that saw the birth of the Norths. They received a five hundred dollar advance for their first effort and never looked back.

Eight more adventures featuring the Troys appeared before they abandoned the series in 1966 (there had been a 17-year vacation from the series between book eight and book nine). The books, laced with wisecracks and filled with screwball humor have the feel of a 1940s movie comedy. In fact, the third Troy mystery, *The Frightened Stiff*, was filmed in 1943 as *A Night to Remember* with Loretta Young and Brian Aherne playing the Troys. They wrote numerous non-Troy mysteries as well and received an Edgar for the 1960 television play, *The Case of the Burning Court*, based on the novel by John Dickson Carr.

William Roos was born in Pittsburgh, Pennsylvania, in 1911, and he was graduated from Carnegie Tech in Pittsburg where he was enrolled in the drama department with an eye toward becoming a playwright. It was there that he met Audrey, who was studying to be an actress. Born in Elizabethtown, New Jersey, in 1912, she had been raised in Uniontown, Pennsylvania. After graduation, Audrey took a touch-typing course (William never learned) and two headed for New York City. Audrey eventually gave up her dream of becoming an actress and decided to write a detective novel. William soon became attracted to the idea as well and initially the two would plot their books over drinks in the evening. At first they wrote alternate chapters and then passed them on to the other for rewrites. Eventually, William wrote the entire first drafts but, with William still unable to touch-type, Audrey always had the last word.

They lived in Connecticut and Spain as well before finally settling in the late 1960s in an old whaling captain's house on Martha's Vineyard, where Audrey died in 1982 and William in 1987. For more information on their lives and collaborations, see Tom and Enid Schantz' introduction to The Rue Morgue Press edition of *The Frightened Stiff*.

THE COLONY THEATRE

BEGINNING
MONDAY EVENING,
NOVEMBER 6, 1939
MATINEES
THURSDAY AND SATURDAY

CLINTON BOWERS
presents
GREEN APPLES
A new comedy
by
GREELEY MORRIS
with
EVE NORTH
Staged by Mr. Bowers
Production designed by Lennox Koy

CAST
(In the order in which they speak)

JESSIE CARLETON	Haila Rogers
TIMOTHY CARLETON	Philip Ashley
MARAINE CARLETON	EVE NORTH
FRANK PHILLIPS	Stephen Brown
DINA	Carol Blanton
GEORGE ROMSON	Benjamin Kerry

Time: The present
ACT I
The morning room of the Carleton house.
ACT II
The terrace of the Carleton house.
ACT III
The Carleton dining room.

FOR MR. BOWERS
Stage Manager ... Thomas Neilson
Assistant Stage Manager ... Phoebe Thompson

CHAPTER ONE

I PUSHED the elevator bell and its feeble pinging sound floated up from the basement. A minute later Jinx, the pop-eyed elevator operator, grinned at me as he slid open the door.

" 'Evenin', Miss Rogers."

"Good evening," I said.

"Tonight the big night?"

"Yes."

"Gonna roll 'em in the aisles?"

"Sure."

"Hang out the old S.R.O. sign?"

"You bet." I began to wish that I hadn't passed all my old copies of *Variety* on to Jinx.

"Where's Miss Blanton?"

"She's sick," I said, "and, incidentally, how's chances for a ride down?"

His eyes popped now like two bright marbles. "You mean she ain't gonna play tonight?"

"No," I said, "she ain't."

In a sort of stunned silence he piloted the elevator down. At the lobby floor he stood back respectfully while I stepped out, then almost knocked me over as he scooted past to get to the outside door. He held it open for me.

"Good luck!" he yelled.

It was a wonderful night. November had begun to take itself seriously and the air was crisp and cold. There was a smattering of stars competing timidly with the glow of Times Square ten blocks down. A perfect opening night. The theater would be walking with ermine and white ties and orchids and celebrities. Backstage there would be that breathless darkness and the smell of grease paint and the quiet rustlings from the front of the house. And up in my little three-room apartment on East Fifty-fourth Street would be Carol, cheated out of her first opening night by a case of laryngitis.

I was still fuming helplessly about it as I turned the corner and started toward the glare of the theater district. If only there had been something to do for her, something or someone to swear at and blame for it. But a voice is a pretty intangible something when you just lose it. If Carol had tripped on a broken step or been hit by a taxi you might have started suit against the building or beaten the driver to a pulp, but you can't be very vindictive about a sore throat.

I turned the corner off Broadway and the lights on the marquee of the Colony Theater popped out at me. "Clinton Bowers," they spelled, very simply and proudly, "Presents *Green Apples* with Eve North." My heart began pounding a nice, familiar opening-night pound and I stopped a second in front of the theater to look at the shiny new pictures that had been slid under their glass covers that afternoon.

Monopolizing nearly all the space, Eve North smiled serenely into the street from three giant photographs. She looked quite young with her hair piled toweringly on the top of her head and the still youthful contour of her chin outlined against the frill of her high-necked dress. Even in black and white you would know somehow that Eve's hair was dull henna color and that her eyes were greenish gray.

You hardly saw the other pictures, completely overshadowed by the almost life-sized ones of Eve; but there were two of Philip Ashley, smirking a little and looking like a handsome, well-to-do retired businessman, and a scowling one of old Benjamin Kerry just beneath him. There were two of Steve Brown and me together, both of us looking pretty silly, and a quite large one of Carol with a sort of tremulous smile on her lips and her hair in close cropped ringlets.

Not much like the Carol I had left on Fifty-fourth Street. That Carol had been a little huddled-up ball in my old terrycloth bathrobe, her face white and miserable under a mop of tangled hair, her lips twisted into a grimace as she tried to down the last of my throat cures. I had made her take everything I had ever heard of in the theater or had learned from my grandmother, who had had a trusty cure for every ailment from common children's warts to beri-beri. It was seven o'clock before I finally gave up, or rather before Carol did. Her tearstained face had jerked out of the pillows. "Call Tommy; call him right away. Say I can't play." Her voice had been a strange, croaking whisper and she had held her throat in both hands as if she were trying to push the words out.

It was then that I had hung out the white flag. I called Tommy Neilson, who was the stage manager for *Green Apples*, at the theater.

"This is Haila," I said. "Tommy, Carol can't play tonight."

There was a pause, then Tommy boomed, "What in hell are you talking about!"

"It's her voice; it's gone. We've done everything we can and it hasn't helped. She just can't play."

"She's got to play." He sounded final, as though his words had settled the problem and now he could hang up.

"Tommy, I tell you she can't! She can't speak above a whisper and not a very pretty whisper either."

I could almost hear him gritting his teeth in exasperation. "All right," he said at last, "McDonald's here. I'll tell her to get ready."

I hung up and went back to Carol, touched her on the shoulder. "It's all fixed. Tommy says Alice McDonald can go on tonight and he says he's sorry and for you to take care of yourself and knock 'em dead tomorrow."

She didn't move except to bury her head deeper in what I suspected was a tear-sodden pillow and hunch lower into the bathrobe. There was nothing for me to say, nothing that wouldn't have sounded trite and fatuous; and I sneaked my hat and coat out of the hall closet and left. She probably hadn't realized yet that I had gone.

I swore silently and walked down the alley to the stage door. Nick, the Colony doorman, was perched just inside it puffing happily at a foul old pipe, opening night excitement reflected in even his old eyes. He beamed at me as I passed him and went up the narrow iron stairs.

Alice McDonald was standing very still before the full-length mirror in the dressing room that Carol and I were to have shared. She had Carol's third act cape, a lovely hooded thing of black velvet, wrapped around her. The hood fell back over her shoulders and her ash-blond hair, as soft and straight as the cape, was drawn like a pale tight helmet around her face. Her eyes were shining and she looked almost lovely.

It was hard for me not to resent her being there where Carol should have been – wearing Carol's dresses, about to play her part. I mumbled some greeting at her as I slipped into a faded old housecoat that had seen me through my seven Broadway shows and wrapped a Turkish towel around my head.

"Clothes fit all right?" I asked.

"Yes. Oh, yes, they're all right."

She was draping the black mass of velvet almost lovingly over a hanger. She turned and, sitting beside me at the table, leaned over and put her hand on my arm. It was cold and the long unpainted nails, a dull pale color like her face and hair, bit into my skin. Her voice trembled with its intensity.

"Haila, I can't believe it! It isn't a dream, is it? It's true! I'm going to play Dina, I'm going to play an opening night again! Oh, Haila, I've got to be good!"

I said, with all the assurance I could muster: "You'll be swell, Alice. Don't worry about it." And mentally, I crossed all my fingers and felt a little bit sick. There wasn't much chance of Alice's being good. We would be lucky, in fact, if she could just pass unnoticed in the part.

She was almost fanatically ambitious, but she was not an actress. From a long line of theater people, many of them great, she had inherited, not talent, only a passionate craving to be on the stage and to take her place among them. And she had no gifts to offer the theater. Her every instinct was wrong; her voice was thin, metallic; her gestures started awkwardly from her wrists; and her words came from her lips instead of stemming from some place deep inside. Even that cold paleness of hers that was unusual and rather charming close up became tedious as it crossed the footlights. But she had had her chance. Four years ago she had snagged the ingenue lead in a play called *Gibbon's Glade*, and the pitiful mess she had made of it had limited her parts from then on to understudies and walk-ons, given her by kindhearted managers who had known and admired her family.

I watched her now as I opened my green lacquered makeup box and began removing tubes and jars and tins of powder from it.

"I'm not going to play Dina the way Carol Blanton played her," she was saying, almost defiantly. "That was wrong. She looked the way Dina should look, but that was all. She didn't know what was going on inside her. I know. I'm going to play Dina the way he meant her to be played, the way he saw her."

I tried not to let my impatience show. "Evidently Carol was doing it the way Bowers saw it. She took his direction beautifully."

Alice looked at me scornfully. "I don't mean Clint Bowers. What does he know about it, about what's going on in Dina's mind? I mean Greeley Morris. I know what he meant her to be when he wrote her."

"Well, Greeley Morris will be in London and Clint Bowers will be out front. If I were you I'd be smart and cater to Mr. Bowers whether his conception of the part is the way you see it or not."

Her eyes filled with quick surprise. "Didn't you know? Greeley Morris is to be here tonight. His boat docked this afternoon."

I sat back abruptly. "When did all this happen? I thought wild horses never dragged Mr. Morris from his native soil."

"He's coming. Even Bowers didn't know until Morris called him this afternoon. He's on his way to Hollywood. They're making *The Thunderstorm* into a picture and he's going to adapt it himself."

I dabbed cold cream on my face and said, "Well!" three or four times. I had left the line rehearsal early to be in time for a last-minute fitting, and the news of Greeley Morris' arrival was a shock. To have Greeley Morris at a New York opening was the next best thing, and the next most incredible, to having Mr. Shakespeare. Although nearly all of his plays had been produced in America, Morris had maintained a calm, snooty indifference to their productions. American acting, he had been quoted as saying, was the worst in the world. Even the maids were played as if it were their nights out. He had never thought it worth the price of passage to see a work of his butchered. Well, now, after all that, he was to be here. Even if it had been the lure of Hollywood gold that had brought him, and not our production of *Green Apples*, it was still an event. Very probably we would go down in the annals of theatrical history as the company that had played for Greeley Morris on his initial appearance in America. And Carol would miss that, too. She would be the girl who missed it because she had a sore throat. Well, when Greeley Morris saw Alice in her part, he would find good grounds for his antipathy toward American acting, I thought bitterly.

In the mirror I saw Alice twisting her hands nervously, her head bent slightly over them. The light had gone from her eyes and she looked tired and helpless as though my words had leaped out of my mind and she had heard them. I was instantly contrite.

"You'd better start ... Alice, what's the matter?" She had dropped her head onto the dressing table.

"Nothing. Just a headache. Nerves, I guess, and all this excitement."

"Would an aspirin help? Philip Ashley will have one. I've played with him before and he wouldn't think of opening a show without his medicine kit properly stocked."

"Oh, Haila, don't bother."

"Shucks. I've been playing doctor all day. I'll run up and get it now."

Philip Ashley's dressing room was on the third floor and as I climbed the stairs I could hear the quiet whisperings and feel the excitement and anticipation romping through the theater. At the light switch Tommy Neilson was giving sharp soft orders and from the second floor, where Benjamin Kerry dressed, came a gentle grumbling. And I could hear

Steve Brown humming nervously and the floating sound of Eve North's laugh, tinkling and unconcerned.

If I hadn't known that Philip Ashley was in New York, I would have still been sure that this dressing room was his. He had been in it only a few nights now, the dress rehearsal and two invitation performances, but he had made it as much his own as a bedroom where he had slept every night of his life. There was the little hunk of Aubusson rug and the wingbacked chair that he carted around from theater to theater with him. His suede smoking jacket was placed carefully over the chair and two gorgeous dressing gowns hung from pegs on the wall. On the table his makeup was laid neatly out on a monogrammed towel, and glass ashtrays and cigarette boxes were scattered on every available slab of flat surface.

In a corner I located his first-aid department, a roll of bandages, adhesive tape, a number of partially filled bottles and jars. I rummaged through them and found a small cellophane package housing two white tablets, the kind that they sell aspirin in at drugstores. I picked it up, pleased that Philip hadn't failed me.

"Put that down!"

Philip Ashley stood in the doorway. He was already in his first act cutaway and he looked handsome and youthful in spite of the silver wings at his temples that were powdered to a brilliant sheen.

"I said, put that down!" I hadn't noticed that his face was white with anger and that he glared at me in a kind of trembling fury. The clipped British voice was shaking. Helplessly, I stared at him and then at the tablets in my hand, so stunned I could find no words to say. Then Ashley strode across the room and snatched the tablets from me.

"I won't have people snooping in my room. I won't have it! While I'm engaged at this theater this is my property and it is personal and private. I shan't have people darting in and out, messing with my things, infringing on my privacy. I shall complain at once to the management!"

"Nobody's darting in and out," I said. Somewhere during his tirade I had found my voice. "I just wanted to borrow an aspirin for Alice McDonald. I never thought you'd mind."

"I shan't have people snooping around," he repeated sullenly.

"All right. All right, I'm sorry."

I went flouncing out of his room, slamming the door hard behind me. The whole thing was ridiculous. Nice, good-natured Philip Ashley putting on a temperament act. During the run of *West Wind* two years before, I had often gone into his room to bum cigarettes or matches or anything that happened to be around; everyone in the company had,

and he had never discouraged us. It had annoyed him when the meticu-
lous order of his things had been disturbed in any way, but he was
gregarious and chatty and his dressing room had been an open house.
The way he had burst out at me now you might have thought I was a
second-story man about to make off with his most prized possession.
Either our ex-matinee idol had a bad case of opening night jitters or, in
spite of his alleged forty-three years, he was growing senile.

Steve Brown was parked on the top step at the end of the hall, laughing at me.

"Caught you that time, didn't he?"

"I've never been so insulted, not in all my years as a kleptomaniac."

Steve chuckled and then became serious. "What's this about Carol?
She can't play tonight?"

"No. Laryngitis. It kills her to even whisper."

"The first night of her first show! Why do things like that have to
happen?" He thrust his hands deep into his bathrobe pockets and walked
glowering down the hall to Ashley's room.

It was always hard for me to realize that Steve was *the* Steve Brown,
scion of the Stephen Munson Browns, the Backest Bay family in Boston and, incidentally, millionaires many times over. Standing there in a
ratty colored bathrobe that must have been presented to him on about
his tenth birthday, with a raveled towel around his neck and his sandy
hair tousled, he had looked like some kid who had run away from the
other side of the railroad tracks to go on the stage. He tried his best to
act like one too, probably to counteract the millionaire publicity he
was getting. Since his advent in the theater, much against the older
Stephen Munson Brown's wishes, he had ticked off about a mile of
space in theatrical gossip columns. Everything he did was news, buying a girl a Coca-Cola, moving to a new hotel, changing his brand of
cigarettes. He took it all good-naturedly but I think at times it made
him sick.

I went on downstairs to my dressing room. Alice wasn't there and I
sat at my table and started smearing a makeup base on my chin. Tommy
opened the door two inches, yelled "half hour" and went on. I could
hear him along the hall and on the stairs, stopping at each room and
banging the doors behind him. Then, before I had got the grease paint
even to my forehead, he was back. I could tell from the pound of his
brogans on the steps and the way he burst into my room that something
was wrong.

"Where did McDonald go?"

"I don't know. Why?"

"Phoebe just saw her tearing down the alley. She called after her but

Alice was going to beat hell and she hasn't come back."

"Probably she went to get a bromo. She had a headache."

"She had her hat and coat on."

"It's freezing out, Tommy."

"She could have swallowed a gallon of bromo by now. The drugstore's only ten steps away." He looked nervously at his watch. "Go call Carol."

"Carol!"

"She should be here in case McDonald doesn't come back. And for some reason I have a hunch she won't."

"Of course she will, this is the chance she's been …"

"We can't risk it, Haila. Call Carol, will you, please?" Tommy's voice rose.

I tried to be patient. "Tommy, she couldn't play if she did come. She can't talk, understand! And there's no use even calling her, because she won't answer the phone; she can't."

"All right, we'll go get her."

"We! But I'm making up, I …" Tommy flung my coat at me and grabbed my wrist and I was being hurtled down the stairs, through the alley, into a taxi. The driver, sensing Tommy's haste, had the cab moving almost before we were in it. I pulled the Turkish towel off my head and made futile swipes at my grease paint with it while Tommy told the driver where to go and to hurry, that it was a matter of life and death. The driver looked back at me.

"I can believe it, buddy," he said.

The Paramount clock leered twenty after eight through the taxi window. Twenty after eight. I groaned and then I was furious. "Tommy, why? In heaven's name, why am I going?"

"Huh?"

"Why are you dragging me along? I have to act tonight! Make up and get dressed and …"

"Listen, Haila!" he shouted. Then abruptly he turned away and leaned forward in his seat, ignoring me. It was as though he had realized his stupidity in dragging me along with him. His brown freckled face was wrinkled in a scowl. The wide mouth that usually turned jauntily upward at each corner was drawn in a straight tense line. It struck me suddenly that this was the way Tommy looked most of the time now. He had stopped being the easygoing, wise-cracking guy that everyone was crazy about soon after rehearsals had got under way and had gone sullen and morose on us. I wondered curiously what had happened to him. Then I forgot about Tommy and tried to think of my first line. At least, I could be ready with that when the curtain went up.

The cab squealed to a stop in front of my apartment and we took the sidewalk and the two steps up to the door in one leap. Jinx was dozing on the imitation oak bench just outside the elevator. I halted the twenty questions that were forming in his master mind.

"If you'll just take us up, Jinx," I told him, "tomorrow I'll come clean as a whistle, so help me!"

I rummaged through my purse for the key and glanced at my watch. It was eight-thirty. Ten minutes before curtain time, and I stood in an elevator fourteen blocks from the theater, not made up, not dressed, a wreck. And all for nothing. Even Tommy would admit it was for nothing when he heard that feeble crackling noise that had once been Carol's voice. It would be Alice McDonald playing tonight or there would be a long line of people getting their money back at the box office.

I unlocked the door and reached for the light switch in the hall. A hand closed over mine as I touched it. Tommy's other hand clutched my shoulder and he said, "Wait!" softly and close to my ear. There was talking in the other room. It was Carol's voice, speaking into the telephone. It was her normal voice and it was loud and clear.

I think I must have squeaked. The receiver went down with a sharp click and Carol stood in the doorway. She had on her dark blue suit, a little turned up hat and under her arm was the patent leather purse that I had given her. For a long moment no one spoke. Carol looked from me to Tommy and her hands tightened on the purse.

"It came back," she said. "It came back all of a sudden. I was calling the theater to tell you ..." She stopped.

I don't know how I knew that Carol was lying, nor how Tommy knew; but we did. Tommy turned and opened the door.

"Let's get going," he said.

CHAPTER TWO

WE clattered up the iron steps at Tommy's heels. With one hand on the doorknob of our dressing room he turned to us. "Can you make the curtain in ten minutes?" I nodded and hoisted myself up the last step. He threw open the door and I saw his eyebrows jerk up. He said furiously, "Where the hell have you been?"

Alice raised her head and smiled. She was wearing Carol's first act clothes, her face made up, her hands lifted to the sleek hair, smoothing it closer over her ears. "I just ..." Then she saw Carol. The smile faded from her lips, her whole body went dead and stiff. She turned slowly to

Tommy. "Is she all right?" Her mouth scarcely moved when she spoke.

Tommy nodded. "She's going to play. What happened to you?"

Alice made no answer. Putting her hands to the lapels of the shark-skin jacket she slipped it from her shoulders. We stood watching her, not knowing what to say or do. Tommy grunted something unintelligible as he stamped out of the room. Carol said timidly, "I'm sorry, Alice."

Alice's eyes, full of bitterness, grazed Carol and she turned her back. The clothes came off mechanically and were hung over the chair. She threw a dressing gown on her shoulders and, without a word, was gone.

Almost before we had found time to move, Tommy was back, banging at our door and yelling, "Five minutes!"

I managed to dress, I don't remember quite how. I know that Phoebe Thompson, a tiny pert-faced girl who was Tommy's assistant, stood behind me buttoning up my back and curling the ends of my hair. I know that Eve North had sent her maid, Amelia, and that she was on the floor shoving on my white buckskin shoes and lacing them. My rouge kept smudging as I smeared it over my cheeks, and mascara ran into my eyes and stung. Beside me, Carol, whose first entrance didn't come until the middle of the act, tried to help me and dress herself at the same time. I stood up and was surprised to find that I was all together and that my makeup job presented a fairly human face. Tommy opened the door.

"Places," he said. "Ready, Haila."

I nodded, snatched one last glimpse in the mirror and followed him to the wings. Against the wall the third act scenery was stacked and I stood back near it, looking out over the stage.

Even with a ladder straddling one of the satinwood chairs and an overalled electrician straddling the ladder, it was still a lovely English morning room. A warm, sunny light filtered through the French windows at stage right and landed on the squat bowls of flowers and the white-shaded lamps and made them glitter. In stage center stood a lemon-colored divan, on either side a chartreuse chair and in one corner under a window was a great desk of blond mahogany. A few other pieces, priceless things that had come from Clinton Bowers' home, completed the room. There was a hint of red in the draperies and the thick plushy rug, and the whole effect was gay and charming. Whatever the critics did to us, I thought, they must give our set a rave.

Suddenly Tommy's hand was at the back of my neck, shoving me forward and not very gently. "Haila! Look out!"

"What's the matter?"

He pointed at the flats behind me, dull green slabs of canvas that would be lashed together to make the third act dining room set. "I told Phoebe to warn everyone," he growled. "The damn painters didn't get enough glue in their paint. It'll come off on you."

I jumped away with alacrity, craning my neck over my shoulder to spot any damage. "I'm all right, aren't I, Tommy?"

"Yeah, so far. But for God's sake be careful." He looked out over the stage, then up at the light board and back at me. "Okay, Haila, let's go. Good luck!"

It was right then, without any warning pangs at all, that stage fright hit me. I knew it from the wet clammy feeling of my hands and the rocking in the pit of my stomach. Frantically I searched for one of my lines, not necessarily the first line, just any line, and there were none. The set bleared before my eyes and I took hold of Tommy.

"Remind me," I said weakly, "never to do this again."

A soft buzz that was the signal from the front of the house sounded and the set was cleared. The curtain lifted smoothly and after a second the telephone rang. I breathed my customary opening night prayer. "Dear Lord, just let me get through this thing tonight and I'll never go near a stage again, never, never, never. ..."

Tommy nudged me and then my legs were somehow carrying me across the stage toward the screaming telephone, my hand was somehow lifting the receiver. The little squeak that I knew was the only sound that could possibly emerge from my tightened throat didn't come out. Something amazingly close to my ordinary voice was saying "Hello!" into the mouthpiece, and when Philip Ashley came in through the French windows and we swung into our first scene, I hastily took back my prayer. I was having a swell time, perfectly swell. I wanted to stay on the stage, especially that stage, for the rest of my life.

Green Apples was a good play too, of the fluffy, English drawing room school that is almost passé in the American theater, but it had an added something that the passé ones don't have. Tea was served only once and horses were completely ignored. Greeley Morris' dialogue was crackling smart and if the characters weren't real they were at least amusing.

I remember that performance only blotchily, as though it had been pressed upon my mind in alto-relievo, some parts of it standing out vividly, the rest fading into the hazy background of an opening night.

I remember the audience, warm and friendly, laughing in the right place, quiet in the right place, glad that they had spent their four-forties and dollar-tens. I remember that first act intermission when the curtain came down on a burst of applause that made us all grin happily at each other as we scampered for our dressing rooms. Old Ben Kerry alone was not elated. Shaking his head in glum surprise he muttered, "Damn thing seems to be going!" and Clint Bowers, watching smilingly from the wings, clapped him on the back and laughed. Phoebe Thompson, her face smudged and her blue smock flying, was on stage before we were off, dodging moving furniture and stagehands and electricians.

Once, as I rushed upstairs to make a costume change, I saw Alice. I stopped and took her hand.

"Alice, what happened? Was something the matter?"

She jerked her hand away. "Nothing's the matter," she said sullenly.

"I only thought I might help."

"You can't." There were tears in her eyes as she turned her head away and stared over the railing. "You ... you wouldn't understand."

Vaguely, I remember costume changes and hurried makeup repairs and tense moments while I waited in the dark wings for my cue and the audience's laughs, big sweeping ones that rolled through the house and little knowing chuckles that crept about cautiously.

And then we were gathered around the long oak table and the third act was ending. Ben Kerry lifted his glass in a toast, a toast to the human race, and Eve answered him in her warm throaty voice. We drank to it, Carol and Philip Ashley and Steve Brown and Eve and I, and the curtain and the laugh came simultaneously. The applause was enthusiastic and prolonged and the curtain made eleven round trips before the clapping died away.

When at last it came down to stay I thought of Jeff, the first time in hours, which was a record. I beat it off the set and made straight for the stage door. He was coming down the alley and he looked tall and, from where I stood, handsome. But of course no matter where I was standing Jeff looked handsome. He kissed me and stepped back, smiling.

"Well," I said, "how was I?"

"Too good, too beautiful! You'll be leaving me in the morning for Hollywood."

"Me! The cinema! Never. How'd you like the play?"

"Didn't see it, only saw you."

"Wasn't Carol wonderful?"

"Sure, swell."

"What did you think of Eve?"

"Wonderful, wonderful. And I think the radio is here to stay if it can be commercialized. C'mon, darling, slip into your civvies and we'll go ashore."

After the last four hectic hours Jeff was like a Coca-Cola on the morning after. I parked him in the hall and left him struggling for standing room in the mob of friends and admirers and unemployed colleagues that was surging toward the dressing rooms. The air was heavy with "Darlings," and "Divines," and "Magnificents," and the modesty emanating from beneath the collective grease paint was stifling.

I took one look in our room and high signed to Jeff to guard the door. Carol was slumped before the dressing table, her arms hanging limply at her sides, and the face that stared unseeingly at me from the mirror was haggard and, even through the makeup, strangely white. She started when she finally saw me and made a halfhearted dab with cold cream. I sat down beside her.

"Carol, what is it?"

She glanced at me and then busied herself almost feverishly at her makeup box, her attention riveted upon it as though she were afraid I was about to demand an explanation now for her returning voice. She looked so miserable that I couldn't. With a forced brightness she said: "I'm all right, Haila. Just done in. I'm going straight up to the apartment and crawl in bed."

"I'd better go with you."

"No, really, Haila. All I need is some sleep and I'll be fine in the morning."

She seemed to mean it and I was anxious to go with Jeff, so I let her win without further argument. We both set to work on our faces in earnest. Through the wall that separated our room from Eve's came the hum of many voices. Outside I heard Jeff telling someone sadly: "I'm sorry, but Miss Rogers can't see anyone. She was attacked about the eyes by a swarm of bees."

Above the hubbub in her room, Eve's voice rose. It was sharp and soft at the same time, the tone one uses to reprimand a child.

"Philip, darling, haven't you had enough acting for one evening? I'm sure all these people have had their money's worth."

"You have the whole play to yourself." Ashley's voice was livid and I was glad I couldn't see his face. "Is it absolutely necessary for you to steal my only scene?"

Eve laughed. "Dear Philip, I have no idea what you're talking about. Really, I haven't."

Jeff slipped into our room, a grin stretching across his face. He jerked his thumb toward the wall and sat close to it where he wouldn't miss a thing.

Ashley was saying: "You know perfectly well. You stood at that table and rattled silver, you rattled glassware all during my long scene. Why didn't you overturn the table, Eve? It would have been much more effective."

"Oh, that!" Eve's words had a dismissing shrug in them. "That was

Tom Neilson's fault, or the little Thompson girl's. I'm supposed to arrange flowers during your speech, and where were they? Was I to stand there like a mummy while you droned through your lines?"

"It's customary to be quiet while another actor is speaking," Ashley said acidly. "They teach that at dramatic school."

"Philip, dear Philip, you must read the script one day. I'm not supposed to be interested, even listening, while you make that endless speech of yours. Philip never reads a script, you know, just his part." There was a roar from Eve's audience while Ashley said something that ended in hell and was punctuated by a slamming door.

"It's over," Jeff said sadly. "Eve by a technical knockout."

I bunched my purse and gloves together and took Jeff by the arm. "C'mon, Jeff. I've had enough of actors for one day." The moment I said it I could have bitten out my tongue for I had forgotten that Carol was still there. But she hadn't heard me.

"Haila," she said as we reached the door, "may I take your key? I guess I must have left mine in my blue purse."

"Of course." I fished through my pocketbook for it and tossed it to her. "Put it on the ridge over the door. Jeff and I may be late. You're sure you'll be all right?"

"Sure, I will. Go on, you two, have fun."

After the sticky warmth of backstage the night outside seemed bitter cold. A few snowflakes fluttered down and lost themselves on the pavement and the Forty-fourth Street wind whisked up stray programs and whirled them toward Broadway.

"What'll we do, Jeff?"

He laughed at me. There was really no question of what we would do; we had an old opening night custom. We would tramp all over town biting fingernails and chafing at bits until the reviews appeared at daybreak. Then, if the notices were bad, Jeff's shoulder would be handy to weep on and together we could curse the critics for their illiteracy and lack of taste. If they were good there would be one more drink to toast them as gentlemen and scholars. It was fine for me, I could sleep all the next day; it was Jeff who took the beating. I asked my usual next question.

"What about work tomorrow, Jeff?"

"I'm on my vacation."

"Vacation!" That wasn't part of the routine. "When did this happen?"

"Today at noon. 'Want to take a two weeks' vacation, Troy?' … 'Anything to accommodate you, sir.' … 'Very well, Troy, see if you can't come back with renewed vim and vigor. You haven't been selling much advertising lately, Troy.' … 'Business is bad everywhere, sir.' …

'Get away, Troy, relax.' … 'I may get away, sir, but I'll never relax.' "

"Jeff, a vacation in November! You're letting Leonard and Milligan impose on you."

"Never. I might let Leonard, but not Milligan."

We were automatically heading toward Ralph's, where theatrical people who can just afford beer and spaghetti convene and where every once in a while a star drops in to prove that the theater is democratic. It is the Sardi's of Forty-fifth Street, the stamping ground of Equity's midnight shift.

"Jeff," I said, trying my darnedest to mean it, "you really should get away. Why don't you go to Florida for two weeks?"

"I've never been to Florida."

"Well?"

"I don't want to break my record."

"What *are* you going to do?"

"Don't know yet. I might just stay in town. Take a trip to Chinatown and wash out some things."

It was early and the smoke at Ralph's was still thin enough for us to find a table. Teddy Hart, whom Jeff considered America's greatest actor since W.C. Fields gave up his career to go into the movies, was at the bar, and Jeff beamed at the sight of him. Jeff ordered Scotch and soda and I went overboard with a Cuba Libra minus the rum.

"Or I might get married," Jeff said, picking up the conversation we had dropped on Eighth Avenue.

"To me?"

"It's time we broke up our friendship."

"Let's."

"I've never been married. Do you know anybody in New York who's married? We could find out about it."

"My father and mother were married."

"And look what happened to them. You." He took somebody else's stray arm off the back of his chair and moved closer to me. "Look, Haila, I love you."

"I love you too, Jeff."

"If only I could save some money! We want to get married right, don't we? We want to be conventional, or unconventional, and have some children, don't we?"

"Yes. Some boys and a smattering of girls."

"And we want a maid so you won't have to give up your career, and insurance, and I want to join the YMCA."

"No, sir, you're not going to hang around the Y nights."

"It'll keep me out of pool rooms."

"Jeff, if the critics come through, I'll be making money for a while. *Green Apples* might run a year."

"No. We've been through that. I'll have to pick up some more money somehow."

"I'd marry you," I suggested modestly, "if you were only making five dollars and fifty cents a week."

It looked for a second as though I was going to get kissed, but Tommy Neilson broke things up by plopping down at our table and losing no time getting tight. He ordered straight rye with a beer chaser and downed both in morose silence. After grunting hello he refused to open his mouth except to fill it.

"Tommy's quite a conversationalist," I explained to Jeff.

"What is there to talk about?" Tommy challenged me.

"Conditions," Jeff said.

"People talk too damn much."

Tommy beckoned the waiter and duplicated his order. Jeff and I tried to ignore him but the blanket was too wet. We were about to make our escape when Phoebe Thompson joined our merry group. She took one look at Tommy and wagged her head. "I see we're off to a big evening."

"Oh, I don't blame him," I sympathized. "It's been quite a night."

"It isn't the night," Tommy said.

"What is it?"

"It isn't the night."

Phoebe shrugged hopelessly. "I don't know. He's cross. When we started rehearsals he was a lamb who drank Sherry Flips. Now look at him." We all looked and Tommy got to his feet, scowling. Jeff put a restraining hand on his arm, drawing him down again. "It's been a tough show. Tommy's worn out."

"It's been a lousy show. The whole damn thing stinks."

Phoebe smiled tolerantly at him. "Nasty, nasty old play! Going to be a hit."

"It stinks. I wish I'd had sense enough to stay out of it. I've been in the theater long enough to know better than to get tangled up in a Clint Bowers production. All of 'em stink."

Phoebe's bright face shadowed. "There's nothing wrong with Clint Bowers' productions. You're drunk."

"Yeah, I know. I'm drunk and Clint Bowers is a genius. A genius who hasn't had a hit in five years. A genius who produces trash for a washed-up, worn-out leading lady, a man of the theater who ..."

Phoebe turned on him and her eyes shot sparks. "Stop it! I won't sit here and listen to you slander him. He knows more about the theater in a minute than you'll know in a lifetime. He … Clint Bowers *is* the theater!"

Tommy said wearily: "Can it, Phoebe, I'm tired. Sure, Bowers is a great guy. Only he produces bad shows with bad people and he does it badly."

Phoebe's lips parted in a quick retort and then closed again, a trembling line. She slipped her arms into her coat and bundled its collar around her neck. "I'm going home. Good night." Before we could speak she was gone, a tiny blue figure losing itself in the bluer haze of Ralph's.

I turned on Tommy. "You should be nice to Phoebe. It's her first show and she's worked hard for you."

"Aw, she's got a bad case of hero-worship. Her first real live producer, so he's wonderful, he can do no wrong. Besides, his name was in a textbook that she used in a course called History of the Theater that she took her sophomore year, so that makes him a god. I'm sick of hearing about him."

"Why are you so down on Bowers?"

"I'm not down on him. I'm tired. I don't like *Green Apples*. Never have. It was a lousy script when I first read it and it still is. Production hasn't helped it any. An ingenue who loses her voice on opening night. An understudy who walks out. The Eve North-Philip Ashley feud. It's a mess, the whole thing's a mess. Even the scenery's painted badly."

Jeff blinked. "I find myself becoming fascinated. Who lost whose voice? Who walked out? Who is feuding with who?"

I told him then, starting with the case of the missing understudy, dramatizing my little battle with Ashley over an aspirin tablet and finishing up with Carol and her lost voice. Tommy went painstakingly on with his drinking career while I talked. Once he came out of it to mutter, "Yeah, tell him about Carol, the little …" I missed the noun but I didn't ask for it again.

Jeff took a long drag on his cigarette and squashed it under his foot. "What do you figure?"

"I don't know. It's terribly strange. She couldn't even whisper when I left to go to the theater and an hour later she was fine. That just doesn't happen, Jeff. But I hate to ask her about it. She looked so shot when we left tonight that I just couldn't bring the damn subject up."

"Maybe it was opening night nerves. Aren't they popular?"

"Nerves! Yaaah." Tommy slouched down behind his glass and scowled at it.

Jeff stood up. "I'm beginning to be frightened by actors. Let's get out of here."

It was only twelve-thirty. We had long hours to kill before the first morning editions appeared on the street. Jeff suggested the inevitable, a movie. On Forty-second Street we managed to find a double feature that only one of us had seen half of.

Jeff awakened me by removing his shoulder from under my head. "Is this where we came in?" I asked.

"I can't remember back that far. Let's get out of here and see what day it is."

Times Square had settled down for its short nap before the sun rose. The newsstands were still devoid of the papers whose notices would spell either food, clothing and shelter for me, or slow starvation. We walked down Seventh Avenue to the Metropolitan and read all the three sheets. The Ballet Russe was due soon. We managed to put all of fifteen minutes more behind us by wandering down to Pennsylvania Station. Time had stopped marching; it was walking on its hands. Finally, Jeff decided we should take a ride and he pushed me into a taxi.

"This is no way to save money, Jeff."

"If we think of some way for me to earn enough to get married while we're riding, it'll be a good investment. Let's see, I could sell Christmas seals."

"Christmas comes only once a year."

"How about *Saturday Evening Posts?* That comes fifty-two times."

"But you might just win a bicycle or a new catcher's mitt."

"I can always use a new catcher's mitt."

"Let's just ride," I said. "You can put your arm around me."

When the meter hit the two dollar mark we got out. We were on Broadway and a hundred and something so we took a subway back to Times Square. The papers were out when we climbed the stairs into the Times Building. We bought them all and lugged them to a Childs.

Over butter cakes and steaming cups of black coffee we read them, each trying to read aloud to the other and neither paying the slightest attention. On the whole they were enthusiastic. Burns Mantle gave it four stars and Brooks Atkinson bequeathed a more dignified blessing. Richard Watts asked who says the theater is dead and nobody answered him.

There were nice things about Greeley Morris' dialogue and about Clint Bowers' direction. Steve and Ashley and old Ben Kerry were favorably mentioned. Even I had a few sweet remarks passed about me here and there. But the orchids went to Carol. She was hailed as a discovery, her notices alone would insure the play a run. *Green Apples* was a hit and we had all scored personal successes. All, that is, except Eve North.

Poor Eve. "Despite a faltering performance by Miss North," was the way the *Times* ran, and one of the tabloids reported: "The old gray mare ain't what she used to be, which is young, but she won't admit it." The *Herald Tribune* was cruel in its kindness. Its only mention of Eve was a flattering description of her second act gown.

Somehow it shocked me. I knew, of course, that Eve wasn't the actress that she had once been, that when her sparkling beauty had begun to fade her talent had oozed away with it, but I had never dreamed she would be received like this. With every play in the last five years she had lost a little ground, but in *Green Apples* rock bottom had come up to hit her. Playing with her it was hard to tell if she were good or bad. She was so much the great lady, above all reproach or criticism, that you forgot to think about her acting. She herself took her talent so much for granted that you began to do the same. I was sorry for Eve North. In spite of a star complex I had found her fine to work with, and once she had been a really great actress.

"Listen to this," Jeff was saying, " 'Miss Haila Rogers gives a performance that is both delicate and charming.' "

"I am delicate! So delicate that I'm going right home to bed."

After gathering the papers together to show Carol, we paid our check and went out into the street. There were faint pink streaks in the dark sky and streetlights and signboards were popping off. A few people hurried along dodging the spray of the sanitation truck that passed. We walked slowly and the pink light in the sky spread and grew and it was daylight when we reached my apartment. The elevator bell rang hollowly through the silent building when I pressed it, but no Jinx appeared.

"Let him sleep," Jeff said.

"Softie!"

We trudged up the six flights dragging our heels and resting at each landing. I felt above the ledge of the door for the key that Carol was to have left there. The ledge was smooth under my exploring fingers. Sleepily, I rattled the knob and the door swung open. Then I stepped back and reached for Jeff. There was a long thin man asleep on my studio couch.

"It's an overworked burglar," I whispered. "Should I scream or can you take care of him yourself?"

"Scream," Jeff said.

The man stood up. I guess he hadn't been asleep. He looked at me and I saw he had nice gray eyes and a sour looking mouth.

"Miss Haila Rogers?" he asked.

"Uh … yes. May I come in?"

"Come in," he said, not very graciously, "and sit down. I'm Peterson. Of the Homicide Bureau."

CHAPTER THREE

"How do you do?" I said charmingly and sat down. Then I stood up again, gaping at him. "Of the what did you say?"

"Peterson," he repeated, "of the Homicide Bureau." He was looking at Jeff. "Who's this?"

"His name is Jeff Troy and he's a very dear friend of mine. And is it rude of me to want to know just how you got in here and what you're doing here and where is my roommate?"

"Sit down." To my surprise I sat down unprotesting. Jeff slouched on the arm of a chair and we waited. Peterson eyed us quietly. "You live here with Carol Blanton?"

"Yes. Or rather, she lives here with me. It's my apartment."

"You're both employed by Clinton Bowers in a play called *Green Apples* that opened last night at the Colony Theater?"

"Yes."

"How long have you known Miss Blanton?"

"Four, no, five weeks. Since the day we started to rehearse *Green Apples*."

"And how long has she been living here with you?"

"Five weeks."

"Since the first day you met her?" he grunted, giving me a quick look. "How come?"

"Because she hadn't any other place to live and because she was broke. I invited her to stay with me and she did."

"What do you know about her?"

"Nothing very much. She's a nice girl who wants to be an actress. Why? What's the matter with her?"

He went right on. "What about her private life? Where's her home and her family? Who are her friends?"

"She's from Salt Lake City and she hasn't any family, but she's never told me anything more than just that. And as far as I know she hasn't any friends in New York. Just some friends of mine whom she's met up here in the apartment and of course everyone in *Green Apples*."

"How long has she been in New York?"

"I don't know exactly. I think about six months."

"Six months? And she hasn't met any people?"

"That isn't hard to do," I told him. "Not when you live in a furnished room and eat in drugstores and spend your days going around to casting offices."

"What about Lee Gray?"

I frowned. "All right. What about him?"

"He's a friend of hers, isn't he?"

"I don't know. If he is I've never heard her speak of him. I've never met him."

Peterson rambled over to the window and stood jingling the coins in his pocket and looking out at the morning. He turned suddenly.

"And you don't know anyone who might want to kill her?"

I jumped up and then thought better of it and sank limply back into my chair. "To kill her!" I said. My voice was such a tiny thing that it surprised me. "Has somebody tried to kill her?"

He nodded grimly. "And damn near made a good job of it, too. She collapsed in the elevator last night and the doctor who was called discovered she had a skinful of poison. He notified us and we managed to get her to Bellevue in time. She's going to pull through."

Jeff spoke for the first time. "What was the poison?"

"Morphine."

"Where did she get it?"

"At the theater. During the last act. It seems you got a scene in your play where everybody drinks a toast. Well, that scene was when it happened. Headquarters says there was morphine in the glass she drank out of. All the other glasses were O.K."

Jeff let out an explosive breath. "Poisoned on stage! God! Poisoned in front of a thousand people and every one of them watching it. Have you been able to trace the poison?"

Peterson scowled. "Trace morphine? Not a chance. Every doctor in the country keeps a supply of it in his office, carries another supply in his bag. Every drugstore has it. You can get it in a hundred different ways." He turned to me. "You wouldn't know anything about how this morphine got in Miss Blanton's glass, I don't suppose."

Jeff said, before I could open my mouth, "What do you know about how it got there?"

Peterson reached for a battered hat that lay on the coffee table and stuck it on the back of his head. "What would I know? I wasn't there. Somebody who was there will have to tell me," he said pleasantly and went out. The door clicked shut behind him and I heard his footsteps fading down the stairs. Jeff gave a long low whistle and I made as energetic a dive as I could muster for the telephone. I called Bellevue. Miss Carol Blanton's condition, they told me, was favorable.

"When can I see her? When will she be able to leave?"

Her condition was very favorable indeed, they said.

"But I want to know …"

"Her condition …" began the white hospital voice. I hung up in disgust and slid the phone across the desk. Suddenly I remembered how Carol had clapped down the receiver when she heard us the night before, remembered her face as she stood watching Tommy and me in the doorway. It had been white and drawn, not with illness nor with the surprise of our being there, but white with anxiety and something very close to fear. And then I knew. I grabbed Jeff by the shoulders.

"Jeff, listen to me! I know why Carol lost her voice, why she would give up her first opening night! It was because she was afraid that something was going to happen to her at the theater and she wanted to stay away!"

"Then why did she finally go?"

"I suppose because we caught her phoning and knew she was all right. And if she had simply refused to play she would have lost her job. Oh, the poor little fool! If she had only told us!"

Jeff frowned and shook his head. "No, I don't think so, Haila. If Carol really thought that something was going to happen to her, that her life was in danger at the theater, I can't see her up and walking straight into it, job or no job."

"But this isn't just a job, Jeff. It's the start of a career, it's a whole new life beginning for her. A life in the theater."

"Not if it's going to end the first night."

I walked aimlessly around the room. "I wish I knew what it was all about. One thing I do know. Voices don't just snap off and on like electric lights. You don't croak like a frog one minute and talk in your ordinary voice the next. I don't think there was ever anything wrong with Carol's. I think she lost her voice so she wouldn't have to go to the theater last night but could still play her part later on. She did it awfully well, but she could. She's one swell little actress."

"I think I'd like to talk to Clint Bowers about it. What time does he get to his office?"

"About eleven usually," I said. "And just what do you think you're doing?"

He had yanked off his tie and was unlacing his shoes. The tie he draped neatly over my little white-potted cactus plant and the shoes were deposited with a bang on my Windsor table. Sprawling out on the studio couch he dug his head into the pillows. I stood over him and raged.

"Do you really mean to lie there calmly and go to sleep while Carol Blanton is in Bellevue poisoned? Listen, Jeff, somebody tried to kill her! Aren't we going to do something?"

"Not till eleven o'clock. Then we go see Bowers."

"And until eleven we just sit here?"

"You sit here. I sleep." He rolled over on one ear and pulled down a pillow to cover the other one.

"Sleep, damn you, sleep!" I said and sat down wearily at the desk. I tried to think of who could have poisoned Carol and why and what I should do about it. I put my head on the red leather memorandum pad and closed my eyes.

It was half past ten when Jeff shook me, and there was the lovely bubbly sound of coffee perking in the kitchen. I took a cold shower, slipped into my old tweed suit and did a hasty job on my face. Then, standing wedged in between the stove and the refrigerator, we gulped iced tomato juice and cups of strong black coffee. It tasted wonderful.

It was cold and bright as we walked down Fifth Avenue to Forty-fourth and over Forty-fourth to the Colony. Clint Bowers' office was on the third floor over the theater and we squeezed into the self-operating elevator and went up.

Before the great mahogany desk that seemed to sag under its load of littered papers, letters and photographs, Bowers was sitting, his head resting on his hand. His face was drawn and grayish and his crisp hair rumpled as though he had run his fingers through it many times. Phoebe Thompson, who did a smattering of secretarial work for him during the mornings, sat across from him, her pencil poised over a page on which nothing had been written. And striding back and forth in front of the one window was our ubiquitous new friend, Mr. Peterson. His head jerked in our direction as we entered.

"Oh, it's you two. You can come in. Sit down."

"Clint," I said, without any preliminary greetings, "do you know how Carol is?"

"I've been calling the hospital. Her condition is …"

"Favorable. I know. I've been calling them too."

Peterson said: "Your friend's all right. Lieutenant Sullavan just made a report on her. She'll be out of there in no time at all. Now, will you sit down?"

We did, on the edge of our chairs. Peterson drew a long breath.

"All right now, let's get back to where we were. Miss Thompson, you said that you have charge of those glasses, didn't you?"

Phoebe nibbled at the end of her pencil. "I ... yes, I do. I take them out of the prop room and arrange them on the table on stage. And I see that they're put back in the prop room after the show's over."

"And last night? Did you do that last night?"

"Yes. As soon as the set had been put up I carried all the things in and fixed the table, the silver and china and glasses. I dusted them and ..."

"Dusted them? You dusted the glasses?"

"Yes, they'd been standing in the prop room all day and they needed it. I dusted each one as I set it on the table."

"And there was nothing in any of the glasses then?"

"I'm positive there wasn't."

"When did you do this dusting, what time?"

"Two ... not more than three minutes before the curtain went up on the third act."

Peterson wheezed with satisfaction. "Well! That's what you call placing the time of the crime, all right. In those few minutes after you dusted the glasses and before the curtain went up someone dropped morphine in Carol Blanton's glass."

"Not necessarily," Jeff said.

"What?"

"It could have been dropped in any time from when Phoebe dusted the glasses until Carol drank the stuff."

Peterson glowered at him. "You mean that one of the actors might have put it in after the curtain went up? While the play was going on?"

"It's a possibility."

Peterson smiled. "I think you better try again, Troy." He turned back to Phoebe. "Who was on the stage while you were fixing the table?"

"Why ... why, nobody."

"No one at all? How come?"

"The company all had costume changes and they were in their dressing rooms. The set had been put up and all the stagehands had gone back to the cellar to their card game. Tommy Neilson was upstairs in the dressing rooms, I heard him calling places. And Amelia, that's Eve North's maid, had just gone into the kitchenette to do something for Eve. I don't know where the doorman was except that he certainly wasn't on stage. There, that takes care of everybody, doesn't it?"

"Everybody but me," Clint Bowers said.

"How about you?"

"I had gone up to Miss North's dressing room. There was a piece of business in the third act I wanted to speak to her about."

Peterson looked again at Phoebe. "After you finished the table, what did you do?"

"Went into the kitchen. I had to make tea. We used colored tea for the wine in the last act, you know."

"And that left the stage empty. Very conveniently."

"Yes." Phoebe's eyes flew eagerly to his face. "Look, Mr. Peterson! There were those few minutes just before Tommy brought the company down when no one was anywhere around. Couldn't someone have sneaked in through the stage door then, poisoned the glass and left again without being seen? Amelia and I in the kitchen wouldn't have been able to notice."

"Sure, that could have happened."

"How about Nick?" Jeff asked. "Wouldn't Nick have noticed a stranger coming in between acts?"

"I've talked to him. He wasn't on the door every minute during the night. He admits someone might have sneaked in that way."

"And there's that door from the front of the house," Phoebe said. In her excitement she had risen. "Anybody in the audience could have slipped through it during the intermission and not been noticed! That could have happened easily!"

"Sure, it could have happened," Peterson repeated. "Only it didn't. Nobody came through that door, nor through the stage door either."

"But why not?"

"Because the person who did this wasn't an outsider."

"You mean that someone in the company poisoned Carol, someone backstage? Oh, no, Mr. Peterson!" Phoebe was shocked. "Who would have done that?"

"Someone," said Peterson grimly, "who knew the setup, the stage and the theater. He had to know his way around, he had to know when the glasses would be put on the table, when he could sneak in and out with the least chance of being seen. And he had to know which glass Carol Blanton was going to drink from. Doesn't sound much like an outsider, does it?"

Phoebe admitted defeat. "No ... no, I guess not. Then ... then that means that someone in *Green Apples* is a potential murderer, doesn't it? That's what you're saying, isn't it?" She stopped, catching her lower lip in her teeth. The rest of us stared at each other and a queer little thrill of horror crinkled through my spine. "Any one of us backstage might have slipped onto the set during those three minutes and poisoned Carol's glass. Any one of us!"

Peterson said, "Yes. One of you did." He turned to Bowers. "Maybe you could tell me, Mr. Bowers, why Eve North would leave town at the crack of dawn this morning?"

"Eve! Leave town?" Bowers' eyes filled with incredulity and his hand reached for the telephone on the desk. "I think you must be wrong."

"Don't bother calling, I've been at her hotel. They say that she's out of town, won't be back until time for her performance tonight. And they don't know where she is."

"But Eve would have phoned me. She wouldn't have gone away the day after an opening night without first letting me know."

"That makes it all the more unusual, doesn't it? Where would she be, Mr. Bowers? Long Island someplace? Westport?" He watched Bowers, obviously waiting for an answer which he didn't get. "Okay. If she isn't back by tonight we'll find her."

"Miss North will be back tonight," Bowers said, smiling. "And in plenty of time for the performance, wherever she is."

Peterson moved back to the window and stood there a moment, contemplating us in silence. Then he slipped two fingers into his vest pocket and brought out a folded slip of yellow paper."

"Tell me, Mr. Bowers, who is Lee Gray?"

"You've asked me that before. And I told you that I had no idea."

Peterson looked questioningly at Phoebe who shook her head, and then turned to me. "Do you know?"

"I've told you before, too, that I didn't."

He tapped the paper thoughtfully against the palm of his other hand. From the way the light fell I could see that there was writing on it. He looked at Jeff and said nothing.

"Why don't you ask my friend Mr. Troy?" I said. "This Lee Gray is more than likely some old crony of his."

Jeff gave me a dirty look. "Never heard the name."

"Troy doesn't know anything about this business last night," Peterson said. "Do you, Troy?"

"No, sir."

"No, he doesn't know anything about it at all. And that's just about as far as I've got on this case. Troy was talking to the check room girl all during the second act intermission. I checked on him as soon as I saw him in your apartment this morning."

Jeff's mouth fell open. "Checked up on me? Why?"

"Because," Peterson said, "you look like the type who would poison a girl."

Jeff stared at him speechless and then at the rest of us for reassurance. We couldn't help laughing and it felt good to laugh.

At the wall mirror Jeff inspected his face minutely, as though he had never noticed it before. He rubbed his chin. "It's because I need a shave.

I always look like the killer type when I need a shave." His confidence in himself seemed to have been restored.

"Peterson," Bowers said, "what is this Lee Gray business about?"

The detective smoothed open the paper that he still held in his hand. "We found this note in Carol Blanton's purse. It seems to be a warning. It says: 'Meet me in front of the Broadhurst, I have got to see you right after the play. I can't tell you in a note what this means.' It's signed Lee Gray. This Lee Gray might have known what was in store for Miss Blanton and this note might be meant for a warning. And then again it mightn't be. But I think it is."

I said sweetly: "Wouldn't it be a good idea to ask Carol who Lee Gray is? After all, it was sent to her; she's the one who's likely to know."

"I'm going to ask her, Miss Rogers. Just as soon as she's able to answer."

We all turned at the creaking of the door. The man who stood there seemed to me the tallest man I'd ever seen. His parents, I thought inanely, must have been Basil Rathbone and a skyscraper. Perhaps it was partly because he was thin and long-necked and held his head so unbelievably high that he seemed so towering. He had brown hair and heavy-lidded eyes that were speckled colored, like tweed, and his mouth was thin and unpleasant.

I heard Clint Bowers say, "It's Mr. Morris, isn't it?" and I felt a nervous little tingle that was quickly followed by a surge of disappointment.

So this was our author. This was England's pet playwright. I hadn't expected him to look like that. He smiled with an obviously forced politeness as Bowers introduced us all to him. The smile didn't make him any prettier. Bowers ushered him into a chair and held out a chromium cigarette box. Taking a cigarette, Morris glanced at the brand and pointedly replaced it. His eyes roved the room and stopped at the detective.

"Mr. Peterson!" Somehow he managed, even when he sat, to give the impression of looking down on the people standing around him. "Peterson of the police. It was you who shattered my ears with a telephone call at ten this morning."

Peterson nodded. "Thanks for getting here."

"I was coming regardless of your request. It's a coincidence, I assure you. Now what is this about someone being poisoned? Someone besides the entire audience, I mean?"

We sat in startled silence. Phoebe turned sharply, her eyes blazing, to stare at him. Even Peterson was stopped by the colossal rudeness of this man who sat smiling, apparently oblivious of the shrapnel he had burst at us.

In a voice not quite level, Bowers said, "Carol Blanton was poisoned last night on the stage. There was morphine in the glass she drank from."

"Blanton? Which one was that?"

"The little girl who played Dina."

A shade of something that might have been annoyance swept over his face. "That's really too bad. She seemed to have some idea of what my play was about."

Peterson had had enough of that. He stood in front of Morris and, with both hands in his pockets, seemed to point a shaking finger in his face. "Who is Lee Gray?"

Morris lit a cigarette that he extracted from his pocket and smiled through a cloud of smoke. "I see. The direct method. Surprise 'em. Page ten of *How to Trap Your Man*. Well, Lee Gray, is that the name? Sorry, Mr. Peterson, I've never heard of her."

We could hear Phoebe catch her breath. "Of her! Of her, did you say? Is Lee Gray ..."

Peterson was eying Morris curiously. "Yes. It's a woman. The hand-writing is definitely feminine. How did you know, Mr. Morris, that Lee Gray was a woman?"

Morris was annoyed. "I choose my pronouns at random, Mr. Peterson. The name Lee is a very common female name in England. So common that I shouldn't think of knowing anyone by that name."

"Is this your first visit to America?"

"Are there people who come here twice?"

From the way the detective looked at him then I could tell he wouldn't be inviting him out for Sunday dinner. Daggers were beginning to shuttle between them. "I'd like you to stay in New York until we get this business straightened out, Morris."

"Sorry. I have other plans."

"What other plans?"

Morris stood up. "I will not be asked rude questions by stupid po-licemen."

"What other plans?"

Bowers was between them. "Surely, Mr. Peterson, you're not trying to connect Mr. Morris in any way with what happened here last night? He only arrived in New York late yesterday afternoon."

"That was in plenty of time."

"He's had absolutely nothing to do with this production. He's never seen Miss Blanton, nor any of the people connected with *Green Apples*, for that matter, before last night. Isn't that right?"

"I assure you," Morris said in a smiling voice, "that if I had, my play should have been very differently cast. Am I suspected of having poisoned this Miss Blanton?"

Bowers interrupted quickly. "Of course not, Mr. Morris. It's merely ... merely police routine more or less. Mr. Peterson has already established the fact that the poisoning was done by ... by a member of our company and not by any outsider. That's so, isn't it, Mr. Peterson?"

Peterson nodded. "Right." He smiled complacently at our playwright. "However, Mr. Morris is not an outsider and I am including him in the company. He knew this play as well as anyone in the company. We know that it was possible for him to have been backstage during that intermission. I'm afraid, Mr. Morris, that right now you are as much a suspect as anyone who belonged backstage."

Morris seemed thoroughly amused. "Really, officer, the only thing in which I'm interested is the theater. And the poisoning of one ingenue wouldn't help the American theater much."

"Apparently you didn't care for our production," Clint Bowers said. The deep hurt stood out on his face and cut through his voice. "It got rather good reviews."

"And Mr. Bowers got raves for his direction!" Phoebe put in staunchly, but her lips trembled at the corners.

"Oh, was it directed?"

Hate flared in Phoebe's eyes as her face went white. The pencil she had been toying with cracked like a birthday party snapper in the silence of the room.

"Tell me, Bowers," Morris continued. "This Eve North. Why? Is she your mother?"

I couldn't bring myself to look at Bowers then, or Phoebe, or anyone. All New York had been asking that question, I guess, but they hadn't used the word "mother." And no one had used it anyplace but behind Clint Bowers' back. When he spoke at last his voice was calm.

"I think that the critics were most unfair to Eve. She held the whole play together without starring herself. If at times she looked bad it was only to make someone else seem good. Eve North is the most unselfish actress I have ever known."

Morris shrugged. "Well, of course, I hope you have a run. After all, it is my play, although I scarcely recognized it."

"We'll try to do better for you tonight," I said bitterly.

"Please do. Only not for me. I'm leaving for Hollywood on the five o'clock plane. They've offered me more money than I knew existed and, although I'm fairly sure I'll loathe it, I'm rather anxious to go."

"You'll stay in town." Peterson sounded like a burlesque on a tough cop, but he didn't look like one. "You'll do me that favor, Mr. Morris, so I won't have to go to the trouble of making you."

Morris looked at him through half-closed eyes. "Very well. Only I make one stipulation. I absolutely refuse to subject myself to another performance of *Green Apples*."

"You don't have to subject yourself to anything but New York."

The policeman flipped his hat on the back of his head and opened the door. Facing him was a pale little girl in a navy-blue suit and a turned-up hat.

We sat and stared at her as if she were a ghost. She put up one hand and grasped the open door but made no other move. Her eyes swept over the room. For a moment I thought that she would turn and disappear as suddenly and quietly as she had come.

And then we came to, and Bowers was dragging out a chair for her and Jeff was trying to make her drink a glass of water and Phoebe fluttered around helplessly. There was a hasty blurred introduction to Greeley Morris and everyone asked questions that no one tried to answer.

Carol said: "There's a taxi waiting downstairs. I didn't have any money."

Jeff took charge. "Let it wait. You tell us why you're running around the streets like this. When did you leave the hospital? Why aren't you in bed taking care of yourself?"

Carol smiled. Under her eyes were dark purple hollows and her mouth seemed tight and thin. "I'm all right, Jeff. And they discharged me at the hospital; I didn't escape. I'm not running around the streets, either. I just stopped in to tell Mr. Bowers that I could play tonight."

"I'm afraid you're not going to play tonight," Bowers said grimly.

"But I'm all right now, honestly I am. Just a little weak and sort of … of tired. But tonight I'll be fine again. Please!"

"It isn't that, Carol!" I cried. "It's that someone tried to kill you, someone right in the company! And tonight they might. …"

I stopped, wishing I could bite off my stupid tongue. Carol's lips trembled and she had a tough time making the corners turn up instead of down. But it came out a smile.

"I know, Haila. They've told me at the hospital. They've told me about the poison and the glass and when it was done. And I … I still can't believe it. There isn't anyone who would … would do that to me." The corners went down this time and she looked scared and little and yet brave too. She took a long breath. "But even if somebody did try to kill me, I still want to play. I've got to! Oh, don't you see? If I didn't play tonight I'd be afraid to tomorrow night. It's sort of like … like going up in an airplane after you've just crashed. I have to do it. I can't spend the rest of my life locked up in Haila's apartment being scared every time the doorbell rings or the elevator stops at that floor. I've thought about it all morning long and I know! I have to go on tonight."

Bowers didn't answer her. He was frowning intently at a pencil in his hand.

I had never dreamed that Carol was made of that kind of stuff. If the poison had been put in my glass, no power on earth could have got me out of my locked and bolted bedroom.

"You'd better let her do it."

It was Peterson speaking from the doorway. He hadn't moved since Carol had appeared and I had forgotten he was still there.

"I think she's right," he said. "Nothing will happen to her at the theater. She's safer there than anywhere else. I'll be there." There was no boast in his tone, just a calm matter-of-factness that made us all feel that his being there would make everything all right.

"Very well," Bowers said slowly.

Carol stood up and rubbed her hand across her eyes. "I'll be at the theater on time."

"I'll go home with you," I said and put my arm around her shoulders. Peterson stopped us at the door.

"Just a second, Miss Blanton." I knew that he was about to go into his theme song. "Who is Lee Gray?"

Carol didn't answer. She looked from the detective to all of us. Peterson stood quietly waiting. At last she said, so softly that you could scarcely hear her, "I don't know."

Peterson had the note between his fingers again. "This was found in your purse. It's from someone named Lee Gray." Carol watched him, not moving. "It was handed to you in the theater last night, wasn't it?"

Carol's eyes leaped up to his. "No," she said slowly. "No, it wasn't. When I came up to my dressing room to make my second act change, it was there. Propped up against my mirror. I put it in my purse. But I didn't see her at all."

I caught my breath. "You … you knew it was a woman!"

She looked at me in surprise. "Yes, of course. The handwriting is a girl's handwriting. But I don't know who she is."

"You didn't meet her after the show in front of the Broadhurst?" Peterson asked.

"No."

"Why not?"

"There was no one there."

He held the note out to her, right under her eyes. "You don't recognize this writing? Never seen it anywhere before?"

"No. Never."

Peterson put the note back in his pocket. He looked down at Carol and his face was very serious. "Look, girlie. This Lee Gray knew something that she wanted pretty bad to tell you. Maybe she knew what was going to happen to you, that your life was in danger. I don't know why she wasn't waiting for you like she said she'd be, unless somebody else knew too and stopped her. Your life's still in danger. But if we could find this Lee Gray, it mightn't be. Everything might get straightened out and you wouldn't need to be afraid any more. Think hard, Miss Blanton. It's important to us, but it's a whole lot more important to you. It may mean your life. Haven't you got any ideas now who this Lee Gray is?"

Carol looked at him quietly. "No," she said at last, slowly and distinctly, "I've never heard of her."

CHAPTER FOUR

I TUCKED Carol's arm under mine and we took the elevator down from Bowers' office and climbed into the waiting cab. With a weary sigh Carol fell back against the leather cushions and closed her eyes. One look at her stilled all the questions that were hopping through my mind.

A traffic light stopped us at the corner of Broadway and Forty-fourth. On the sidewalk a young man I didn't know, but who was too obviously an actor, nudged his companion and pointed to Carol whose eyes were still closed. Around the corner swung a girl. She hesitated, then joined the men and, whispering among themselves in awe, the three inspected Carol as though she were a museum piece. In a moment, as so often and miraculously happens in New York, there was a crowd on the curb, staring into the cab. I leaned forward trying to shield Carol, to keep her from noticing, but as the car lurched into gear she sat up and saw the gaping goons.

"What are they looking at?"

"Nothing, darling."

"Oh, yes, I see. I'm a celebrity now, aren't I? One performance in New York and I'm famous already. But it isn't quite the sort of fame I dreamed about. I wanted my picture on the theatrical page, not the front one."

"You've seen the papers, then?"

"Only on a newsstand." She leaned back again.

"But you got raves, Carol. You did make the theatrical page. They wrote about you, not about Eve or the play."

"It doesn't seem to matter so much now."

"Carol, do you want to talk about it?"

In a flat, tired voice she said, "I don't care."

"Then ... who could have done it, Carol?"

She shook her head. "Haila, I don't know. Mr. Peterson says it was someone in the company, someone who knew the play. And I've been trying to think ... taking each person ... everyone, separately, and trying to remember every word that ever passed between us. But it's no good. I don't know why anyone should hate me enough to kill me, or even hate me at all. They've all been so good to me, from Mr. Bowers to ... to Nick the doorman. I ... I thought they all ... well, liked me." She looked straight at me and the puzzled expression on my face made her cry, "Haila, you don't believe me!"

"Yes, I do. Of course I do. But ..."

"What?"

"Well ..." Then I blurted it out. "You knew something was going to happen, didn't you? You were afraid to go to the theater last night, you ..."

Her eyebrows drew together and bewilderment filled the lovely blue eyes beneath them. "Afraid?"

"Weren't you afraid of something? Isn't that why ..." I stopped, flustered.

"Go on, Haila, please."

"Carol, when I heard that you had been poisoned, I thought that was why you lost your voice, that you only pretended you were sick so you could stay away from the theater. I don't blame you, darling, only you should have stayed away. You shouldn't have gone at all. ..." My words died in my throat as I saw her bewilderment change to sudden comprehension. She turned from me and leaned against the window.

"I see."

We rode in silence until we had crossed Madison Avenue. Then she reached over and laid her hand on my arm. "Haila, that wasn't it. Please believe me. I did lose my voice and it did come back. It sounds strange, I know it does, but that's what happened. About half an hour after you left, it just was there again, that's all. I dressed as quickly as I could to make the curtain. Then as I was leaving I realized that I should call the theater and tell them ... and that's when you and Tommy came in."

"Oh."

"I don't suppose anybody'll believe me."

"I do, Carol. It's just that I didn't understand. I ... I hoped that I was right. It wouldn't all be so mysterious and horrible if you knew who might want to ... Carol, isn't there someone in the company whom you've known before someplace?"

"No. I never saw any of them until we started rehearsing."

"And you don't know why one of them would ..."

"No. I don't know."

The cab swung into Fifty-fourth Street off Lexington Avenue. I looked at the meter and started groping in my purse for the right amount of change. "Carol, there must be an answer to this. Think back; there must be someone who ..."

She stopped me. "I've thought back ... that's all I've been doing ever since ... and I can't any more! I've tried and tried and it always ends up the same. I don't know who wants to kill me or why. Please let's not talk about it any more now, Haila, please!"

The taxi meter, which had been going since Carol left the hospital, had ticked its way up over four dollars and I just about made the grade. Carol leaned heavily on me as we walked to the elevator. Fortunately the day operator was on and not Jinx, the human interrogation point.

The shadows under Carol's eyes had grown darker and her face seemed even paler than before. I unlocked the door and she almost fell into the nearest chair. I insisted that she get some rest if she expected to play that night."

"I'm all right, Haila, honest I am." She tried hard to sit up straight and look ready for anything, but it wasn't very good. Firmly I led her into the bedroom, made her lie down. I opened a window four inches and pulled down all the shades.

"Would you like anything? A cup of tea?"

"No, thank you, Haila. You're so kind. All I want is to sleep and forget that stomach pump. ..."

She was practically asleep already. After covering her with Grandma Rogers' afghan, I tiptoed back into the living room. Jeff had promised to follow us and I walked aimlessly about the room waiting for him, switching the radio on and off, dealing hands of solitaire and messing them up before they were half played. Every sixty seconds I went to the window to see if Jeff was coming. I knew what was the matter with me and finally I admitted it. I was scared.

It was all right now, bright afternoon in my own apartment, six floors from the street and the door locked. It was the night to come that frightened me. When night came Carol and I would go to the Colony Theater and spend four hours there with a murderer. We'd be in his dressing room, maybe, talking about the crime. We'd play a scene with him or stop him in the wings to bum a cigarette. We'd meet him on those long dark stairs. Him or her ... or it. And we would all be thinking the same thing, all scared of each other, watching each other, and waiting breathlessly to see what would happen to little Carol Blanton.

Little Carol, I decided, was made of sterner stuff than I. If someone had put morphine in my glass, wild horses and their big brothers couldn't drag me within ten blocks of the theater that night. I'd start packing immediately for the handiest nunnery.

It was nearly five o'clock when the Troy rat-a-tat sounded at the door. He came in looking as though he'd just eaten a flock of canaries. On toast. His smile stretched from ear to ear and the sight of all this calm happiness made me furious.

"Where've you been? Seeing a movie while I sat here petrifying with fear?"

"How's Carol?"

"She's sleeping, thank heaven."

"Good. Well, sweetheart, I've found a way to spend my vacation."

"That's nice. Drop Carol and me a card. In care of the morgue."

"Somebody trying to do away with you too, Haila?" He didn't seem the least worried. I knocked his feet off the coffee table.

"You're doing your best."

"*Au contraire*, kid, to the contrary. I'm about to start solving the Colony Theater Attempted Murder Case. I'm going to see that no harm comes to Carol or you. Or anybody. That's the unselfish way I'm spending my vacation."

"I feel better already. What are you gabbling about?"

"I'm a detective. Just call me seven-seven-two-nine. Regent seven-seven-two-nine. Clint Bowers engaged me."

"What, dear?"

"Bowers engaged me as a private detective."

"Why?"

"Because *Green Apples* and Bowers will make a pile of money if some unknown doesn't continue to make passes at his ingenue's life. Murder stalking around backstage doesn't encourage long runs. And Bowers wants Carol in the cast; he doesn't want to replace her because he knows that it isn't the script and it isn't Eve North that'll keep the old S.R.O. sign out. It's Carol. And you, darling, and you."

"Uh-huh."

"Furthermore, Bowers doesn't like to see his acquaintances lying about in cold blood."

"Shh! Carol may not be sleeping!"

Jeff obligingly lowered his voice. "So he has accepted my offer. We have a gentlemen's agreement. He's going to make it worth my while if I clean this matter up."

"Didn't you talk him into signing a contract?"

"I said we had a gentlemen's agreement."

"Gentlemen always agree on paper."

"You're being cynical, Haila, very cynical."

"Well, if the police can't take care of this, I don't see ..."

"The cops can't get very interested in an attempted murder case. They have too many bona fide killings to worry about."

"What about Peterson?"

"This isn't the only case he's working on. And I promised Clint I'd give it my undivided attention."

"You a detective! It's ridiculous."

"Why?"

"Just deciding to be a detective doesn't make you one. I suppose if you picked up a saxophone you could play it."

"I couldn't if I didn't pick it up. Anyway, I can play a sax, I used to before I met you."

"All right, a xylophone."

"You don't pick up a xylophone, you play it while it's lying there on its back. You know a hell of a lot about music."

"And you about detecting! Taking a man's money ..."

"I don't get it until I ... I crack the case."

"You talk like a detective, and that's something a good detective never does."

"Why are you sore at me?"

"I'm not. I'm just nervous. Poor little Carol and ... well, maybe I'm being self-centered, but Carol and I are roommates; we drink out of the same bathroom glass."

"You know my interest in this isn't purely financial even if it does mean that we can get married if I succeed. I don't want anything to happen to Carol. Or to you either, except momentarily."

"I know, Jeff. I hope you can do something."

"I've done something already."

"What?"

"I had ideas about all this before I talked to Bowers. I ... Look, has Carol said anything to you about it?"

"Just that she doesn't know who or why or anything. I can't understand it. The fog's as deep around her as it is around the rest of us. My little theory that she was afraid to go to the theater last night and played possum because she knew what was going to happen to her is smashed to pieces. She says her voice *did* go, and it *did* come back and she was calling Tommy Neilson when we came in and found her."

"Yeah, I checked on that. Phoebe says that the phone rang about eight-thirty and that someone asked to speak to Tom Neilson and then, a second later, hung up. She knows it was Carol."

"Well, that fixes that. Now what do *you* know?"

"Not much. But there are a lot of things I'm going to find out. Like who in hell is this Lee Gray?"

"You have a neat little task there. What else?"

"Why is the great Greeley Morris so bored by this whole business? And why did he know that Lee Gray was a woman?"

I shook my head. "I don't think there's anything there. He's bored because that's the kind of a person he is, and he called Lee Gray 'her' because that was the first sex that flashed into his head."

"He doesn't impress me as ever saying the first thing that flashes into his head. He says the best thing."

"He's a rat!"

"I like him."

"All right, you like him. What else?"

"I want to know why Alice McDonald made such a hurried exit last night as soon as she found out that Carol wasn't going to play."

"You mean as soon as she found out that she was going to play Carol's part."

"My way is more significant. But all right. Another thing, where is Eve North today?"

"I think I know, Jeff."

"If you do you can be my assistant. Where?"

"In her apartment," I said smugly. "I could have told Peterson if we hadn't been in Clint's office when he asked. I couldn't say it in front of Clint. But where would you be if you were Eve North this morning after you had opened your papers and saw that every critic in town had roasted you unmercifully? If you saw that practically everyone in the show had got a rave but you? You'd be locked in your apartment with orders to your maid that you were at home to no one. You'd be sulking or crying or pacing up and down and cursing the critics to Topeka and back. And that," I said conclusively, "is where Eve North is."

"Except she isn't."

"Huh?"

"I've been to her place. The Alexandria. It's an apartment hotel. The man at the desk said she was out."

"Of course she'd leave orders that …"

"Wait! I wrote her a note and when the guy put it in her box I could see that there was a telegram there."

"Well, Monsieur Poirot?"

"Telegrams aren't left sitting around. They're delivered if possible."

"Yes," I said doubtfully.

"I wasn't satisfied either. I used deceit. Very degrading, being a detective. I said to the clerk, 'I see that Auntie Eve didn't get my wire!' "

"Auntie Eve! She'd love that."

"The clerk raised his eyebrows. Miles. 'You are her nephew?' he inquired politely. 'I am,' I replied. 'That's why I call her Auntie Eve.' The clerk lowered his eyebrows. 'I have come a long way,' I went on, 'without food and water and I am dying to see my Auntie Eve. She is my father's sister.' At that the clerk melted. 'And how is your father?' he asked."

"Jeff, stop having such a good time. Remember you're trying to save Carol's life."

"Well, the clerk fell for my gag and told me that Eve and her maid had left early this morning. The maid was carrying a traveling bag."

"But that doesn't mean necessarily that she was going to leave town."

"No, she could have gone to the Bronx Zoo and the bag could have been filled with peanuts, except that I asked the doorman and he remembered that Eve's maid had told the cab driver to go to the Pennsylvania Station."

"But it still may mean nothing."

"Sure, maybe she has a secret son at Princeton. That's something I'd be ashamed of."

"Don't be so Dartmouth."

"When an actress gets up early in the A.M. after an opening night and leaves town, it means something. An actress getting up early makes me suspicious. It makes me want to know."

"You can ask her tonight at the theater."

"If she's at the theater tonight."

The telephone shrilled at my elbow and I jumped. This business was getting me. It was Philip Ashley calling. He had just read about the poisoning and his crisp English voice was anxious and strained. I answered his solicitous questions coolly, remembering that I should maintain a dignified aloofness until he had apologized for his childish rudeness of the night before. Then something clicked in my mind. I made quick excuses to Philip and hung up.

"Jeff, what does morphine look like?"

"It's a white powder."

"Could it be in tablet form?"

"It could be."

"Like aspirin?"

"Oh. Philip Ashley and his aspirin."

"Yes! Why should he turn savage on me if it was just aspirin?"

"Because it wasn't? Because it was morphine?"

"Yes."

"No," Jeff smiled tolerantly. "I don't think our man would leave his morphine where you could find it."

"But he wouldn't have gone into a foaming rage if ..."

"Tell me what you know about Ashley."

I didn't know a great deal. He was one of those English actors who come to New York in a London play, then get another engagement here, and another, and finally stay, gladly forsaking the British theater for the higher American salaries. The first time I had ever seen him was in a play with Eva Le Gallienne. He had played supporting roles with Nazimova and Ina Claire and Blanche Yurka. He was a good, dependable, uninteresting actor and I suppose the big names liked him because he didn't detract any attention from them. Philip Ashley couldn't have stolen a scene from a snowdrift. I had met him several seasons ago when we were both working for Max Shuman in *West Wind* and since then we had been casual friends. The past year he had spent in Chicago playing a series of classical revivals. Bowers had rescued him from that to play opposite Eve North in *Green Apples*.

"Hmmm," Jeff said when I finished my résumé. "He's been in Chicago all year. Carol's been in New York only six months. They couldn't have met in New York before *Green Apples*."

"Contrary to local opinion, New York isn't the only place in the world."

"Carol grew up in Salt Lake City. Philip Ashley is an Englishman. I can't see much possibility of a connection between them."

I had a feeling I was licked. "Well, how do you explain his behavior last night over an aspirin tablet? I suppose it's a coincidence!"

"Probably indigestion. Have Carol and Ashley been especially friendly during rehearsal or vice versa?"

"Friendly, but not especially. They used to play two-handed rummy during waits at rehearsals, that's all. Jeff, it's too much for me. Somebody tried to kill Carol, but there's nobody that could want to! Nobody ever saw her until five weeks ago and they're all still just mere acquaintances."

"There's someone. Murder isn't like love, it doesn't happen at first sight."

"Then it's someone with a reason so deeply hidden that not even Carol knows it."

A low terrified whimper came from the bedroom. Jeff leaped to the door and flung it open. Over his shoulder I could see Carol, still sleeping. As we watched, she twisted nervously and one arm flopped across her eyes. She sighed deeply, then the regular breathing of a slumbering child went on.

"Bad dreams," I said.

Jeff closed the door quietly. "I wish she'd talk in her sleep and tell us who Lee Gray is."

"But, Jeff, she doesn't know!"

"Maybe her subconscious does."

CHAPTER FIVE

As if the weather had been anxious to provide the proper atmosphere for murder, late in the afternoon the day darkened, not with the creeping dusk of an early winter evening but with the quick unnatural blackness of a storm. The sky lowered to meet the steepled tops of skyscrapers and crushed down past them sullenly. At five the snow began. Carol sat curled up on the window seat now, her face pressed against the pane, watching it.

I snapped on all the lights and built a little cannel coal fire in my miniature fireplace. In the kitchen, as I threw together all the odds and ends I could find in the refrigerator, I hummed loud and determinedly. Carol had drawn the butterfly table up close before the fire and we sat down and made a fairly brave pretense of eating.

Neither of us was very successful. Somehow the cheerfulness of the apartment with its lamps glowing warm and yellow and the fire's cozy crackle seemed only to stress the bleakness of the night outside and the horror of those hours stretching before us.

We walked to the theater. That was Carol's idea. I think she was trying desperately to postpone her arrival at the place where she had been so near to death the night before. We trudged toward Broadway silently and the snow felt dry and soft as it landed in our faces. The buildings on either side of the street looked strange and unfamiliar through the snow, their outlines wavering vaguely, and the street lights blurred as though we were seeing them through some thick gray scrim.

Peterson and a mountain of a man with a round fat face were standing just inside the stage door talking to Nick. We heard them as we stopped to shake the snow off our coats and out of the brims of our hats.

"No one," said Peterson, and his voice was even sterner and more authoritative than I had thought it could be, "no one at all is to be allowed inside this door tonight other than members of the company."

Nick banged the ashes out of his pipe. "No one to come in," he said, nodding.

"And no one is to leave until the play is over, and then not until I say so."

"No one to leave."

There was something in Nick's voice that made the policemen look at him sharply. It wasn't contempt, he was too docile for that, but it was a kind of ill-concealed disdain. Nick had been guarding stage doors for over thirty years and his life revolved around them. He called producers by their Christian names, the numerous first ladies of the theater were all "honey" to him, and his respect for anyone not in the profession was negligible. His irritation at being given orders about his work, even in this emergency, shone plainly on the wizened old face. I could understand, but the detectives obviously thought the old man sullen and codgery.

The man mountain said gruffly, "You understand that?"

Nick shifted his feet to the radiator and tilted back his chair. With his pipe between his teeth he looked hard at the men. "No one in and no one out."

I felt Peterson's eyes following us as we walked across the stage. I thought, this isn't the same theater that I came to last night. It's something that we've wandered into by mistake. Last night this had been a thrilling place, a place that housed in a part of one small block all the glamour and excitement that the world could hold. Now it was cold and dismal, full of shadows and unfamiliar sounds. The second act furniture piled in back of the set made a grotesque heap in the semi-darkness. A stagehand looked curiously at Carol and then quickly away again, as though he had been caught staring at a cripple. She saw him too and her hand was cold as it reached for mine.

Jeff was ensconced in our dressing room, lounging contentedly in one chair, his feet stretched out on another. He looked lazy and ineffectual and very, very comforting.

"Ha!" I said. "It's Nero Wolfe. Miss Blanton, Mr. Wolfe."

"Sit down, girls." He planted himself more firmly on the only two chairs.

I hung my coat on a hook and stuck my limp hat over it. "Jeff, have you seen her? Eve, I mean?"

"She hasn't come in yet."

"Then you don't know anything more?"

He looked at me with indignation. "Plenty more. What do you think I've been doing all evening? I've been sleuthing. Or rather, I've been helping the police sleuth. And we've discovered some very interesting facts about the mysterious Miss Lee Gray."

Carol's eyes jumped to his face and she watched him breathlessly. "Do you know who she is?"

"Jeff, have you found her? Tell us!"

"I don't know if I should trust you with a thing like that."

"Jeff, stop it! I swear I won't breathe a word to anyone."

"Well," he lowered his voice and looked around, "I'll tell you then. It isn't you."

"That's enlightening. Is that all?"

"No. It isn't Eve North or Alice McDonald. It isn't Phoebe Thompson. They thought that note might have been written by one of the women in the cast and signed with a fictitious name. But specimens of all their handwriting show that none of them compares with Lee Gray's."

"So Lee Gray isn't one of us?"

"Apparently not."

"Well, that's swell. You're getting along fine. Now get off those chairs. Carol and I have a show to play."

Jeff obligingly went and stood in the corner while we made up. I glanced at Carol in the glass. Her hands shook a little as she dabbed on rouge and purple eye shadow and dotted her lashes with mascara, but long before the call for places came she was ready, waiting with her hands folded in her lap. Except for a tiny tense line around her mouth that powder hadn't been able to conceal, she looked like any pretty ingenue whose greatest worry at the moment was to remember her lines.

Peterson opened the door and looked around the room. "Feeling all right, Miss Blanton?"

She nodded briefly and managed a smile.

He said, "That's fine. Now don't worry. Everything's going to be okay tonight. Nick understands that nobody is to go through that door, either in or out, and I've got Lieutenant Sullavan watching the door into the front of the house and keeping an eye on things in general. I'll be near you all the time."

Jeff said, "Me, too, Carol. All you have to do is reach out your hand to touch me."

Peterson grimaced good-naturedly. "Yeah, Troy's playing cop now, too. It's okay with me. But pretty soon there'll be more detectives around this theater than actors." He turned to go and stopped abruptly. "Look,

Miss Blanton, it isn't too late for us to help you a great deal if you've managed to remember anything about Lee Gray."

"I told you. There isn't anything for me to remember."

"Even if you could tell us where you've heard the name before," he persisted.

Carol said wearily, "I'd never heard the name before."

Peterson, with a foggy shake of his head, went out.

It was nearly eight-fifteen when Eve arrived. We heard her running lightly up the stairs, Amelia's sonorous footsteps close behind her, and the door of the dressing room next to ours clicked shut. Jeff went out quickly and I followed him, watching as he knocked at Eve's door. It opened only a crack, which Amelia's bulk filled amply, and Jeff said, "I want to see Miss North."

"She can't see you."

"Only for a second," Jeff said firmly.

"She don't have a second, she's late now. She has to dress." The door shut in his face. He waited a moment and lifted his hand to knock again. Then apparently he thought better of it and came back.

"Congratulations," I said.

He scowled at me. "When does that sea lion named Amelia leave her side?"

"Almost never. Sit down and stop fretting. You won't be able to see her now until intermission. She's on nearly all of the first act."

We sat there saying nothing and pretty soon we heard Tommy at Eve's door asking if she were ready and Amelia telling him to go ahead. Then he was in our room. "Places," he said. There was questioning and pity in the look he threw Carol, but Carol didn't see it. She fluttered the powder puff across her face and didn't seem to be aware of his presence. Tommy turned and went out. I whispered to Jeff: "Watch her. Watch her every minute." He nodded and I followed Tommy down the stairs. Peterson had stationed himself outside our dressing room and Sullavan had taken his position on stage left.

That first act was a nightmare. I had known our performances would be uninspired, but I hadn't expected a weird burlesque. And that was what *Green Apples*, acclaimed and lauded by the critics in the morning, amounted to that Tuesday night.

Anxious to show, I think, how completely unaffected he was by all this mystery, Philip Ashley overacted until he might have been playing the dagger scene from *Macbeth* instead of a quietly humorous British professor. Steve was jumpy too, the unhurried, gangly quality that gave his work such charm gone completely. And as usual when he was under any strain whatsoever, old Ben Kerry forgot his lines and Phoebe's

The audience seemed cold and hostile to us from the first and we
hated them for it. We threw our funny lines in their collective faces
with a there-that's-funny-laugh-now-damn-you air. We could hardly
expect a warm reception for the antics that were thrust before them on
the stage of the Colony Theater that night, but stubbornly we blamed
them for our failure. The applause, when the curtain fell at last on the
first act, was scattered and painfully polite.

I looked at Carol standing behind the chair at stage left and drew a
breath of deep relief. That much was over anyway. That much was
behind us. I took her arm and we went upstairs together, Peterson following us. Over the banister I caught a glimpse of a black-clad figure
hurrying across the stage toward the prop room.

As we went into the dressing room Peterson, having told Jeff to
stand by for a few minutes, went clattering back down the stairs.

"I just saw the sea lion on stage," I told Jeff after the detective had
disappeared. "I think she's getting Eve some tea or something. Now's
your chance, M. Poirot. I'll take care of Carol."

He was out before I had finished. I heard his knock on Eve's door
and her "Who is it?" I slipped out of the white sport dress and into the
lamé evening gown, trying to keep my ear against the wall. Eve's voice
rang out astonishingly clear.

"I don't see people during a performance! Please leave."

Jeff said, "You don't see people hardly any time, Miss North. But
I'm afraid you've got to see me now."

Eve was resigned and patient. "Well, what is it?"

Carol turned from her mirror and opened her mouth to speak. I ges-
tured toward Eve's room and she stopped and sat up straight listening,
too, her eyes riveted on the wall in front of her.

"It is none of your concern, Mr. Troy," Eve was saying in a voice
cold with repressed fury, "what I was doing at that table. It's outra-
geous that you should ask. I won't tolerate this ... bursting in and questioning me about my acting ..."

"I don't want to know anything about your acting," Jeff said. "Last
night you inserted some business that wasn't acting around that table.
And when there is the question of murder ..."

There was a toppling sound as though someone had clutched at something and it had seesawed before steadying itself. Then, after a pause,
Eve's voice came again, almost a whisper.

"Murder!"

"You didn't know?" Jeff was surprised.

"No, I didn't. It's ... it's a shock to me."

"You've been out of town all day so you couldn't have talked to anybody from the theater, Miss North ... but surely you've seen the newspapers."

Eve said very quietly, "I haven't seen any papers since the first editions this morning. I think you can understand that, Mr. Troy."

"I understand," Jeff said. "Then you wouldn't know about Carol. She was poisoned last night in the dining room scene. There were four grams of morphine in the glass she drank out of."

The wall trembled slightly, Eve must have leaned against it. We waited an eternity for the sound of her voice. "Morphine in her glass ..." She breathed the words. I could scarcely catch them.

"Yes," Jeff said. "So you must see why I'm anxious to know why you were doing things, unrehearsed things, at that table. I know you did. I heard Mr. Ashley speaking to you about it last night. He said you rattled glasses."

Eve said falteringly, "There were no flowers on the table, there was nothing for me to do." She broke off suddenly and laughed. "Oh, I see, Mr. Troy! I do see what you're getting at! You think that possibly I was doing something else at the table, perhaps slipping ... morphine, did you say it was? ... into Carol's glass!"

"I'm merely asking questions, Miss North."

"That would've been a clever idea! While a thousand people were watching, to have dropped the poison in the glass before their very eyes and not to have been seen doing it!" Eve laughed again, almost hysterically. "That would have taken a good actress! And even you must know by now, Mr. Troy, that I'm not a good actress. For further details see your favorite newspaper." The bitterness drained from Eve's voice and she went on, sounding very old and very tired. "No, I didn't do it. ... I didn't poison Carol Blanton. ... I ... I ..."

If Eve said anything more, Tommy calling "Places" at our door drowned out her words. He went next door and we heard his incredulity at finding Eve still in her first act costume. Then we heard Clint Bowers in the hall outside talking to Tommy, telling him to hold the curtain a few minutes. Jeff came back looking grim. There was only time for Carol and me to take hasty, unseeing glances in the mirror and run out. Alice was outside the door and Carol said as we passed: "Don't go away, Alice. We may need you yet."

It was said lightly, jestingly, but the tight-lipped smile that accompanied the words showed what an effort it had been.

The second act went some better. The detectives were still keeping vigil but they were listening to the lines. Sullavan seemed frankly puzzled by Greeley Morris' brilliant display of wit, but Peterson smiled in the right places.

Philip Ashley had toned down his performance and the rest of us gradually took his pace. I trembled when Eve made her entrance in that act. Her first act performance had been smooth but there had been no reason for it to have been otherwise. Now, knowing what the rest of us knew, feeling the horror and suspense that we were feeling, I wondered if she would be able to hold up.

From the moment she swept on, her hand tinkering at the collar of the icy white jacket she wore over her evening dress in a gesture that had long ago been famous, I knew that it would be all right. Eve had trouped too long and too hard to let anything ruffle her stage composure. Her voice, as she threw her lines away, might have been a little tense and her mannerisms a little stilted, but not enough for an audience to notice. I knew I had been waiting nervously for that moment when she entered, and her serenity was reassuring.

It wasn't until we were three quarters through the second act that it happened.

Carol had got through her big scene nicely and at her exit applause had started in the orchestra and thundered solidly through the whole house. I realized then that our audience was not as lethargic as we had supposed, but that suspense was hovering over them as well as us. They waited, as we were waiting, for the evening to end safely. That hand had been for Carol's courage as well as for her acting.

Through the wide French doors I could see her in the wings making toward the stairs, both Peterson and Jeff close at her heels. Almost two thirds over now, I thought gratefully. Carol had one more scene, a short one that she played with Eve and me, and that would bring the curtain down on the second act. Almost two thirds over and Carol was still safe.

There were only Eve and old Ben Kerry and I on stage now, and in a moment Eve followed Carol through the door on stage right. Kerry lounged in the chair beside the big golden oak desk where I sat writing what was supposed to be a passionate love note. I scribbled, "Green Apples, Green Apples, Eve North in Green Apples" and rushed through my few lines with Kerry. He rose now, heavily, and with an avuncular pat on my shoulder started for the door.

The act was nearly over now, a little scene with Eve, then Carol's entrance and then the blessed respite of an intermission.

It was the half-smothered sound he made that caused me to look up from my desk and stare at old Ben Kerry and wonder hysterically if he had gone mad. Instead of exiting through the door right he had closed it softly and turned and taken one faltering step back into the room.

And then I saw his face.

For one terrifying moment I thought it wasn't Kerry's face at all. In spite of the florid makeup that he used, it had somehow the look of a plaster cast, numb and frozen. But his eyes darted wildly around the stage, stopping for a moment as they rested on me and seeing nothing.

I searched frantically for something to ad lib. "Back so soon?" rose inanely to my lips and I smothered it and could think of nothing else. I had to get the old man off the stage. Eve wouldn't make her entrance until I had. I tried to catch his eye and motion toward the door. He stared at me and made no move to go. Silence pressed down in cold stifling clouds over the house and then was stabbed by a titter in the audience.

I got out of my chair at last and took Kerry by the shoulders, turning him forcibly around to face the door. The titter spread to a running laugh, rolling through the audience, the balcony, the boxes. I said, trying to fight the laughter, "Good night, Uncle George," and in Kerry's ear I muttered, "For God's sake, get out!" I held the door open for him. It was then, I guess, I screamed.

Before I touched the shapeless mass on the floor at my feet, even before I saw the sharp glimmer of the knife beside it, I knew that she was dead. I knew from the way the thick velvet of the cape fell over her body and from the terrible stillness of it. I knew it and yet I screamed, "Carol, Carol!" and I tried to lift her.

I saw the jacket then, the shimmering white jacket that was splotched now with thick green stains and crumpled under her head. With feverish fingers I tore the big black cape from her shoulders. My arms went limp and numb with horror.

The back beneath the cape was hideously shriveled, the arms and shoulders a network of ancient brutal scars. Somehow I managed to put my hand under her head and turn it toward me. Eve North's dead eyes stared up into my face.

CHAPTER SIX

It was half past four when we left the theater. Carol sat between Jeff and me in the cab, her hands working spasmodically in her lap at the little ball of felt that had, much earlier in the evening, been a hat. I noticed dully that it was still snowing, or maybe that it was snowing again, and that our cab was creeping cautiously along the icy street toward Broadway.

Jeff stuck a cigarette in his mouth and fumbled for a match. The driver crooked his arm back over the seat and held a lighter for him. A very courteous driver. I glanced at the framed identification hanging in front of us. Your driver, it said, is Fred Neblico. A very courteous driver, Fred Neblico, and a very careful one. I looked above the name at his picture, but it wasn't Fred Neblico's picture that I saw. It was Eve North's face staring at me still. I closed my eyes and tried to let the comfortable numbness that had crept through my body long ago take over completely.

It was no good. If I could blot out Eve's face there would be Carol's. Not Carol now, white and tired, but Carol as she ran down from her dressing room when she heard my scream, and stopped and stood there above the grotesque figure in her velvet wrap. I was crouching over Eve, staring up at Carol. I had waited for her to faint or to cry, but not to laugh. She had reached out her hand to lift a fold of the black velvet and to finger it, as though a sales girl had just pushed a bolt over the counter toward her, and she had laughed. Then Jeff slapped her, hard, for the print of his hand was white and then red across her face. He put his arm around her and led her away. She was crying then and the long choking sobs were almost as awful as that first terrible laughter.

It was Amelia's face that was the worst of all. There had been no grief nor horror on it, just a cold look that made it seem as dead as Eve's. Only once had Amelia shown any emotion. When she had started to go to Eve and Peterson's hand shot out to grasp her wrist, she had wrenched herself free as easily as if her arm had been imprisoned in a filmy spider web. Kneeling beside her mistress she had lifted the cloak and thrown it over Eve's back and shoulders. Slowly she stood up. "You've killed her," she said. Each word was an icicle. "Don't stare at her now. She'd rather you kill her than stare."

I rubbed a clear space in the steamy window glass and peered out. We were passing Forty-eighth Street. Could it have been only last night, only nine hours ago, that Carol and I walked past this street on our way to the theater? My mind went hurtling back over those hours, seeing it all in gruesome detail; I couldn't stop it. That static moment after Amelia's outburst which had been jabbed by Peterson's quiet cursing and Sullavan's rough voice barking into the telephone. The men trooping in from the radio cars. Blue uniforms dotting the stage, herding us into corners, standing over Eve's body. Orders in brief, sharp tones. The door swinging wide to admit more men in uniform, more plain-clothes men, the coroner, photographers. They kept on coming, a steady one-way stream through old Nick's stage door. And in the alley outside the mumbling of the quick-gathered crowd and the yammering of the newspapermen.

I had answered questions, the same questions, until the words I spoke had taken on an unfamiliar sound and my throat grew dry and bitter. Over and over I told my story, how I had taken poor Benjamin Kerry by the shoulders, how I had opened the door on stage right to push him through it, how Eve's body had lain crumpled behind it. I told it to a man with beetling brows and a ridiculously gentle voice who was the Inspector, and the police stenographer's pencil flew across his notebook as I talked. I told it to a fat detective sergeant and to a skinny red-haired one. I droned through it again for the two special investigators from the District Attorney's office, one who fumed and snapped at me, one who seemed to hardly listen.

And all through the relentless prodding was the murmur of the crowd outside, the incessant talk around me, the voices at the telephone demanding headquarters or the police laboratories, the spit and flash of the camera lights. From every angle Eve's lifeless body had been photographed, her green-stained jacket and Carol's blood-smeared wrap. They had turned the camera on her dressing room, the wings in which she had been stabbed, the set on stage, the door she had been about to go through.

Those hours had the timelessness of a nightmare. When for a moment I had stood alone watching the coroner examine Eve, it seemed that all of it had been squeezed into a few brief seconds. But when I faced the barrage of seemingly endless questions I felt that my whole life had been spent on the stage of the Colony Theater and that those words were the only ones I had ever spoken.

We had heard the newsboys on the street yelling about the "Big Theyater Moider" before they had let us go.

Now it was over. Eve was dead and Carol was alive. There had been no arrests. I leaned my head wearily against the icy pane and it felt good. There had been no arrests. Then it wasn't over. Eve was dead but it wasn't over. Somewhere, someone was still waiting to kill Carol.

The cab stopped in front of our apartment and we went in. Jinx was sitting crosslegged on the bench in the lobby, half asleep. He jumped up with a start when the door slammed closed behind us and his bland, sleepy face told me that no word of the Colony murder had reached his ears yet. None of us wanted to inform him; we'd had enough of murder for one night.

Jinx winked one of his popping eyes at Jeff. "I see you ain't scared of riding with me no more," he chuckled.

Jeff made a noble attempt at lightness. "You're the safest pilot I've ever known, Jinx. I never know fear with you at the stick."

"You musta been scared Sunday. You walked up and down."

"I wasn't here on Sunday," Jeff said.

"Sure, you was, Mr. Troy."

I said, a little sharply, "There wasn't anyone here Sunday, Jinx. You've got your dates mixed."

He looked puzzled. "Yeah, I guess so. Sorry."

We went into the apartment and it was a warm and pleasant contrast to the bitter cold outside. I went straight to the cabinet under the built-in bookcases and put a bottle of Scotch on the coffee table. "I want a drink," I said. "A good, stiff drink. Do you?"

"Yes," Jeff said.

Carol reached into the cabinet and brought out a bottle of brandy and a shot glass. She filled the glass to the top and gulped it down. It was Courvoisier and very strong. Without even a grimace she refilled the glass and swallowed. When you'd been through what that girl had, I thought, you probably couldn't feel anything. Suddenly she set the glass down, walked slowly to the window and stood staring out.

"If I hadn't left my wrap on the stairs, Eve wouldn't have put it on. Eve wouldn't be dead. Eve would still be living and I ..." She stopped and covered her eyes with clenched fists.

Jeff poured another shot of brandy and followed her. "Drink this."

She brushed it away. "They thought it was me in that big black wrap. The hood over her head, they couldn't tell. I would have been there where she was in a minute. They thought they were sticking that knife in my back. It was almost as if I killed her, letting her wear my wrap, not wearing it myself. ..."

"Don't talk stuff, Carol. You didn't let her wear it. It wasn't any of your doing that she leaned against the damned scenery and messed up her own jacket. It wasn't your fault that she picked up your coat."

Carol said, her lips quivering: "And then when I saw her ... I laughed! I laughed! I stood there and ..."

Jeff took her roughly by the arm. "Drink this. Or do I have to hit you again?"

Carol tipped back the glass and drained it. Her hand went limply down on the table and the glass rolled across the top, stopping with a clink against the china book end. She watched it for a moment, then turned toward the bedroom. I started to follow her but Jeff caught me by the hand, holding me back. "Let her alone."

I sank down beside him on the studio couch. My eyes were burning with a tired ache, my whole body felt cold, somehow, and detached. Jeff was looking hard at the door through which Carol had gone.

"Jeff, who did it?"

Jeff quirked an eyebrow. "Do you think I know?"

"You know something. You listened to them talking. The police, I mean. I didn't. I tried, but I couldn't. They talked in circles."

"They were going in circles."

"But they must know something, they have something to go on. It isn't like the poisoning. They have the knife. ..."

"The knife came from the kitchen. Tom Neilson recognized it at once; he saw it in the cabinet drawer the first day of rehearsals at the Colony. He hasn't noticed it since, nobody has. Anybody could've sneaked it out of the drawer, any time. No," he went on quickly as I opened my mouth, "no fingerprints. Wiped off clean."

"But they must have some idea ... about someone ..."

"The only idea they have is who didn't do it. That's as far as they can get."

"Who do they think didn't do it?"

"You. You were on stage. Ben Kerry. He was on stage."

"That couldn't be all!"

"Not quite. Carol's eliminated."

"Of course."

"I mean she has an alibi because Peterson and I were with her from the moment she left the stage until you screamed."

I said in disgust: "Those three eliminations are a lot of help. Nobody else?"

"Listen, Haila. There were twenty-seven people backstage tonight when Eve North was murdered. They say nobody came in and nobody went out. Twelve stagehands, six people in the cast, Alice McDonald, Tommy Neilson and Phoebe, Clint Bowers, and the doorman, Eve North's maid and Peterson, Sullavan and I. You and Kerry and Carol are out. The detectives and I are out. Nobody else."

"Eve North is out," I reminded him.

"Yeah, and that leaves twenty. Tommy Neilson brought the curtain down the second you screamed. So he was near the rope at the other side of the stage from Eve. But he has no witnesses to his movements between the time of Eve's exit and your scream. Phoebe Thompson was on that side of the stage, but even she can't check on Tommy. She says she was standing in the wings with her eyes glued on you, trying to think of some line to throw you to get you out of the mess Kerry had stuck you in, and she didn't see Tommy, didn't know he was there until he lowered the curtain. And Tommy can't check on Phoebe, so neither of them has an alibi."

"What about Sullavan? He was on that side of the stage."

"Sullavan's no help. In the dark he couldn't tell Steve Brown from

Phoebe in her slacks. There were twenty-seven people moving about
backstage. Nobody can remember when or where they saw anyone
else. The police finally gave up on that point. They can figure out where
everyone was when you screamed – that was something definite – but
Eve was killed a minute, or maybe four minutes, before you yelled.
And in thirty seconds, just for instance, Steve Brown could have gone
from the stage all the way to his dressing room. Peterson nearly went
nuts before he realized that this was one murder that wasn't going to be
solved by placing people at the time of the crime."

"But, Jeff, there must be some alibis!"

"Not enough of them to help much. Five of the stagehands were in
the basement and they alibi each other."

"And where were the rest?"

"Around someplace. At the light switch, in the prop room, on the
stairs into the basement. No alibis. Bowers was sitting on that pile of
first act furniture in back of the set, and he saw people moving about.
But that's all they were, just people, no specific persons. It was too
dark. He thinks he saw Amelia coming out of the kitchen when you
screamed, but he isn't even sure of that."

"What about the rest of the cast, Jeff?"

"Well, Philip Ashley was in his room on the third floor making a
change. Alice's room is next to his and she was in it, but that doesn't
give either of them an alibi unfortunately for she had her door closed
and was 'wrapped up' in a script. Neither of them saw or heard the
other. Steve was in his dressing room too, on the second floor, but
Kerry has the room next to his and Kerry was on stage. So that leaves
Steve minus an alibi."

"Stop, Jeff, I'm dizzy."

"You and me too. And Peterson. He finally ended up with fifteen
suspects. And I'm adding another one for good measure."

"Who?"

"Greeley Morris."

"But he wasn't at the theater, Jeff!"

"Nobody saw him at the theater, you mean."

"But the doors were guarded!"

"Right. But the first chance I get I'm going to find out where and
how he spent the evening."

"It was quite an evening!"

I went to the table and poured another drink. The Scotch was beginning to tingle through my cold insides and fuzz over the sharp ache
behind my eyes. I shot some soda out of the siphon and stirred it noisily.

"Jeff, her back and arms. Eve's, I mean. What was it?"

"Burns."

"From long ago?"

"From very long ago. More than twenty years. A theater fire in Detroit."

"Are they … are they as terrible as they seemed to me?"

"Yes. Pretty awful."

"And yet no one knew?"

"No. Amelia told us. Eve had been such a beautiful woman. She could never reconcile herself to the fact that her neck and arms and back were ruined. Instead of getting over it or used to it she only became more sensitive as the years went on. She was still going to skin specialists, taking treatments all over the country. It was completely hopeless, but Eve never stopped hoping. She was going now to someone in Philadelphia, going twice a week. That's the mysterious errand she was on this morning."

"And that was why she took Carol's wrap?"

He nodded. "She must have leaned against that scenery, and then, realizing what she had done, whipped off her jacket to see the damage. There was a lot; the back of her jacket is thick with the stuff. I don't suppose she thought there would be time to get another wrap from her dressing room. She couldn't wear the jacket and she couldn't go on without something. Carol's cloak was there on the banister, almost beside her, and she must have thrown it on and stood there waiting for her cue. It was then that she got it, there in the wings where Carol would have been a moment later, in Carol's black wrap with the hood up over her head. It was a pretty easy mistake. They're about the same height, the same build."

I said, thinking back over all the times I had seen Eve North on the stage and off: "She always wore such high-necked dresses and long flowing sleeves. I thought it was an affectation and really …"

"Yes. She lived in dread of being discovered. I think Amelia was probably very right. Eve North would rather have been killed than stared at."

"Poor Eve," I said.

I hadn't heard any sound from the bedroom nor the opening of the door, and I almost leaped when my eyes fell on Carol standing quietly in the doorway bundled up in my terrycloth bathrobe.

"I can't sleep and it's worse in there alone. May I … do you think I could have another brandy?"

I was at the liquor cabinet pouring it for her when a soft sly pecking sounded at the door. Jeff turned sharply and we watched him with apprehension as he moved to open it. He had only pulled it a cautious inch before Jinx pushed his way in, closed and locked the door behind him and faced us, his eyes bulging.

"There's a man out in the hall!" he whispered.

"No!"

"Yes! He's been settin' on the steps for an hour. Should I call the cops?"

"Why?"

"I just read in the papers about the murder. This guy looks suspicious. He might be the one after Miss Blanton."

"Don't be silly, Jinx," I said.

"Awright, what's he settin' there for?"

"Have you spoken to him?"

"Not since I read about the murder. When he first come in I spoke to him. I asked him what he wanted. He said he wanted a little farm on Long Island."

"Is he drunk?" Jeff asked.

"Not so's I could notice, Mr. Troy."

"Did you ask him who he was?"

"He said he was Admiral Byrd. But he ain't, I seen pictures of Admiral Byrd."

"Jeff," I said, "you go talk to him."

"I don't want to talk to him."

"Please."

Jeff stepped into the hall and shouted, "Hey, you!"

Slow footsteps dragged down the corridor. Jeff leaned against the door jamb and waited. A short swarthy individual in a blue serge suit appeared opposite him.

"Yeah?" the individual said.

"Won't you come in and have a drink?"

"Jeff!" I said.

"It's okay, lady. I can't drink on duty."

"Duty?"

"Sure. Peterson sent me up to keep an eye on Miss Blanton."

We all turned to Carol. She attempted a smile. "Well, if you're going to keep an eye on me, shouldn't we meet?"

"My name's Lugotti."

"How do you do, Mr. Lugotti?"

"I'm terrible. How would you be if you'd been followin' people for twelve years?"

"It would depend on who you followed," Jeff said. "I'd feel swell if it was Madeleine Carroll. But awful if it was Jess Owens. He goes too fast!"

"Madeleine Carroll, that'd be nice. But that would never happen to me. You should see some of the characters I been assigned to. It's usually some politician with the jitters, or if it's a woman ... well, not only my feet take a beatin' but also my eyes."

"Your eyes won't take no beatin' from Miss Blanton!" Jinx said stoutly. We had forgotten he was there. I thanked him in behalf of Carol and suggested that he was now free to look after his elevator. He left reluctantly.

"The kid's right," Lugotti said. "I imagine I will have some competition. I bet a lot of guys follow Miss Blanton without gettin' paid for it." His leer at Carol was a work of art.

"Listen, Mr. Lugotti," I said. "I hope ..."

"Don't worry, lady."

"Don't call me lady!"

Jeff laughed. "It's just a figure of speech, Haila. You misunderstand Lugotti. He is probably married and has five or six children."

"No, I ain't married. I never get close enough to anybody to marry them. I spend my life fifty feet behind everyone."

"Are you going to watch me all the time?" Carol asked.

"I'll be takin' turns with Jimmy Rosen and Crowley. And listen, Miss Blanton, you could do Crowley a big favor when he's on duty. You could stay off busses. Busses make Crowley sick."

"Everywhere I go, I'm to be watched?"

"That's right, Miss Blanton."

Her voice rose shrilly. "Then tonight isn't the end! Mr. Peterson thinks they're going to keep on trying to kill me! Of course! Everybody knows it. They poisoned me and they tried to stab me and they won't stop now until ..."

I put my arm around her trembling shoulders and urged her toward the bedroom.

"It's all right," Lugotti said in what was supposed to be a soothing voice. "Nothing's goin' to happen to you with us around. But look. If I was you I'd stay right here in your apartment. I wouldn't go out at all."

"She won't," I assured him.

"And, Miss Blanton," he went on, "you can go to sleep now without worryin' at all. Because I promise you I won't go to sleep."

CHAPTER SEVEN

CAROL and I were on our second cup of coffee and Jeff well into his fourth when Peterson appeared that morning. Dangling from the corner of his mouth was an unlighted cigarette that looked as though it had hung there for the last twenty-four hours. His face was as tired and worn looking as the cigarette, but his voice was still a policeman's voice. Brusque, but comforting.

"How are you, Miss Blanton?"

"Still here."

"Atta kid!"

"Thank you for Lugotti. And Crowley and Rosen."

Peterson grinned. "You're welcome to them. You can have them for keeps. If Lugotti gets fresh, and he probably will, tell me."

"Do you think I need all that protection, Mr. Peterson? Don't you think that after last night they'll stop?"

"I wish I knew. But if it'll relieve your mind any, you aren't being trailed for your protection. Technically, it isn't our job to prevent crime, our job is to catch criminals. And that's what those mugs are doing primarily. Of course, they're going to take care of you, too. Now listen, Miss Blanton, I want you to go on living as if nothing had happened."

Carol was puzzled. "But Lugotti told me to stay in."

"He what? Why, that lazy flatfoot, I'll ... don't you listen to him, Miss Blanton."

"But I thought it was good advice."

"Wait till I see Lugotti! What he's trying to do is fix things so all he has to do is sit out there in the hall. He's arranging himself a little vacation."

I spoke up. "Mr. Peterson, you want to encourage another attack on Carol!" Peterson made deprecating sounds but I went on. "It's just inviting disaster for her to go out. You saw what happened last night! There must be some other way ..."

"Now, listen, Miss Rogers!" There was a noticeable lack of affection in his attitude toward me. "If you know a better way, tell me. This case is a stone wall. Even Miss Blanton can't help me. We have one clue, Lee Gray. And even on that she can't give us anything."

"But really, I don't ..." Carol began.

"You and I will discuss that later. And alone." He turned back to me. "Who knows if there'll be another attempt? If there is, it might be next Sunday or next year. Miss Blanton can't spend the rest of her life in hiding, can she? I don't say that anything will come of my boys tagging her. But if anyone behaves strangely, if somebody is too interested in her comings and goings, we'll know about it. Troy!"

"Yes. sir?"

"I don't mind you sticking your nose in this case. God knows we cops need all the help we can get. But I said help, not interference. If you know anything, or find out anything, you tell me. Quick."

"Of course."

"Yeah, but you won't. And you'll probably get hurt. But I'd be wasting my breath to warn you. Now, you take your girl for a walk. Miss Blanton and I want to be alone, don't we?"

Carol smiled and waved us away, but I thought I heard her catch her breath and saw her hands clench slightly as we closed the door.

At the corner of Fifty-fourth and Lexington Jeff stopped. "What do you think the chances are of Bowers being in his office now?"

"Fair."

"Then we'll go see him first."

"First? Does that mean you're going detecting?"

Without even smiling modestly he nodded and we headed for the office in silence. Under the bright cold day the pavements were rapidly drying and there was no vestige of last night's storm but the already black-jacketed piles of snow along the curb. I snuggled my chin deep into my collar and concentrated on keeping up with Jeff. We met Philip Ashley in front of the Colony Theater and the three of us turned down the alley together.

Inside the stuffy elevator I rummaged through my purse for my compact and lipstick. I would be stopping to powder my nose before venturing into a producer's office, I told myself ruefully, when I was ninety. If you were an actress you remembered to powder your nose even if in the last forty-eight hours you had had practically no sleep, very little food and a great deal too much drink; even if your roommate had twice been whizzed past sudden death and your leading lady brutally murdered ten feet from where you stood. A producer's office is a producer's office and it doesn't matter that you've got the job and played the part and it's over and done with. I snapped shut the enameled box and dropped it in my purse.

"It's fairly crass of me," Philip Ashley was saying, "to barge in on Clint at a time like this, I suppose, and to demand just what is what. But I thought it possible that he might want to close the show."

"Quite possible," Jeff said shortly.

Philip loosened the gay colored scarf that muffled his throat. "That's what I thought. Nevertheless, I have to know definitely in order to make my plans. I don't mind telling you that Hollywood's been after me for some time now. In fact, I had a good offer from Metro just last week. They'd snap me up in a second if they knew I were free. It would be a damn good thing, too. Get out to the coast while this thing blows over. You know," he added warningly to me, "this isn't going to do any of us any good. Bad publicity. Very bad."

We stepped into the reception hall that fronted the office. It was empty, Phoebe's desk unopened and the door marked "Clinton Bowers – Private" closed. I put my hand on the knob but I didn't turn it. In the office someone was speaking and there was something in her tone that made us stop abruptly and look at each other.

"Please, please, Mr. Bowers," Alice McDonald was saying. She might have been reading for a part and overacting badly. "Let me try it. Just let me try it! You must know what it would mean to me! Oh, you've got to let me, you've got to give me this chance!"

"I'm sorry, Alice." Clinton Bowers' voice was very patient and very weary. "I have decided definitely to close the play at once. There will not be another performance of *Green Apples*. That is final."

"But you don't have to close it," Alice said eagerly. "I can play Eve's part. It's the kind of a part I've always prayed for. I'll show you what I can do with it, I'll show everyone! You'll never regret it, Mr. Bowers, I promise you."

"I'm sorry, Alice. No."

"But I'm up in it. I'm letter perfect. There wouldn't have to be a single rehearsal for me. I could go through it this minute."

"No."

Anyone but the stage-crazed, thwarted girl that Alice was could have told he meant it. She said, "But, I …"

"This play is closing. No one is going to follow in the part that Eve North created here."

"Created!" Her voice exploded loud and scornfully. "Created! If you call mangling one of the most beautiful parts ever written creating! If you call babbling through it with a lot of tricks and phony mannerisms creating! No one's going to follow in her part, you'll see to that, won't you? Yes, you'll see to it all right and I know why, Mr. Clinton Bowers! Because any decent actress who followed in the part would show Eve North up too badly, wouldn't she? She'd show what a stinking sloppy mess she made of it! She'd show that your great Eve North was nothing but a ham, she's …"

"Alice!" His voice wasn't patient now; it was cold and threatening. "Get out of my office, Alice. Get out!"

His door swung open and we tried to look as though we were wending an uninterrupted way to the office, but I don't think Alice even saw us. She dashed straight into the elevator and the door slid quickly past her pale furious face.

Bowers hadn't risen from his desk. He sat hunched over the disorderly mass of papers, his head bowed in his hands. When he lifted his face to us, I was shocked at its gray haggardness. Philip coughed a forced, stagy cough.

"We … we couldn't help overhearing, Clint. *Green Apples* is closing, then?"

Bowers nodded. "Yes. Definitely."

"Then … I suppose it will be all right for me to accept any offer that might come my way? I'm considering Hollywood."

"It'll be all right so far as I'm concerned. The police, however …"

Ashley smiled with a sort of grave amusement. "I hardly think there will be any difficulty there. After all, my long record on the American stage …"

"Your long record on the American stage!" I repeated indignantly. His calm assurance made me sick at my stomach. "What's that got to do with whether or not you tried to kill Carol?"

"Relax, Haila." Jeff put his hand on my shoulder.

"It's quite all right," Ashley said, oozing with patronage. "We're all horribly upset and overwrought. It's been a frightful experience, this … this …"

"This murder," Bowers said quietly.

We had all been chanting "Murder" for the past twenty-four hours. It had become the prime word in our vocabularies and had almost lost any connotation. But when Bowers said it now, so quietly and bluntly, it found its place again, and Eve's horrible dead body and Carol's scared white face were with us in the room.

Jeff moved uneasily. "I'm afraid I didn't exactly live up to my recommendation of myself."

"No," Bowers said. "You couldn't help it. Don't blame yourself, Jeff. I asked you to watch Carol."

"I might have watched … a little further."

"You couldn't know that Eve would pick up Carol's cape and stand there, where in a minute Carol would be standing, looking like Carol. …"

"Madness," Ashley said.

"Eve didn't think. She needed something to cover her scars, and she took the first thing she could find. She didn't think about murder; she thought about her entrance. Eve was like that. No, Jeff, there was nothing anybody could have done."

"Darling, you did your best," I said. "Clint knows that. Why, even Peterson couldn't prevent it."

"My responsibility was greater than his. He was doing a job that had been assigned. It was routine for him. I was trying to do a job that I'd made for myself. And I failed." He stopped and took a deep breath.

"Well, the point is, I'm going on. And you can forget that money was ever mentioned yesterday, Clint."

Bowers looked at him for a long moment. "We won't forget anything, Jeff. Since last night … since Eve …" He swung his chair around so that his face was turned from us.

No one spoke. It was as though all of us were searching our minds for the right thing to say and there was no right thing. At last Philip coughed again and stood up.

"It's a beastly business. I wish there were something I could do. I know there isn't. Just … if ever you have anything for me again, Clint, I'd consider it a privilege to play for you."

"If ever I produce again."

"But of course you will! And soon, old man, very soon." Philip patted him on the shoulder.

"Without Eve? I haven't produced a play in five years without Eve. No play comes into this office except some agent thinks there is an Eve North part in it." He wasn't talking to us; he was thinking out loud. "I've built every production around her. Everyone in the cast a contrast to her. Every set a background for her. I … I wouldn't know how to go about producing without Eve."

He stopped and his eyes, soft and sad, turned bitter. He stared unseeingly at the sheaf of papers on his desk. We made mumbled exits that Bowers scarcely noticed.

I walked between Jeff and Ashley up to Broadway, breathing the crisp air gustily as though I might expel with it the tragic atmosphere of that office over the Colony. Philip was going on again at greater length to explain how Eve's murder was inconveniencing him personally. At Times Square a delivery truck pulled up to a kiosk and dumped a bundle of papers. I slipped away and bought one to see what was being said about the case. Jeff flicked the front section from me. I turned to the theatrical pages while Philip droned away, seemingly unaware of our lack of attention.

In the notes of coming productions I saw something that made me gulp in astonishment, and it was a minute before I could collect enough breath to speak.

"Jeff! Jeff, listen to this! 'For his next production, *Though Heavens Fall*, Vincent Parker has engaged Morgan Thomsand, Marge Flint and … and *Lee Gray!*' "

Jeff ripped the paper from my hand. I pointed to the item and he read it aloud as if he expected the name, if it had been there at all, to be gone by now. "… Morgan Thomsand, Marge Flint and Lee Gray. Haila, who is Vincent Parker? Does he have an office? Where is it?"

"It's in Radio City. I know him."

"C'mon," Jeff said, "let's get moving."

"Just a second." Ashley put his hand on Jeff's arm. "Are you ... are you going to Parker's office now? Immediately?"

"Sooner than that. C'mon, Ashley, walk up with us."

"No, thanks. I wouldn't be seen in Parker's office. I couldn't afford to. Besides, I've a terribly important appointment downtown."

"Wall Street, no doubt," I said maliciously.

"As a matter of fact, it is Wall Street. Taxi!"

Ashley stepped into his cab and I had to run to catch up with Jeff who was halfway across Broadway by that time.

On Sixth Avenue he didn't even stop, as he usually did, to make sure the khaki colored men digging the new subway were getting along all right. Breathless, I grabbed his arm and pulled myself abreast of him. "Jeff ..."

Jeff snorted and two middle-aged women gaped at me. Automatically, I still raised my voice to a shriek on Sixth Avenue to combat the roar of the El trains that were no longer extant.

I tried again, in a softer tone, "Jeff, shouldn't Peterson know about this?"

"He probably does. Save your air. We should've taken a cab."

"What's the rush? Parker won't forget who and where Lee Gray is before we get there."

At Radio City we took one of those rocket ships they call express elevators and I answered the operator's questioning look. "Sixty-two." He punched the button with a flip of his knuckle and leaned back against the wall, waiting for the car to fill. When he had become convinced that no one would ride in the same elevator with Jeff and me, he took off for the sixty-second floor.

The doors slid open and we stepped out. Jeff started to say something, then stopped. I glanced in the direction he was staring. Backing slowly into the next car, while the crowd settled in the rear, was Philip Ashley. The doors closed. It was impossible for Ashley not to have seen us, but his eyes gave no flicker of recognition. His face was deadpan.

"Well," I said, "so this is Wall Street."

"Yeah."

"But why should he do that?"

"Maybe he wanted to find out about Lee Gray before we did. We'll see."

Parker's secretary announced me over the telephone without first asking my name. That made me feel fine and smug. That girl and her colleagues had almost nipped my theatrical career in the bud until one day I had managed to slip past her, and Vincent Parker had given me my first part in New York.

Mr. Parker would see me in a few minutes. In answer to Jeff's question, the secretary told him that Philip Ashley had not been in to see Parker within the last few minutes or, as far as she knew, ever. Jeff sat down beside me.

"Haila," he said, "let me do the talking about L.G."

Vincent Parker opened his door and beckoned to me. He looked like five and a half feet of rainbow with his dark blue shirt, yellow knitted tie, brown tweed suit and very conservative battleship gray spats. His face split in a grin that shook his ears. When Jeff followed me into the office he flattered me by looking disappointed that I wasn't alone.

"She's my girl," Jeff explained. "I never leave her alone with strange men."

"If you think I'm strange you oughta see my brother!" Parker said. When he had stopped laughing I introduced Jeff to him and we seated ourselves, Parker behind his huge, streamlined desk, Jeff and I on a luxurious divan that Vincent must have bought secondhand from some insolvent Caliph. It took me a while to figure out that what was missing from the room was a pair of Ethiops standing in back of Parker and fanning him with purple palm trees.

"Nicely appointed chamber," Jeff said. He had nearly broken my neck to get us up here and now he was being the suave, casual Philo Vance type. "Who decorated your office? Billy Rose?"

"Billy Rose? Naw. Great little fellow, though. I knew Billy when he was shorthand champion of the world. Billy thinks a lot of me and I've always admired him, too."

"I understand you're going to do a play, Mr. Parker," I said, trying to get Jeff to the point.

"When you call me Mr. Parker, Haila, I don't know to who you are referring. The first name is Vincent. It ain't as if we were mere acquaintances. I give you your start on Broadway. Tell me if I'm wrong."

"You're right, Vincent."

"May I call you Vincent, too?" Jeff asked. He pulled a cigarette out of his pack.

"Any friend of Haila's is a friend of mine, Jeff. Maybe you'd be interested in trading that cigarette in for a cigar. Right there in that humidor. How do you like that humidor? Seventy-five dollars. You don't see a humidor like that every day. It's imported. From abroad."

"Vincent," I blurted, "who is Lee Gray? What is she, where is she?"

Parker beamed. "You want to know, too, huh?"

"Too!" Jeff barked. "Who else has been asking?"

"The cops. One of the drama-page boys on the *Post* tipped them off when he seen my press release. I figured it would raise plenty of comment."

"Well, who is Lee Gray?"

"Frankly, Haila, I don't know."

"You don't know!"

"That is, I don't know yet, Haila."

"But you've been in touch with her," Jeff said.

"Frankly, Jeff, I ain't."

"Do you know anything about her? Anything at all?"

"Frankly, between friends, like I told the cops, no."

"But what the hell!" Jeff shouted. "You announced her for your cast!"

"That was one of the cleverest strokes of genius I ever committed! Lee's name is on the lips of New York, the lips of the country! We'll pack them in! My show will clean up! Don't you get the angle?"

"But, Parker," Jeff said desperately, "you must know *how* to get in touch with her!"

"I wish I did. If you should find out anything about her, will you let me know immediately?"

I leaned back on the sofa. I felt like crying. But I should have known. I knew Vincent Parker. Jeff was regarding him with amazement mingled with distaste. "I still don't get it. You put Lee Gray's name in the papers. What did you expect? Why?"

"She ain't in no other show, is she? So she needs a job! Okay. When she sees I hired her, ain't she gonna be elated and come to see me?"

"Then you're taking it for granted that Lee Gray is an actress?"

Obviously no other possibility had occurred to him, but that only stopped him for a second. "If she ain't an actress all I got to do is talk to her in a persuasive manner. Who don't want to be an actress? Is there someone?"

Jeff gave up. He went to Parker and extended his hand. "Vince, let me shake with you. You're right, you are a genius."

Parker clasped Jeff's hand warmly. "I appreciate that, Jeff, coming from you. You didn't tell me, Jeff, what line you're in."

"My line is – I'm in advertising. But right now I'm on my vacation."

"Advertising, huh?" Parker made a note. "Who you with? I'll talk to one of my friends there and get you put in a better spot."

Jeff managed not to laugh. "C'mon, Haila, we'll be going."

"You ain't detaining me," Vincent said. He turned to me. "Haila, I'm glad you dropped in, maybe you can tell me. I'm thinking of Carol

Blanton for the part of the girl in my show. I seen her in *Green Apples* and she was good. But what I want to know is this: Was her performance indicative of her talent? I mean, was it typical?"

"I'd call it typically indicative," Jeff said.

I frowned at him. This would mean at least two weeks' rehearsal money for Carol even if the play flopped, as Vincent's usually did, and it would be an opportunity for her to be seen in another part.

"Carol is a fine actress," I assured Parker. "And that isn't sentiment."

"I figured she might be. But I wanted to be sure that the part she played in Bowers' show wasn't just her dish. Know what I mean? That she ain't just a one-part actress."

"Oh, no, Vincent. Carol has a wonderful sense of character."

"Sure," Jeff put in. "She's got everything. Especially a voice. It gets me. It's exciting."

"I'd like to have her read for me."

"There's just one thing about her, Vincent, and that's it," I said. "She gives a terrible first reading."

"Professional jealousy!" Jeff jeered.

"Don't be silly, Jeff."

"Were you there when she first read for Bowers?"

"No, but one night some agent sent a couple of scripts over to the apartment and Carol and I read them to each other. She's really pretty bad, reads a part as though it were a timetable. She admits it herself and worries a lot about it. I just told Vincent because I don't want him to judge her by her first reading. She works into a part beautifully."

Parker looked mortally wounded. "Haila, have you ever known me to misjudge talent? Ain't that always been one of my fortes?"

"That must be one of Clint's fortes, too," Jeff said, "if he cast Carol despite her reading."

"Uh-huh, Clint and Vincent are both famous for their casting ability. Aren't you, Vincent?"

He smiled modestly. "The only difference between Bowers and me is that I got showmanship. For instance, not only do I want Carol Blanton because she is perfect for the part, but with all her publicity about the poisoning and murder, we'll pack them in! With her *and* Lee Gray it can't miss."

"What!" I felt a little sickish. "Vincent, you're not going to exploit Carol's ... murder publicity?"

"That's showmanship! It'll be a cleanup!"

"But, Vincent, Carol won't stand for it!"

"When she reads the script ... if she's an artist ... Look, let me tell you about the script! *Though Heavens Fall*. That's the title. The kid that wrote it is a genius. It's his first play. He's only twenty-one years of age, ain't never even voted. His grandmother is a millionaire. She's backing me to the hilt. I predict that *Though Heavens Fall* will revolutionize dramatic writing. It's in five acts."

"People are used to three acts," Jeff said. "They might leave after the third."

"Not a chance! This show is gripping! It grips you. It's the story of a violinist that loses an arm fighting for free speech. He can't play the fiddle any more, even if he felt like it. He gets bitter and joins the Communistic Party. He sells his only Stradivarius and donates the money to the Reds so they can stage a demonstration. His father is killed in the demonstration. His mother never wants to see him again."

"The father?" Jeff asked.

"The son. The two of them have a terrific scene in which the mother says, 'I never want to see you again.' His girl's going to have a baby and he thinks the only reason she don't throw him over is because of the baby, since they ain't married. That's how bitter he is. See? There's a beautiful scene in Central Park. In fact, the entire action of the play takes place in Central Park."

"It sounds wonderful, Parker, revolutionary," Jeff said.

"And that's only the first act!"

"Don't tell me how it ends, you'll spoil it for me."

"Okay, Jeff. What do you think, Haila?"

"I still don't think Carol will let you ..."

"Now, wait a minute, Haila! She needs a job, don't she? Bowers has closed his show, ain't he?" Parker shook his head sadly. "The chance of a lifetime falls in his lap smack, and he closes. With all the publicity, he could run a year and make a million. Don't misunderstand me. Clint is a prince among men, but he ain't a showman. There's very few of us left any more."

"I doubt, Vincent, if even you would have the showmanship to make a million out of the murder of one of your dearest friends."

"Haila, you know there ain't no place for sentiment in show business. That's why Bowers slipped. Eve North was washed up years ago and Bowers he never seen it. His eyes were blinded with the sand of sentiment. When Eve had the appeal of youth she was a box office attraction, a draw. But when she lost her youth – and who don't, I ain't criticizing Eve – she didn't have nothing left. She was never an actress; she was to look at. Bowers never seen that Eve was through, and that's what ruined him."

"Ruined? You talk as if he's living in the poorhouse," Jeff said.

"Remember his address is still Gracie Square."

"Vincent means ruined artistically," I explained.

Parker shook his head. "I mean Bowers don't have a nickel to rub against."

I stared at him, thinking of Clint's lavish productions, his cars, his apartments, his clothes. Everything about him murmured affluence. I said incredulously, "You mean Clint Bowers is broke!"

"In little pieces. He's in debt past his ears."

"But he has the reputation of being a wonderful businessman."

"It takes one hell of a wonderful businessman to keep on producing shows and living at Gracie Square when you're flat. Personally, I don't care for Gracie Square. It ain't business acumen that ruined Bowers. It's like I said, sentiment and no showmanship."

"It's a strange combination," Jeff said. "The shrewd businessman and the sentimentalist."

Parker shrugged his shoulders. "Even J.P. Morgan got married."

"It's tough," Jeff said. "*Green Apples* would have been a hit and saved Bowers."

"Sure, it was his comeback. That's what I told him when I seen him Sunday night after the invitation performance. All the show needed was a third act twist to be a smash. And I had a wow of a twist for him. I walked all the way up Lexington with him and the kid he's got stage managing for him ..."

"Tommy Neilson."

"Yeah. I tried to give Bowers my idea, not sell it to him. But he wouldn't see it. I finally give up when we got to Zollers and went in and had a drink. I even offered to buy him one, but he refused – the kid, too. No wonder Bowers is all washed up. In show business you got to be receptive. Now look at me ..."

Jeff motioned to me and we started edging toward the door. Only after Parker had thrust a copy of *Though Heavens Fall* under my arm and extracted my promise to read it and talk to Carol about it did we manage to escape.

When I reached for the Down button Jeff said, "Wait!" He led me over to the board that listed the tenants on Radio City's sixty-second floor.

"If Ashley didn't sneak up here to see Parker," he mused, "who did he see?" He began reading down the list. "The Grayson Company, Lithography. Ernest Horowitz, Attorney-at-law. Leather Novelties. Lincoln Photographic Supplies."

I took over. "Mallon Sporting Goods. Madame Mantillini, *Corsetière*. Wendell Drug Company. And Zenith Displays. Well, Jeff?"

"Hmmm. I better get myself a notebook."

"He might've been to any of three or four of those places."

"Or all of them. Maybe he was passing out calendars with his picture on them. And then again," he added, trying to sound like Ellery Queen, "maybe he wasn't."

CHAPTER EIGHT

THE big brownstone building with its neat half-curtains in the windows, the inevitable sign of a female establishment, looked somber and quiet as we climbed the steps. Halfway up Jeff stopped and looked at me with a puzzled frown.

"Is this the Rehearsal Club? *The* Rehearsal Club?"

"Yes. It isn't swank, it's economical."

"Oh." I reached for the bell and Jeff touched me on the arm. "But why does Alice live here?"

"Where do you think she should live, Jeff?"

"I mean hasn't she any family?"

"No. She's all there is of the McDonalds, there isn't any more. And like real troupers, they died broke."

"That's tough."

"Sure, but don't you go loaning Alice any money." I pushed the bell and in a moment a maid answered the door, then went to fetch Miss McDonald while Jeff and I waited in the hall. A little blonde ingenue whom I had never seen on the stage but often in the Penn Astor drugstore flitted past. She said hello to me with her eyes on Jeff.

"Guess I look all right today, don't I, Haila?" Jeff said.

He watched Blondie go up the stairs. At the top she passed Alice who came shuffling down in a pair of old fuzzy bedroom slippers that threatened to fall off at every step. She wore a pale yellow smock that covered all but a few inches of a dirty tweed skirt and there was a brown-backed manuscript under her arm. She was holding the place with one finger. Alice was always reading the works of weird young dramatists who wrote plays about the Bronx in blank verse. She stopped on the landing.

"What do you want?" Her voice was chilly.

Jeff beamed at her. "I'm *Detective* Troy now, you know, Alice, and I'd like to ask you a few questions. No third degree stuff, just some nice friendly little questions."

"I must finish this script. The author wants my opinion on it as soon as possible."

"Mr. Bowers told me he was sure everyone in the cast would cooperate with me. Let's sit down and have a cigarette."

"I don't smoke." She didn't budge from the landing.

"I wanted to talk to you this morning when we met in Bowers' office, but you seemed in a hurry."

She looked at him sharply and her teeth bit into her pale lip. "Oh! You … you overheard me then. You know what I told him and what he said to me. I thought you had." She stopped and then went on again defiantly. "I don't care though. It doesn't matter to me what eavesdroppers think."

"If you don't like people to overhear you, Alice, you should keep your voice down to a shout."

"And you think it was ruthless of me, don't you? Maybe it was. But I could play Eve North's part, I could play it beautifully." She faced him squarely, daring him to contradict her. "That play doesn't have to close because of her. She wasn't a good actress, she never was. I've watched her for years and she was a phony clear through. I saw her in the play my father was doing when he died. It was *King Lear* and she played Cordelia. She was young then, and beautiful, that's why my father engaged her. But even back then she wasn't good. My father knew it, everyone did! And she never got any better. But look! They're taking *Green Apples* off the boards because of her! That shouldn't happen, I tell you! *Green Apples* shouldn't be closing because a second-rate actress like Eve North was killed by mistake."

"You can't blame Bowers for not wanting to go on."

"I'll never act for him again, never!" Jeff opened his mouth to speak but took a drag of smoke instead. Alice's lips twisted into a thin smile. "You were going to say that I never did act for him, weren't you?"

"You almost did. That was a bad break you got opening night, Carol's voice coming back like that. Funny thing, laryngitis."

"Laryngitis couldn't make much difference to Blanton's voice."

I had rather liked Alice until she made that crack, at least I had been sorry for her. My resentment must have shown for she turned away from me, excluding me from the conversation.

Jeff said, "I think Carol has a swell voice. It's sexy."

"That part shouldn't be sexy. It's a girl who's in love for the first time, and the last. She should be timid about love, it's delicate and beautiful to her and …" She concluded her character analysis abruptly. "It was horribly miscast. I could have made something of that part."

Jeff smiled. "You're sore because Bowers wouldn't let you play all the parts. You're not Cornelia Otis Skinner."

I smothered a chortle but Alice didn't move a muscle. I was afraid she was about to gouge Jeff's eyes out. "I was promised that part," she said.

"What!" I squeaked. This was one conversation I was enjoying being safely out of, but this was too much news for me.

"Yes. I read for Bowers and he liked me. I was to sign the contract the day that Blanton walked in and swept him off his feet. With her sexy voice."

"Okay, Alice, you are Cornelia," Jeff said, laughing. "You could do anything in the show."

"Evidently Bowers thought so or he wouldn't have engaged me as general understudy."

"Quite a coincidence that you should almost get to play Carol's part after all. You would have if you hadn't left the theater just before curtain time. That was a foolish thing to do, Alice."

Jeff's invitation to confidence was so obvious that I blinked and even Alice looked at him with contempt. Her mouth settled in a straight line.

"What did you want to ask me, Mr. Troy?"

"Oh, just a few routine questions," Jeff said airily. "Can't we sit down somewhere? I'm much better at this sort of thing sitting down."

Taciturnly, she stepped down from the landing and led us across the hall and into an adjoining room where she sat straight-backed on a piano stool, her eyes on the wall opposite her. With a sigh of bored resignation she said, "All right. Play detective, Mr. Troy."

Jeff smiled with difficulty. "Where were you, Alice, when Eve North was stabbed last night?"

"I've told the police at least a hundred times. Must you ask stupid questions like that?"

"Sorry. I must."

Alice sighed again and started reciting. "I was in the extra dressing room on the third floor. I was reading a script and my door was closed and the first thing I heard was Haila shrieking bloody murder. I opened the door then, went out on the stairs and looked down. There was such a crowd by that time I couldn't see what had happened. Then someone stepped back, Mr. Peterson I think, and I saw Eve's body. That's all I saw or heard or know. Satisfied?"

"Not quite. Do you know anything about this Lee Gray?"

"Mr. Peterson's little Sir Echo, aren't you?" she taunted. "No, I don't. Until Peterson asked me I'd never heard the name. Apparently nobody else has either. I'm beginning to doubt that there is such a person." She laughed suddenly. "This is a productive interview, isn't it? Is that all? May I go now?"

"No, there's one thing more. Why did you rush out of the theater on opening night?"

The laughter died in her face. "That's none of your business."

"I think it is. It might be very important to know why you would throw up a chance you'd waited years for at the very last minute. Why did you do it, Alice?"

"I tell you it doesn't concern you. It wasn't anything at all." She turned to me. "If you and Tommy hadn't got hysterical it would have been all right. I was back in plenty of time."

"You should have told Tommy that you were going."

"He ... he wouldn't have let me go," she mumbled.

Jeff said, "I think you had better come clean, Alice. It will help in the long run. The police aren't very sympathetic toward people who keep secrets."

She stood up, her back to us, and slid the palm of her hand discordantly over the piano keys. "The police don't know about that. Tommy won't tell them. And unless you or Haila ..."

"Haila wouldn't tell on you," Jeff said. "But I would."

She turned and her eyes went to Jeff's face and then, uncertainly, to mine. She opened her mouth and closed it. At last she said: "No, it's none of your damn business why I did it. It's important only to me. I don't know who poisoned Carol Blanton, though God knows there ought to be plenty of people who'd like to. A little parasite who uses the theater as a stepping stone, who cares nothing about it ..."

I was tired of hearing Carol kicked around. "Carol loves the theater and she loves to act. You've got her all wrong, Alice."

"Have I? What about Tommy Neilson?"

Jeff looked at me questioningly. I shrugged my shoulders. "Alice will have to tell us what about Tommy Neilson. I don't know."

"Don't be naive," Alice snorted. "Tommy is eating his heart out for Blanton and she's stringing him along, playing him for all he's got."

I almost laughed aloud at her accusation. "That isn't true, Alice, it's absurd. When a girl goes out gold digging she doesn't pick one of the poorest people in all New York. And poor Tommy doesn't have a thing."

"That's what makes it so horrible. I suppose you think she's capable of loving him for himself."

"Loving Tommy!" I did laugh then. "Why, Alice, she hardly knows him. He's no more to her than Philip Ashley or Clint Bowers or Nick, the doorman."

"Alice, tell me something," Jeff said quietly. "Are you and Tommy ... are you just real good friends?"

"I should have known you'd think that! No. We like each other;

we understand each other. Tom's a real person; he's going to mean something to the theater one of these days. That's why I hate to see him thrown around by a scheming little parasite like Blanton, a cheap little ..."

"Alice, you're going to make me think that you hate Carol, and hate, you know, leads to murder. Hate and jealousy. You can't prove that you didn't poison Carol and murder Eve, just like a lot of other people can't, so if I were you I wouldn't talk this way."

Alice clenched her fists, her face deathly pale. "I'm not jealous of her and I don't hate her. I wouldn't take the chance of ruining my life by killing her. She isn't worth it. Now please leave me alone."

She almost ran from the room. We could hear her stumbling up the stairs and a second later a door slammed above us. I looked at Jeff.

"C'mon," he said. "There might be some fresh air outside."

There was too much. The wind, zipping viciously down Fifty-third Street, caught me with my hands up and a taxi driver stopped his cab to watch me collect my skirts. Jeff strode up to the grinning moron.

I shouted: "No, Jeff! Don't make a scene!"

"You made the scene," Jeff flung over his shoulder as he gave the driver Tommy Neilson's address, the Hotel Bristol.

"Are you under the impression that you're tracking down the criminal?" I asked sweetly when we had got under way.

"I'm anxious to see the expression on your face when I solve this thing," Jeff growled.

"When that happens my face will have gone to claim its just reward."

"Look. I admit I didn't find out why Alice left the theater, but I did all right at that. The girl poured out her heart and soul to me."

"She poured out a lot of nonsense. I don't believe that Bowers ever promised her Carol's part, and as for the stuff about Tommy! He took Carol to lunch once or twice, he knew she was broke, and brought her home a few times, but that's all there was to it."

"We'll see what Tommy has to say," Jeff said.

But we didn't. Tommy was out. From the Bristol Jeff called Greeley Morris, but Mr. Morris, according to the operator at the Gotham, was not to be disturbed. Back in the cab Jeff directed the driver to the Alexandria.

"Next on our list, Amelia."

"But Jeff, why of all people, Amelia?"

"Why not?"

"All right, she might have poisoned Carol. But she never would have mistaken Eve for Carol no matter what Eve was wearing. She's been with Eve for a century. Why, it's just preposterous that Amelia … Jeff, surely you don't think she could have done it?"

"I don't know who did it. But Amelia's been around the theater all the time. Eve didn't keep her busy, she had nothing much to do. She sat around and listened and watched. You've told me that. You've called her the Sphinx with the seeing eye. She might be able to tell me something. She might have a clue, a clue deluxe, with tinsel, and not even know it."

We pulled up in front of the Alexandria. In the lobby Jeff pointed out with great pride the clerk who had been so helpful on his previous visit.

Amelia opened the door and when I saw her I was sorry I had let Jeff come. It would be cruel to bother her with questions and pryings. It would be completely heartless. Her dark ugly face was filled with grief, her eyes swollen with crying. The old bulwark of strength and capability that had been Amelia was gone and in its place was a tearstained tired woman. She showed no surprise at seeing us. Probably there had been a hundred others barging in before us. In the center of the room I saw a wardrobe trunk half packed and one of Eve's long flowing negligees was crumpled over Amelia's arm.

Jeff said very gently, "Could we talk to you for a little while, Amelia?"

"Yes." She indicated chairs for us and stood watching us with a weary patience.

"We want you to help us if you can."

"Yes."

"If we can find the person who tried to kill Carol Blanton, we'll know who killed Miss North. You understand that, don't you, Amelia? And we think you can help us if you'll try. You've been around the theater a lot, at rehearsals and performances. You might have noticed something that none of the others did."

She watched Jeff intently, her lips moving with his in silent repetition. "I'm always around the theater when Miss North is playing. I took care of her. All the time I took care of her."

"I know you did, Amelia. You were doing something for her that first night when the poison was put in Carol Blanton's glass, weren't you? Between the second and third acts, do you remember?"

Her head bobbed slowly up and down. "I was putting on water for her tea. She always liked a cup of tea between the acts. She didn't have an entrance until late in the third act so I was taking my time."

"When you crossed the stage to the kitchen that night, Amelia, did you see anyone?"

"Lots of people. Almost all the crew were there working."

"Anyone else?"

"Miss Thompson. She was setting the table."

Jeff's hopeful face took a tumble. "Oh. Then you crossed before the dirty work was done. And what then?"

"I made the tea and in a minute or two Miss Thompson came in. Then I went back up to Miss North's dressing room with the teapot."

"Was anyone on stage when you recrossed it?"

"I didn't go through the set, I went behind it. I didn't see anyone, nobody at all."

"And last night you were in the kitchen again when Miss North was stabbed, when Haila screamed."

"I was just coming out. I was crossing backstage when she started screaming. Mr. Bowers saw me, he was sitting there. He jumped up when the scream came and ran right past me. I know he saw me."

"Yes, Amelia, he said he did." Jeff leaned forward and said earnestly: "Amelia, haven't you ever noticed anything strange in connection with Miss Blanton? Anything at all? Did anyone seem to be watching her a lot or following her around? Did …"

She wasn't listening. Her unfocused eyes drifted around the room as she said in a monotone: "When I got back they were all around her, looking at her poor back. Nobody saw that but me. I was her nurse in the hospital after it happened. In the hospital in Detroit. I left off nursing to stay with Miss Eve. I've always been with her since then, every day. Miss Eve paid me, I worked for her. But I was her friend. Maybe I was her only friend. She knew lots of people but they weren't her friends. She didn't go to parties. And she didn't give them. Not like other actresses always running around. She didn't like men, she didn't want them near her. They made her remember that she wasn't beautiful all over, that her back was all burned. I was her only friend."

"What about Mr. Bowers, Amelia?"

She looked at him dully and Jeff repeated his question. Amelia shook her head. "Mr. Bowers was her manager. Every star has her manager. That's the way it is in the theater. An actress like Miss Eve can't be bothered with business. Mr. Bowers was good to her, she wouldn't act for anybody but him. He would never ask her to wear a dress that showed her back. He would change a whole play just so she wouldn't have to."

"Then he knew about her accident?" I asked.

She hadn't heard me. "She'd only act for Mr. Bowers. He was good to her. He could understand what it meant for a beautiful woman to be partly ugly. Sometimes I thought Miss Eve wanted me to be around her all the time because I'm ugly."

Jeff tried to swing the conversation back to Carol. "Amelia, did Miss North ever seem frightened of anyone? Did she seem to avoid any one person in the company?"

"I remember when they brought her to the hospital, so beautiful and so horrible then. It was the only time I ever cried when I was a nurse. I made the doctors keep it a secret about her scars. And when she left the hospital, I went with her."

"Amelia," Jeff said.

"I never even left her for more than I could help it. And then it was to do something for her. She didn't want me to be away long. I think she was always afraid, afraid that someone would find out. Now she's all alone in a funeral parlor. They're taking her to Michigan to bury her. To Minden City, Michigan. She doesn't know anyone there, she was born there, that's all. I remember the day when they brought her into the hospital. I was a nurse ..."

I touched Jeff's arm and we slipped out. As I closed the door behind us I could see Amelia folding the burnt orange negligee over a trunk hanger.

Last night there had been horror and tragedy, but it was garish and fantastic. This aftermath was real, heartbreakingly real. I almost ran out of the building, away from that bleak place where Eve North had lived and where now a tired old woman was putting Eve's house in order.

CHAPTER NINE

THE thought of facing the devastation of England's leading man of letters had left me weak. Secretly I was praying that Mr. Greeley Morris was still not to be disturbed. The desk clerk squashed my hopes, however. After a brief bit of phone-play, he announced brightly that Mr. Morris would see us. I followed Jeff unwillingly into the elevator.

"But why do we have to see him, Jeff? I don't want to."

"Just a social call. Hands across the sea."

"Well, why do I have to go?"

"You strike the social note. I, the sleuth, will hide behind your charm."

"But it's so useless! You know that he'll just ..."

"Shhh! The operator may be in his pay. Twelve, operator!"

We stood outside the door numbered 1211–3 and I started to grope nervously in my bag for a cigarette. Jeff shook his head at me. The door opened and Greeley Morris blinked in our faces. He was still in his pajamas.

"Good afternoon, Mr. Morris!" Jeff's accent on the good was terrific.

The playwright looked at us for seconds while I grew crimson and small. When he had finally reduced me to something that must have looked like a scarlet pygmy, he said, smiling with just his lips: "Do come in. It's so very nice to see you."

Trying to act as if I hadn't noticed that he was in his pajamas, which was a slightly difficult task, I followed Morris into the room.

Jeff said blithely, "I'm sorry we had to intrude like this."

"I'm sure that you had no alternative. Do you mind if I clean my teeth?" He disappeared into the bathroom. I was about to bolt. I must have shown it, for Jeff plunked me into a chair and stood over me.

"This will be over before you know it. I just want to find out what kind of a guy he really is."

"He doesn't look like a murderer in his pajamas. Jeff, do you have a pair like that?"

"Where would I get a pair like that? They probably cost nine pounds, ten and a half. With only one pair of pants."

"Are you going to be embarrassed when Morris asks you what the devil you want?"

"I want his autograph." Jeff was leafing through a large flat book that he had found on a corner table. On the third page he began to roar. "A scrapbook! And here's another one! Haila, there must be seven of them. Greeley Morris, the world's number one Sophisticate, keeps scrapbooks! They must go all the way back to a nursery rhyme he said in kindergarten."

Jeff was still chuckling, but he had managed to replace the books and move away from the table before our host returned. His dressing gown made me gasp; in fact, all his clothes had me wishing that I were a man.

After he had called room service and ordered a pot of coffee, he lit one of his long peculiar looking cigarettes and turned to Jeff with a question in his eyes. The telephone buzzed. Morris answered it and it was evidently an interview. His civility amazed me.

"You want to know how I like America? A very alive place, very. Even the people seem alive ... lovely women, beautiful. When I see a homely one I turn and stare. In England when a man sees a beautiful woman he is so startled he marries her. Marriage is all right, of course, but it has a tendency to increase the population. ... Oh, but yes, I love children ... when they're grown up. ... I was a boy once and I hated it. My first ambition was to have gray hair. Now my ambition is to have hair. Of course ... I'm delighted that you called. I've been lonely, terribly lonely ... that's because I haven't had a moment alone."

He hung up and Jeff prepared for an attack. But again the phone rang, nipping it in the bud. This time it was a girl named Gladys, and Morris chatted quite amiably with her, or more specifically, at her. Gladys didn't get many words in, even edgewise. The waiter came in with the coffee and Morris described him in minute detail to Gladys while he fluttered around waiting for his tip. At last, red-faced and wild-eyed, he fled, leaving Morris in gales of laughter. A moment after he had hung up Gladys called again. She wanted to know why Morris had phoned her. A ten-minute debate on who called whom followed.

It was over at last and Morris poured his coffee. He seemed vaguely surprised that Jeff and I were still there. "Well?" He smiled ironically. "Why did I want to kill Miss Blanton? Why did I stab Miss North? It's only fair, you know, that I be kept well informed."

Jeff thumbed through a sheaf of clippings. I could see they were reviews of *Green Apples*. Morris crossed his legs, lit another cigarette and waited. You could hear the traffic screaming in the streets below, accenting the stillness of the room. I closed my eyes and plunged in.

"It's too bad, Mr. Morris, that your first visit to New York should turn out to be so unpleasant for you. You must hate our fair city."

"Your fair city hasn't aroused me to any emotion, let alone the strenuous one of hate. And as for your murders, we have them in London, too. However, in London we are permitted to ignore them."

Jeff tossed the clippings on the table. "Look, Morris, why do you act so bored by this murder?"

"I am bored. Must I be intrigued by the death and the attempted murder of two American actresses who are famous for nothing but their death and attempted murder? I noticed in the paper last night that a man named something or other was killed in a place called Pennsylvania. That bored me, too. I didn't peruse the grim details to their finish. Death bores me. I don't imagine I'll even appreciate my own."

Jeff looked disgusted. "It doesn't ring true. You're being detained here by the police for this murder. You happen to be a suspect. You should at least be mildly interested. Your boredom is a little too elaborate, like a character in one of your plays."

"A compliment, I assure you."

"You are a suspect, you know. It was possible for you to have poisoned Carol Blanton."

"So I've gathered from Peterson. However, it wasn't possible for me to have stabbed your leading lady, since I wasn't at the theater last night."

"You mean you weren't seen at the theater last night."

"I wasn't seen?" Morris was puzzled, then he smiled. "Oh, yes, of course! I had forgotten that I'm able to turn myself into a pumpkin at will. Was a pumpkin seen at the theater last night, Mr. Troy?"

"Where were you between nine-thirty and ten-thirty, Mr. Morris?"

"Do you really care?"

"I'd like to know."

"After a very bad dinner which was brightened only by the fact that I was alone, I walked. I walked and walked. Probably from eight until midnight."

"You just walked? That's all?"

"Occasionally I skipped. I love to skip."

"I mean you didn't stop to talk to anyone? Or for a drink?"

"No."

"Do you know where you were about ten o'clock?"

"Yes. That place ... the Battery. Watching the ships leave for England with tears streaming down my cheeks."

"Nobody saw you?"

"With my eyes all red and swollen! I hope not!"

"I mean," Jeff said, with admirable patience, "you don't have any witnesses that you were where you say you were when Eve North was murdered?"

"No, of course not. Of course not. I could stone myself. One should always have a witness while walking. But I left all my witnesses in London. In mothballs. So careless of me."

I could have kissed the telephone for ringing that time. Morris was having too much fun at Jeff's expense. Jeff reached over the table and swung the receiver to his ear. "Hello. Yes, yes, put her on." He turned to Morris. "Some pest. I'll get rid of her for you. Hello ... yes ... this is Greeley Morris ..."

Morris made a quick movement toward the phone. "I'm quite capable of ..."

"Damn it!" Jeff yelped. "She hung up! Operator! Operator!"

Morris snatched at the phone then and Jeff held him off with one hand while he clicked frantically with the other.

"Operator!" He was shouting into the mouthpiece. "Operator, trace that call! Trace it right away! Yes, you can. Damn it, stop talking and do it! Listen, baby. Have you heard about the Colony Murder Case? Have you read about a girl named Lee Gray? Oh, you have! Well, that *was* Lee Gray on the wire! Now, for God's sake," he pleaded, "*will* you trace that call?"

He dropped the phone into its cradle and turned to us.

"She'll call me back. Miss Lee Gray calling Mr. Greeley Morris! What about it, Mr. Morris?"

"A very ingenious trick and fairly amusing. However, I have no idea who the lady is nor why she should be calling me. If she was."

"Jeff," I said, "what was her voice like?"

"Like … I don't know. All she said was one word: Greeley."

"She calls me Greeley, does she?"

"Yes, and you don't know her, do you? Like hell you don't."

"I've heard shopgirls call His Majesty George."

In a remarkably short time the phone rang again. Jeff answered it. He listened for a moment, said thanks and hung up.

"Well, Jeff?"

"She called from a pay station in a drugstore at four fifty-four Madison Avenue." Jeff was disgusted. "A drugstore pay station! A lot of good that does us. But she called Mr. Morris and that's something."

"Yes, isn't it?" Morris said. "But what?"

"I wish you'd tell us who she is."

"I don't know," he said wearily.

"And I don't believe you," Jeff said. "And as for your walking alibi, I don't believe that either. I doubt if you've walked fifty consecutive steps in your life. If you had, you wouldn't look so bilious. C'mon, Haila."

CHAPTER TEN

LEE GRAY. The girl no one had ever seen, or knew, or even heard of. The police, for all their unlimited facilities, could find no trace of her. And yet she was in New York; she must eat somewhere and sleep somewhere, and somewhere in these seven million people must be those who were her friends. She had slipped into the Colony Theater two nights ago and left a note for Carol Blanton, and at five minutes before one o'clock today she had entered a drugstore at Madison Avenue and Fifty-fourth and telephoned to Greeley Morris. How had she managed to elude the nets thrown out for her by the police and why, if, as they believed, she had known of Carol's danger and had even tried to warn her of it, hadn't she come forward of her own accord?

And the Lee Gray enigma was only one of many. Two short days ago we had been, ostensibly at least, a normal group of people working together toward one objective, the success of *Green Apples*. Then suddenly the once affable Philip Ashley was quarreling with Eve North and snarling at me when I ventured into his dressing room. The once gay, irresponsible Tommy Neilson now scowled and swore and drank too much. Carol had lost her voice and miraculously regained it. Alice McDonald, almost madly ambitious for success, ran away from it and refused to tell why.

If Carol had not been poisoned, if Eve had not been killed, might all these mysteries have passed unnoticed before our unsuspecting eyes? Or could they be in some inexplicable way, as Jeff seemed to think, all links in this chain of murder that was tightening around poor Carol?

I tried to shake off these questions that kept recurring through my thoughts and to which no answers were forthcoming. I wanted a respite, however brief, from the derisive banter of Greeley Morris, from Amelia's stunned grief and Clinton Bowers' brooding sorrow, and from the desperate courage of Carol that was heartbreaking to see. If only for an hour I wanted to creep back into my little world where all these things were inflections in an actor's voice and frightened faces come off with cold cream and Kleenex.

As I turned the key in the lock a tall hawk-nosed man stepped out of the shadows at the end of the corridor.

"Wait a minute there, sister!" With long, quick strides he was beside me, peering down into my face. "Oh, it's Miss Rogers, huh? That's okay, sister, you can go in. I'm Crowley." His hand made brief contact with the brim of his hat and he was gone, lost in the shadows again.

Carol shuffled the hand of solitaire she was playing when I came in. Sketchily I told her of our morning's interviews and she listened in silence. Her eyes flew to my face when I spoke of the telephone call at the Gotham.

"Oh, Haila!" she breathed. "If they could trace her through that call, if they could find her …"

"If they could find her we'd probably know all there is to know."

"But will they be able to? A drugstore! Does anyone notice who comes into a drugstore?"

I shrugged. "I don't know. Jeff went up to tell Peterson about it. We'll find out when he comes."

We lapsed into silence, Carol dealing out hands of solitaire and playing them methodically. I stretched out on the studio couch and smoked cigarettes.

It was after four when Jeff arrived, looking tired and woebegone.

"Nothing new," he said in answer to our excited inquiries, "nothing at all. Peterson says he'll do all that's in his power to trace Lee Gray through that phone call, but it's next to hopeless."

"But what about Greeley Morris?" I protested. "He knows something about her, I'm sure of it!"

"He says he doesn't. I tagged along with Peterson back to the Gotham.

Morris still doesn't know Lee Gray, never saw her, has no idea why she should be calling him. That's his story and he's sticking to it like adhesive tape. What can they do?"

"They could third degree him. Did they?"

"No," Jeff said wearily.

"Why not? I'd like that."

"On account of the war debt. They're afraid England won't pay."

There was a rap at the door and I answered it. A thin individual in a pinkish tan camel's-hair coat and a pearl-gray fedora stood there. It took me two looks to see that this individual was Jinx, almost unrecognizable in his civvies. At his side was Crowley.

"Miss Rogers, tell this here gentleman," Jinx said, indicating Crowley, "who I am."

"Mr. Crowley, this is Jinx."

"Thanks, Miss Rogers. And would you tell him what I do here?"

"Jinx runs the elevator. Night shift."

"Thanks, Miss Rogers. See, I gotta talk to Mr. Troy about important private business. Will you tell this here gentleman it's okay?"

"Do you want to see him, Mr. Troy?" asked Crowley.

"Sure," Jeff said. "Come on in, Jinx."

Jinx triumphantly stepped in and closed the door in Crowley's face, then said in a whisper, "Talk low, he might be listenin' through the keyhole."

"There isn't a keyhole," Jeff said.

"There ain't?" Jinx was disappointed.

"What's on your mind, Jinx?"

"They been grillin' me, Mr. Troy. They was up to my house this mornin', they got me outa bed and grilled me."

"Who's been grilling you, Jinx?"

"Mr. Peterson. And he had a Mr. Sullavan helpin' him. But I didn't crack, Mr. Troy," he added reassuringly.

Jeff was amused. "What were they grilling you about, Jinx?"

"They was sweatin' me about suspicious characters lurkin' around the premises. I wanted to tip you off, Mr. Troy, 'cause I might crack under their constant grillin'."

"What are you talking about?" I asked. "Have there been any suspicious characters around here?"

"Only Mr. Troy. I wanted to warn him so he can beat the rap if they put the heat on him."

"Jinx, talk English!" I said sharply. "Stop playing gangster."

He ignored me. "Mr. Troy, you better get outa town an' lay low. If you get caught, crime don't pay. I know, on account of several week-ends behind the bars. Or maybe you got the dough for a good mouth-piece."

"What did I do, pal?" Jeff asked.

"You was up here Sunday night gettin' into the apartment."

"He was not," I said crossly. "We told you last night you were wrong about that."

"It ain't him bein' here that makes him a suspicious character; denyin' it is what does it."

"But I wasn't here Sunday night, Jinx."

"Nobody was here," I said.

"Are you serious? If you are serious, you are wrong. Someone came in here Sunday night, I seen him. I thought it was Mr. Troy. That's why I been withholdin' evidence from the police. I don't wanna double-cross Mr. Troy."

"He's talking nonsense," I said to Jeff. "There wasn't anyone here. Why, that was the night we were going to the Scriveners' party, re-member? And you called me at the theater and said you couldn't make it. I came home with Carol right after the play. And we both went straight to bed, didn't we, Carol?"

She nodded, her eyes on Jinx.

He said: "Well, there was a man here. I know a man when I see one; I wasn't born yesterday. It was just before you two got home, a little after twelve, I guess. I stopped at this floor to put a new bulb in one of the hall lights and this here man was at your door. He had a key, too. I thought sure it was Mr. Troy and I couldn't figure out why he walked up instead of ridin' with me."

"It was probably someone at the wrong door."

"No, ma'am. It wasn't the wrong door. Because he unlocked it and went in. And closed the door behind him."

Carol said impatiently, "You must be wrong, Jinx. There was no one here when we came in."

"Then he musta gone out again." Jinx was stubborn.

"Are you sure, Jinx?"

"Sure, I'm sure."

"Then why didn't you do something about him?" I demanded. "What do you mean by letting strange men run in and out of my apartment?"

"I told you I thought it was Mr. Troy."

I looked at Jeff. "Do you think we had a burglar? He couldn't have been a very good one. Nothing's missing that I know of."

Jinx said, "You sure was lucky!"

"After this, Jinx," I warned him, "you beat any man who tries to get in here to a pulp."

"Okay, Miss Rogers. G'night." He started for the door. Jeff stopped him.

"Wait a minute, Jinx. What did this guy at the door look like?"

"Like you. Sorta tall. Sorta thin. You know."

"What was he wearing?"

"Regular clothes. Hat and coat."

"What color hat and coat?"

"Well, sorta darkish. I couldn't see good. On account of one of the hall lights bein' out. And I only seen him a second. But I think it was darkish ... sorta, anyway."

"Listen, Jinx, would you know this fellow if you saw him again?"

Jinx considered. "If it wasn't you ... naw, I don't think so. The light was ..."

"Okay, Jinx, thanks." Jeff turned to us as Jinx closed the door behind him. "Haila, I want you to think back. Did anyone at the theater know that you were going to the Scriveners' party?"

"Why ... why, anyone *could* have known, I guess. I talked a lot about it."

"Did anyone know that Carol wasn't going, that she was coming back here after the performance?"

"Yes, I suppose so. I kept coaxing her to go all evening. I made something of a fuss about it and Carol kept refusing."

"And then, try to remember this, Haila, did you tell anyone that you ... yourself ... weren't going after all?"

"I ... no. No, I'm sure I didn't. You called just as I was leaving the theater. I decided that I didn't want to go without you and I rushed down the street to catch up with Carol. We walked home together."

I saw then what Jeff was getting at. Carol knew, too, for she was staring at him, her lips parted slightly and her hands clenched around the brandy glass.

"How many keys are there to this apartment?" Jeff asked.

"Two. I have one and Carol has the other."

"Where are they?"

"Mine's in my purse. I used it tonight when I came in." I looked in my purse just to make sure, and I held the key up in front of Jeff.

"Where's yours, Carol?"

She looked at him startled, as if she hadn't been listening and was trying frantically to piece together the bits of conversation that she had overheard.

"Carol," I said, "your key! Where is it?"

"It's ... it's in my blue purse, I think. Yes, yes, that's where it is."

"Go look," Jeff said.

Her purse was on the table in the vestibule and I brought it in and handed it to her. She began emptying it, slowly at first – a handkerchief, compact, a little change purse. Then the things came out flying – lipsticks, a mirror, cards, cigarettes. But no key. And she raised her eyes, unbelievingly, from the stuff spread out before her. She said, "It … it isn't here."

"When did you have it last?"

"I … I don't remember."

"You had it Sunday night," I said. "Just as we were leaving for the theater I gave it to you. I picked it up off the mantel and you slipped it in your purse … that purse."

Carol nodded. "Yes, that's right."

"And after Sunday night?" Jeff asked.

She closed her eyes in an effort to concentrate. "I can't think, Jeff, I'm so tired, I …"

I said slowly, "I used my key Sunday night when we came home. And Monday … Monday night at the theater you borrowed mine, Carol!"

Jeff said, "You haven't seen your key since Sunday night then, Carol!"

"I … no, I guess I haven't."

"But Sunday night you took it to the theater in that purse?"

"Yes."

"Where was your purse?"

"In our dressing room. On my makeup table."

"All evening?"

"Yes."

Jeff sat down and whistled softly. "Everyone at the theater knew, or could have known, that Haila was going to a party and that Carol was coming home … alone. Anyone could have sneaked into your dressing room while you were on stage and taken the key. Then he could have got up here before Carol, let himself in and waited for her."

My spine turned to ice. "Then Monday wasn't the first time that Carol was in danger? The man who stole her key and came here … came here to …"

"I'm afraid so," Jeff said.

Carol's voice was loud and harsh, protesting: "No, Jeff! No! There was no one here when Haila and I got home, I tell you!"

"From that window," Jeff pointed, "he could see you coming down the street. He could see that Haila was with you. And there was plenty of time for him to leave. By the stairs … or even by the fire escape."

"No, that isn't it, I don't believe it! Won't you please stop talking about me getting killed? You sit around and figure out ways! It makes me … I can't …"

She rushed into the bedroom. I started to follow, then stopped, knowing how futile my comfort would seem to her. Jeff was beating a nervous tattoo on the windowpane. When he spoke the excitement in his voice startled me.

"Haila, when we were up at Vincent Parker's today, he said something about seeing Clint Bowers Sunday night, didn't he?"

"I don't remember, Jeff."

"Of course you do! He said they walked up Lexington Avenue together, they …"

"Oh, yes! Parker had an idea for the third act. It was after the invitation performance."

"Right! And they separated outside of Zollers. Just down here around the corner. There isn't another Zollers, is there?"

"Not that I know of. Jeff, you don't mean … that Clint was the man Jinx saw at our door! He couldn't have mistaken Clint Bowers for you, he's so much heavier and …"

"Wait! Who did Parker say was with Clint?"

"Tommy. … Tommy Neilson! No, Jeff! It couldn't have been! Tommy wouldn't sneak in like that and … oh, Jeff, no! Not Tommy!"

"Grab your coat, Haila!"

"Why? Where are we going?"

"To see Clint Bowers. To find out where he left Tommy. Tommy fits Jinx's description as much as I do. It could've been Tommy!"

"But we shouldn't leave Carol alone just now."

"She won't be alone."

He opened the door and Crowley's tall shadow fell across the rectangle of light that spilled out of the living room. I snatched up my coat and followed Jeff past Crowley to the elevator.

CHAPTER ELEVEN

OSUGA, a Japanese boy whom I had seen occasionally at the theater, ushered us into the library of Clinton Bowers' penthouse apartment and in his soft lilting voice explained that Mr. Bowers was busy with a young man and would we wait here, please.

The library was the sort of room that they photograph for magazines, to make you dissatisfied with your own home. It was Clinton Bowers from start to finish, a man's man's room.

One side was nearly all glass and through it the East River seemed so close and inviting that you wished you were a Dead End Kid. Books lined the other walls from the parqueted floor to the high oak-beamed ceiling. A davenport stretched itself luxuriously before a fireplace that had the look of being always lighted and the mantel over it was of some shining reddish brown wood that defied my knowledge of the tree family. Three huge chairs covered in warm dull red leather begged you to accept their hospitality. Close to the windows stood a desk, not littered, but not forbiddingly neat. You felt that those things on it, old pipes, a letter opener that was bent and greenish tinged, a bronze figurine with one arm chipped off, had been through college with Clint. The whole room had been designed for comfort and much living.

I walked around it hugging the book-lined walls, taking a volume down here and there and glancing through them in a desultory fashion, my mind filled with fears for Tommy Neilson. "Don't let Tommy be the man with the key, don't let Tommy be the murderer. If it has to be someone I know, let it ..."

I was interrupted by a long whistle from Jeff as he stopped before a shelf to the right of the fireplace, a shelf that held a line of books all bound alike in handsome Moroccan leather. They were plays – *Twelfth Night, Julius Caesar, Sakuntala*, a dramatization of Dostoevski's *The Idiot*, Ibsen's *Rosmersholm*, two plays by Pirandello, Chekhov's *Sea Gull*, one early Eugene O'Neill and three or four others that were not familiar to me.

Jeff ran his hand over them with something close to awe. "Bowers didn't buy these books in a drugstore!"

All of the books were beautifully bound but these were super. I wondered if this shelf held his favorite plays of all time, and then, looking at them again, light suddenly dawned.

"Why, these are all the plays that he produced himself. Of course! I saw *Sakuntala*. My whole high school class trooped over for a matinee. And that same year he did *Caesar*."

"How did he manage to star Eve North in *Caesar?*"

"That was before Eve. That was when Bowers was roaring through the classics with no stars at all, being the white-haired boy of the American theater."

I looked around for the plays that had starred Eve North and knew even as I looked that they would not be there. There was no place in this library for the lightweight stuff that they had been.

Stepping back in a corner I tried greedily to take in all the room at once. "I would like," I said, "to spend a solid year here."

"Any year at all, Haila."

Bowers was in the doorway, his eyes tired and his face drawn, but he smiled at us with appreciation. At his elbow was the young man of whom Osuga had spoken and that young man was Steve Brown.

Immediately Jeff gave me the high sign, so high it almost went completely over my head, to take care of Steve, and I wheeled him into sitting beside me on the couch. Over his shoulder I could see Jeff and Clint talking softly by the desk, their heads together.

Steve said, "How is Carol, Haila?"

"Brave. Honest, Steve, she's been swell."

"I know." His hands clenched. "God! Who'd want to do that to a kid like Carol? What could she have ever done to anyone? Why should anyone want to hurt her at all, let alone want to murder her?"

"That's what we're all asking ourselves. And Carol most of all."

"I wish ..." He broke off and stood up impatiently. I cast a despairing glance at Jeff and he and Bowers stopped talking. I could read nothing from their faces. They looked discouraged and troubled, but there was no hint of anything else. Steve rambled uneasily over to the big chair beside the window and slouched down in it. There was an uncomfortable silence that the ringing of the telephone shattered. Bowers reached for the phone.

"Yes? Oh, yes, Peterson. ... Yes, we have what we call a working script. Everything's in that. ... Yes. Well, Phoebe Thompson has that. ... Yes, of course you may have it. I'll telephone her right away. ... No, not at all. Good-by."

He turned to us with a puzzled expression. "Peterson is anxious to see the working script of *Green Apples*. Apparently he's in a great hurry to get hold of it, too."

Jeff nodded. "I think I know why, I was talking to him this afternoon. They're working on the poison-put-in-on-stage angle. I suppose he wants to see which of the actors could possibly have been close enough to the table for a long enough time to have done it."

"I'm afraid they won't find much there. Everyone goes to the table for one reason or another during the third act." He reached under the desk for a phone book, opened it and began to run his finger down a page. "Thompson ... God, there are a million of them! Where does Phoebe live, does anyone know?"

I was glad for a chance to be helpful. "She lives across the street from me, right next to the Esquador Hotel. Two forty-nine, I think it is."

Bowers snapped the book shut and dialed a number. We could hear the long buzzes as Phoebe's phone rang and then the sound of Phoebe's voice.

"Hello, Phoebe! It's Clint Bowers. Look, you still have the working

script of the play, haven't you? The police want to have a look at it. …
Yes. … No, Peterson's sending a man to your place to get it; he just
wanted you to know that he had my permission. It'll be a plainclothes
man, name of Crowley. … Yes … you're to give it to him. Thanks,
Phoebe."

I jumped up. "Crowley's the man who's taking care of Carol now!
That means Carol will be left alone! Jeff, don't you think we should go
back?"

Jeff shook his head. "Peterson wouldn't send Crowley away without putting someone else on guard. She'll be all right, Haila."

I sank back again, not terribly reassured, however, and lit a cigarette.

Steve broke the silence that followed. "How are things going, Jeff?
Know anything new?"

"Nothing much."

"Am I one of your ten best suspects?" He grinned and looked more
like Jimmy Stewart than ever.

"Sure, why don't you confess, Steve?"

"What do you want to know?"

"Well … who is Lee Gray for instance?"

"Good old Lee Gray! She does my laundry."

Clint Bowers made a sudden movement and a quiet fell over us
again. This case didn't mean Carol to Clinton Bowers; to him it meant
that Eve North was dead. We needed to force jokes to prevent madness
from setting in, but he was a man bereaved, a man in mourning.

We tried not to watch him as he went to the fire and poked it more
than it needed poking and kept his back to us. I closed my eyes tight to
discourage any tears. Steve got up with a groan.

"If this damn thing would only get cleared up! This stuff in the
papers, all this foul publicity, this …"

He stopped when he realized I was glaring at him in disgust. So that
was the main worry of *the* Stephen Munson Brown, Jr. So that was the
cause of his agitation, that was why he hated this mess. Somehow I had
never figured Steve Brown that way. "You and Philip Ashley!" I heard
myself muttering.

"You … you don't understand, Haila," he stammered. He looked
from me to Jeff and then to Bowers. No one spoke. Bowers lit a cigarette with studied nonchalance, Jeff's eyes were glued to the window.
Steve said, "Oh, hell!" and then picked up his hat. The door clicked
behind him before any of us opened our mouths. Then I said: "Steve
Brown! The boy I used to point out as the swellest fellah in all New
York. I suppose the Back Bay Browns haven't admitted yet that there
is such a nasty thing as murder."

"Steve's all right," Clint said, but there was disappointment in his voice.

"Sure, Steve's all right," echoed Jeff, still looking out the window.

I remembered then what had brought us here. "Jeff, was it Tommy who ..."

Jeff walked across the room and sank into the big chair that Steve had vacated a moment before. "No, it wasn't Tom."

I felt ten years slip from me. "I knew it couldn't have been."

"Tom Neilson and I walked home together Sunday night," Clint said. "At least we walked as far as Seventy-fifth Street together. When we parted it was nearly half past twelve and Jeff tells me this man ..."

"Yes, it was just after twelve that he was at our place. It couldn't have been Tommy."

"If Jeff is right, if the man at your house was the murderer, that eliminates a few people. The main point is that it eliminates all the women. And Tom Neilson. And old Benjamin Kerry. No one in his right mind could mistake Ben for Jeff. Not that anyone had any very serious suspicions of him, of course."

Jeff dug his hands deep into the leather sides of the chair and scowled. "I guess I'm glad it wasn't Tom," he admitted. "But it would have been so easy."

"Not for Tom," I said.

"No. You know it's a damn lucky thing for me that I was with Peterson and Carol last night when Eve was murdered. If it weren't for that the finger would sure be pointing at me now."

"Why?"

"As far as I knew, Carol was going home by herself, I didn't know that you were going to decide to go with her. I could have sneaked into the theater and snitched her key. And God knows no one could look more like me than I do."

"Nice work, Philo," I said. "Prove that you did it. Hang yourself."

But Jeff was already off on a new tack. Leaning back in the big leather chair he turned frowningly toward Clint.

"There's one little thing I'm curious about, Clint, and I might as well get it straightened out while I'm here. It's about Alice McDonald."

Bowers merely raised his eyebrows and waited.

"Had you promised her the part that Carol played in *Green Apples?*"

"Promised her the part?" He seemed surprised. "No, not promised it to her by any means. Alice read for me and I rather liked her. She's not really a good actress but she seemed to have a surprising grasp of that part and I was at wit's end to find the person for it. I had practically decided to give her a contract that day that Carol first read for me. I don't think Alice ever knew it though. Naturally, I never told her."

"She knows. And she's pretty bitter about it."

"I'm sorry. I know, of course, that she expected the part. I expected to give it to her. But after I heard Carol read she didn't have a chance. I knew in thirty seconds that Carol was the girl to play Dina and that was all there was to it. In fact, I ..."

Clint's words were left hanging in midair. A startled grunt had burst from Jeff. He pulled himself up from the depths of the chair and stared unbelievingly at something that lay in the palm of his hand. When I craned my neck to see, he closed it in his fist.

"Haila!" He was almost whispering in his excitement. "Haila, what does that key of Carol's look like?"

"Just like mine, of course. You've seen it."

"Is this it?"

I frowned at the key he dangled in front of me. "Yes. Yes, I think so."

"Make sure you have yours. You might have dropped this."

Mine was in my purse and the two keys proved to be identical.

"It was in this chair," Jeff said slowly. "And Steve was sitting here. So unless ... Clint, has anyone connected with the play been in this room since Sunday night?"

"No."

Jeff put on his hat. "Where does Steve Brown live?"

"At the St. Moritz," Bowers said. "I'm going with you."

"Me, too." I slipped into my coat.

We were silent on our way down to the lobby. The doorman's whistle brought a taxi to the canopied entrance and we started across town to the St. Moritz. I began to be sorry that I had come. To find Eve North's murderer and Carol's would-be assassin had become my utmost desire, but to see Steve Brown confronted with the damaging evidence of Carol's key ... I didn't want to be there. Steve and I had had too much fun and too many heartbreaks looking for jobs together; we had been comrades on the barricades of Broadway.

I was thinking that I could make my escape at Fifty-ninth Street and walk the rest of the way home when Jeff leaped up from his seat. He pounded furiously at the window that separated us from the driver. I looked at him in astonishment. His face had suddenly been drained of all color and was twisted in an expression that frightened me.

"Driver! Go to two forty-three East Fifty-fourth Street and go like hell!" His voice was like his face too, tense and white.

The driver threw his weight on the gas and pulled out of line to get around a bus. He swung into the curb and passed a car on the right that had already halted for a red light. We roared through it. A policeman's whistle shrilled, and we went faster.

"Jeff, what is it? Why are we going to my place?"

He said, looking straight ahead, "If Crowley did leave Carol alone, if nobody was sent to take his place ..." He crouched forward, talking to the driver in low tones.

"Jeff! You mean that Steve went there, that Steve knew she was alone! Jeff, you don't think ..."

"I think that if this cab doesn't break all speed records, we may be too late."

I sank back and closed my eyes.

Jeff was afraid! Jeff was afraid of what I was afraid of. It wasn't my imagination going dramatic on me. It wasn't my mind playing tricks. Steve Brown was on his way to my apartment, he was on his way to Carol.

And Steve Brown was the man with the key.

Oh, we should have known, we should have guessed. Steve looked more like Jeff than anyone else in the company. The same height, the same build. He had a brownish overcoat.

If we hadn't been such blind, stupid fools. If we had even warned Carol against him. But Steve! No one had even thought of him. He was sweet and awkward and likable. Carol was fond of him. She wouldn't believe that he had tried to murder her; she would open the door when he called in that it was Steve. She'd open it without fear or alarm. And she would be letting in her murderer.

I looked at Jeff. His hands pushed hard against the driver's seat as if to help the engine get us there in time. There was a look on his face that I had never seen before.

"If our cab doesn't break all speed records," he had said. "If our cab doesn't go faster than the one Steve Brown is in," that's what he meant. We had to beat Steve Brown. We had to get to Carol before he did.

"If our cab doesn't go faster than his," my mind kept repeating. The street was filled with honking, creeping cars, turning out in front of us, stopping, lagging, holding us back. We were pushing through them at a maddening crawl. Every traffic light was red and every traffic light stayed red interminably.

There were tiny arcs in the palms of my hands where my nails had dug into them.

We were on Fifty-fourth at last. We were at Madison, at Park. I took a deep breath to pull myself together. They would need me, maybe, when we got there ... if we got there in time.

A block and a half to go. Another long red light. A cab making a U turn before us. A car swerving ahead to bring us to a dead stop.

Before the brakes had been jammed on, Jeff was out of the taxi. Clint Bowers was close behind him. The elevator door slid open as I reached it. Jeff held the key in his hand while we were taken up. A bell rang on the third floor.

"Don't stop," Jeff said. "Go on up."

The boy looked at him and opened his mouth. But the elevator went on past the third floor. At the sixth I looked with a prayer for Crowley's bulky figure. The hall was empty.

My heart dropped with a dull, sick thump. We went down the passage and Jeff slid the key into the door and opened it.

Steve Brown was there, standing in the middle of my living room. Close to him was Carol. Her arms were clasped around his neck and Steve's head was bent over hers and he was kissing her.

CHAPTER TWELVE

I LEANED back against the wall and snorted. My knees were wobbling and I was out of breath so the snort was a feeble one, but they heard it. Steve raised his head, startled, and then a sheepish grin crawled over his face when he saw us. Carol flushed and made an effort to pull away but he held her firmly to him with one arm around her shoulders. Putting his hand under her chin he tilted her face up to his.

"The jig is up, Carol." He turned to us. "Are you following me by any chance?"

"By any chance!" I hooted. "We followed you here hellbent to keep you from murdering Carol!"

He stared at us incredulously. "From murdering Carol!" he repeated, pulling her closer to him. "I'm not going to murder Carol. I'm going to marry her."

"We're ... we're going to be married," Carol echoed in a small voice.

"You're going to be married ..." My echo was even smaller.

"I certainly hope so," Jeff said primly. He flopped into a chair and expelled all the breath he had been holding for the past ten minutes in a gigantic sigh of relief. I still couldn't manage to get as far as a chair.

"Congratulations, I'm glad," Clint said, his face lightened in a smile.

"Be happy, children," Jeff said, "and have children, but please bring them up to take better care of their keys."

Steve frowned before his face broke into an embarrassed grin. "Oh. Carol's key. I thought I might have lost it at Clint's."

"You did. And I found it. And we've been chasing you with a long rope to put around your neck."

"I just heard about it from Carol. How Jinx came up with his tale of a man at the door. She should've told you it was I. If you'd asked me, I would have."

"You mean Carol knew all the time?" I managed to gasp.

"Sure she knew. She gave me the key Sunday night. Incidentally, I did just what you figured I had done, Jeff, walked up the stairs, let myself in and waited by the window, watching for Carol to come. And when I saw that Haila was with her, that she hadn't gone to that party after all, I scrammed. But you were awful wrong on one point. I didn't come to kill Carol. I came to praise her and, incidentally, whip up some Texas hash."

"Texas hash," I repeated, somewhat hysterically. There was a pause while Jeff and Clint and I all looked at each other mumbling "Texas hash."

"Yeah," Steve said, "Texas hash. You eat it. It's delicious. And it's a nice thing to cook when you're alone with your girl; you don't have to watch it."

"Look," Jeff said. "Let's all sit down and Steve will start at the beginning." We sat, Steve on the studio couch beside Carol. He reached for her hand and their eyes met and said things to each other.

"The beginning," Steve said, "is that Carol and I fell in love, almost at once. We want to get married, and there are ... well, there are obstacles. The obstacles are my family. Not that they'd disapprove of Carol once they met her; they'd love her, but it's just that they're so dead set against the theater. You probably know what a row they raised when I got my first job. Well, I'm afraid that's what it would be all over again with Carol, and I don't want that. So we hit upon a plan and it was a pretty damn good one, too. We were going to keep our engagement quiet, not let a breath of it slip out until this show was over, and then I was going to take Carol home and she was to play dumb about the theater until they'd sort of got to know each other. The gag's a million years old, I know, but it's still good. It might have worked."

"But all this secrecy ... did you have to go in for that?"

Steve grimaced. "Yes. You know, Haila, what the papers do to me. They grab at any damn thing at all. If Carol and I had lunch together more than twice, if we walked down the street, if I took her home from the theater, the gossip columns would have it. We didn't even want to take that chance. We hated it, but ..."

"And that was what you meant about the lousy publicity. I thought ..."

"I know what you thought," Steve said, smiling. "Shame on you, Haila."

I was ashamed; I should have known Steve better than to think what I did, and he saved me from turning brick-colored by going on quickly: "It meant an awful lot to us to have our plan about my family work. Those gossip columns would have ruined it. That's why we've tried to be so careful all during rehearsals. Then, after the opening night ..."

"After that night," Carol interrupted, "I wouldn't let him tell. He wanted to. He wanted to tell everyone and marry me right then and there and ... and take care of me."

"And why not?" Jeff wanted to know.

Carol's teeth bit into her lips. "Don't you see? I can't do it now, not while this thing is hanging over me, not while I don't know from one day to the next if I'm still going to be alive! That's no way to start a new life. It isn't fair to Steve. His life might be in danger too!" She stopped and I knew that she was perilously close to tears. "Haila, I should have told you. It was nasty of me. You've been so swell and I owe you so much; I at least owe you my confidence. But I've got to keep Steve out of this if I can. I've got to!" She buried her face in his shoulder and he held her tight and touched her hair with his lips. I went and put my arms around them both.

"It's all right, darling. Of course I understand. I think it's brave and swell of you. And this mess will be cleared up in no time at all and you'll be strolling down the center aisle perfectly disgustingly happy."

"But in the meantime," Clint Bowers said from the other side of the room, "I wish I could make head or tail of this key business."

Steve smiled over Carol's shoulder. "It's pretty complicated, Clint. You see, we knew that Haila would be out late Sunday night and we were coming here. We've done it before. It's about the only place we ever get to see each other alone. And Carol gave me the key. I was coming up first and concoct some Texas hash." We all laughed. "What's funny about Texas hash? It's my specialty. And I did just what I told you, sneaked in with my groceries, and then, when I saw Haila, sneaked out again.

"I took the key with me when I left and on Monday night Carol had to borrow yours. She didn't want to ask me for the one I had because my sister and some friends of hers were in my dressing room after the show and she ... well, it's the old secrecy story again. Then we forgot all about it, both of us, in the excitement that followed. That is, we forgot until this afternoon when Jinx turned up with his story and Jeff promptly made a murder clue out of it. And poor little Carol was ..."

"Petrified," Carol said. "Oh, I should have told you, Haila. But it all happened so suddenly, I … I didn't know what I was doing. When Jeff said that the man with the key was the murderer and I knew that man was only Steve, I was so upset and worried I just ran away. After I'd thought it over I realized how stupid I'd been, letting you think that, and I came out to tell you the truth. But you and Jeff had gone and I didn't know where and, well, there didn't seem to be anything to do but wait until you came back and … and confess."

"We had Tommy Neilson practically in the electric chair. And then Steve. And when we realized Crowley had left you …"

Carol laughed. "Yes, he told me he had to go, just for a few minutes, though. He made me promise not to move one step out of the apartment and not to let anyone in. He waited outside until he made sure I'd locked myself in. I wouldn't have let anyone in, either, Haila. But when it was Steve, of course, I …" She stopped and, coming over to me, touched me timidly on the arm. "Haila, please, forgive me for not telling you long ago. You do understand?"

"Of course I do. And I'm delighted about you two. This calls for a drink. Jeff, you do the pouring."

"No, wait a minute," Steve said. "This calls for more than a drink, it calls for a celebration. I feel so swell about telling you, I'd like to give a party. How about a dinner tomorrow night with toasts in champagne and an official announcement for just us, the five of us? Would you like that, Carol?"

She didn't have to answer. Her eyes were sparkling and for a moment she looked like any girl whose engagement was to be announced in toasts and celebration. Then the light faded from her eyes. "We can't, Steve. People would see us, they'd know."

"I wish to God they would!"

"No! Not yet, Steve. Please!"

"Well, there's no reason why we can't celebrate here, is there?"

I said: "Of course not. I'd love that."

"All right, tomorrow then for dinner. Let's all meet here at five. Carol can give me her key again and I'll sneak in and get things ready. You'll come, Jeff? And Clint?"

Jeff said he would be there in person but Clint demurred. "You young people …" he started to say.

"You're coming!" Steve said. "We'll have champagne and lobster thermidor and …"

"Texas hash?" Jeff asked innocently.

"Caviar," Carol pleaded.

"Absolutely! Last week Carol made an astounding discovery! Caviar!"

Jeff grimaced horribly. "Caviar! The undeveloped young of careless fish!"

Carol said, "It's wonderful!"

"I wish that fish would hide their children where they can't be found."

"Oh, be quiet!" I said. "You don't have to eat it."

Carol went to the window and threw it open, letting the wind ruffle her hair and the lacy collar of her dress. When she turned back to us she was smiling. "I feel happy again and not afraid. Just telling you about Steve and me has done it. And a party, that helps too. It makes me feel almost … normal." I thought: "She's really just a little girl. There's going to be a party, a party with caviar, and so everything is all right."

Steve followed her to the window. "If we told everyone and got married, you wouldn't need to be afraid at all. Nothing could hurt you with me around you all the time. I wouldn't let it."

"No," Carol said, turning away.

"We could get away from here, take a cruise, go to Bermuda. Anything you wanted."

"No, Steve."

"Darling, it would be all right. I promise you it would be all right. We'd make my family understand. And as for anyone hurting me, it's ridiculous. It's a crazy idea of yours."

He broke off and they stood just looking at each other, forgetting the rest of us existed. "Keep going, Steve," I rooted silently. "Keep at her, old kid. She's wavering." She was, too. It didn't take much insight to see the struggle she was having. Then her eyes fell upon a crumpled newspaper. She picked it up and turned, appealing to us, thrusting the paper in our faces.

"Look! Look at that! Pictures of me all over the thing. Your family would like that, Steve. My name in headlines. The Murder Girl, that's what they're calling me now. Steve Brown weds the Murder Girl. Your family would be sure to love me. No, no, I won't have it!"

"But, Carol …" Steve pleaded, his eyes begging her to listen.

"No, Steve."

He shook his head hopelessly. "You talk to her, Haila."

"I will, Steve."

Bowers cleared his throat. "I think you should marry him immediately, Carol. That's my opinion and, having given it, I'll run along. I'll stop in at your party tomorrow."

"Wait, Clint, I'll go with you," Jeff said.

"Where?" I asked.

"Anywhere," he said morosely. "Steve shot my pretty theory out from under me and I've got to dig up another one. I'll call you tomorrow. G'by."

He opened the door and I saw that Crowley's reassuring figure was stationed outside it once again. When I turned back to Steve and Carol, they were sitting on the floor close by the fireplace and I mumbled a good night that neither of them heard and slipped into my bedroom. I was done in.

I filled the tub with steaming water and in it I poured half a bottle of pine-scented crystals. My bath was wonderful, everything was wonderful. The hot fragrant water lapping right up against my chin, the brisk dryness of the Turkish towels when I hopped out, the warmth of my old corduroy robe. And best of all were the cool sheets and the eiderdown that I pulled up to my shoulders.

With a pile of pillows behind my back, I switched on the bedside lamp. "This," I thought, "is my first peaceful moment in seventy-two hours. Something grisly may happen tomorrow, more murder, more horror, more dread. But for tonight everything is fine. Steve Brown is in the living room with Carol. He loves her. He'll see that nothing happens to her. Bulldog Crowley is in the hall outside. And Jeff is hounding the criminal. Good old Jeff. Jeff will catch the criminal."

I opened the script that Vincent Parker had given me that afternoon. Skimming through the list of characters I found the one that he had marked for Carol. I turned to page one.

CHAPTER THIRTEEN

UNDER Jeff's surveillant eye I finished the last morsel of Childs bacon and eggs and lit a cigarette. I was thinking happily that there was nothing in the world like the first drag of the day's first cigarette when Jeff said, "You smoke too much."

"It keeps me busy," I said in defense. "I don't have a husband and a home and children to keep me occupied like other girls."

"If you stopped smoking you might. Nicotine's a drug."

"You smoke."

"It's all right for me. I'm a drug addict."

"If you'd hurry up and solve the murder we could get married and I'd have a home and children. And a husband, too. Then I'd give up smoking."

"I'm solving the murder."

"Oh, are you?"

"I'm getting along fine."

"I'll say! You know that the murderer must be either a man or a woman."

"That never occurred to me. Wipe the egg off your chin." I raised my napkin to my face. "The other one," Jeff said.

"The other what?"

"Chin."

"You're sore at me, aren't you, Jeff?"

"Look, Haila. Today's Thursday. Monday night the murderer strikes at Carol and misses. Tuesday night, murderer restrikes, re-misses, gets Eve North instead. Wednesday I don't catch culprit. Police don't catch him either. Today's Thursday. You give me hell, wax sarcastic. G'wan back to bed."

"I'm sorry, Jeff." And I was. I hadn't realized that it was only three nights ago that *Green Apples* opened. It seemed so far back now that I could hardly remember it. Jeff was still scowling at me. "I *am* sorry, Jeff. It's just that I want to marry you."

"I'll have this case solved in twenty-four hours."

"Promise?"

"Bowers will give me my check and we'll be married as soon as the law allows. Satisfied?"

"Yes. Forgive me?"

"No. It's a lucky thing for you we're being joined." He shouted across the restaurant, "Won't you join us, Tommy?"

I looked up and saw Tommy Neilson approaching us. He dragged a chair from another table to ours and sat down heavily. He had been job hunting and there didn't seem to be any producers who wanted any stage managers.

"The theater is dead," Tommy grumbled. "I wish I were."

"Why don't you go see Vincent Parker, Tommy?" I suggested. "He's doing a play."

"Yeah, I know."

"Well?"

"He's got a stage manager. Bobby Reed. The rat!"

A waitress appeared and took Tommy's order. I asked for more coffee. When the girl had gone I said to Tommy: "You can act. I've a copy of Parker's play, and the cast is enormous. There might be something in it for you."

"I'm not an actor."

"You're good enough," I insisted. I had played with him in stock a couple of years before at Martha's Vineyard.

"Naw. How could I get a part in New York anyway? I'm not an Englishman."

I laughed. That was the first attempt at a wisecrack I had heard Tommy make in weeks. Jeff didn't get it and Tommy tried to explain. "There are more English actors working in New York than there are Americans. But then of course I'm not even an American. I was born in Brooklyn."

"What d'ya mean more English actors?" Jeff stuck his chin out. He loved to argue on subjects he knew least about. "What English actors?"

"Shall I name you just a few?" Tommy asked, smiling.

"Yeah. Who besides Evans?"

"And Philip Ashley and half a hundred more," I said.

"Philip Ashley isn't English."

My coffee cup clattered in the saucer as I set it down and stared at Tommy. Jeff was almost out of his chair.

"What's the matter with you two?"

Jeff's voice was sharp with excitement. "Did you say Ashley isn't English?"

"Yes. He isn't."

"How do you know?"

"One of the old-timers at the Lamb's Club told me. Ten or twelve years ago Ashley went to Toronto for a season of stock. When he came back he was English. And he's worked steadily ever since. New York loves English actors."

I was astounded. To me Philip Ashley had always been the very spirit of Trafalgar Square or Piccadilly or whatever it is that is all British and a yard wide.

"Where was Ashley born?"

"Salt Lake City."

Both our cups clattered into our saucers that time. Jeff's hand closed over mine. "Are you sure, Tommy?"

"Positive. Some of us were going to expose him once just for the fun of it, but we decided it wouldn't be so funny to him. We found out then that he was born and bred in good old Salt Lake City, U.S.A."

"C'mon, Haila." Jeff scooped up my purse and gloves and hustled me out to the sidewalk. Through the window Tommy stared at us open mouthed.

"Jeff, why …"

"Why do you think I yanked you out of there?"

"To stick Tommy with the check. Pretty clever."

He rushed back into Childs, slipped a bill into the cashier's cage and was beside me again. "Where does Ashley live?"

"Downtown someplace, I think."

I had to almost run to keep up with him. He ducked into a drugstore on the corner and leafed through the telephone book. Ashley lived in the Village, on Perry Street. I followed Jeff out. "Are we going to see Ashley? Listen, Speedy, maybe he won't even be home. We can talk to Carol. She'll tell us if she knew him in Salt Lake City."

"I'd rather talk to Ashley."

We took a Lexington local to Grand Central, shuttled to Times Square and got on a Seventh Avenue express. Jeff seemed to have forgotten I was with him. I poked him with my elbow. "Don't forget to ask him about those pills in his dressing room and what he was doing in Radio City."

"You ask him."

"All right, I will."

We got off at Fourteenth Street and walked south to Perry. Ashley's house was an old four-story brownstone with a brave little fringe of evergreen bushes struggling up between it and the sidewalk, and some brownish ivy hung limply from boxes at the windows of the first three floors.

We climbed the front steps and Jeff pushed the button under Philip Ashley's engraved card and waited for the answering click of the door. There was none, and I rang again. I couldn't stand his not being home, the letdown would be too much.

"I guess he isn't home," Jeff said. He tried the door; it was locked. Then he rang a bell marked T. Baumer.

"Jeff, what are you going to do!"

"I don't know. Something'll come to me."

The door buzzed and Jeff opened it and started up the stairs. I kept right behind him. A woman's voice from somewhere above shouted, "Is that you, Milly?"

"Say yes," Jeff whispered to me, still on his way up.

"No," I whispered back.

"Milly, is that you?" the voice repeated.

"Milly who?" Jeff yelled. By that time we were on the third floor landing. A stout woman with brilliant blondined hair and scarlet fingernails was standing in the doorway of her apartment. Jeff smiled fetchingly at her. "Oh," he said, "I didn't know Mr. Ashley had a wife."

"I didn't either," said the woman.

"Are you his sister, then?"

"Hell, no! I ain't related. I wouldn't be! My name's Baumer. You must've rang the wrong bell."

Jeff snapped his fingers in disgust. "Yeah, I must have. What a dope!"

"That's okay. Ashley lives on the top floor." She inspected me over Jeff's shoulder.

"Is he at home?" Jeff asked.

"Your guess is as good as mine. Go and see. One flight up."

"Thanks."

I knew Philip's door when I saw it. There was a knocker on it shaped like a tiny black cat. Jeff marched right past it and started climbing another flight of steps, steep and narrow. Panting, I followed him. He pushed open a door at the top of the stairs and pulled me through it after him. We stood in the shadow of a chimney on the gravel roof.

"Jeff!" I wheezed. "What are we doing here?"

He moved to the edge of the roof and looked down. "We're using the fire escape. That would be it and that would be Ashley's window. C'mon."

"Jeff, you can't! You get ten years for that!"

"Not if you catch a murderer."

"But somebody will call the police! Or take a shot at us!"

"Who?" We looked around over the adjoining roofs. There was no one in sight but a little boy with big unhappy blue eyes. He was leaning on the parapet across the shaftway. In his hands was an enormous home-made kite. He was waiting for some wind. "Hey, kid," Jeff said, pointing to the fire escape, "is this the way to Perry Street?"

"I don't know," the little boy said.

"He'll tell his mother on us, Jeff, and ..."

"My mother isn't home!"

"See, Haila. Let's go."

I didn't feel quite like it. "Jeff, the window won't be open."

"It would be if you hadn't said that."

I eased myself down the iron steps gingerly after Jeff, until we stood on the balcony outside Ashley's window. Jeff put his hands against the pane and turned his head to me. "Cross all your fingers, Haila." I did. Jeff pressed upward: nothing happened.

"Damn!" Jeff said.

The little boy said helpfully, "The next one to it is open." We looked and he was right, but it wasn't on the fire escape. The sill was a good three feet from the rail of the fire escape.

"No, Jeff!" I said. "You'll kill yourself!"

"Don't be a sissy!" the little boy shouted.

Jeff grinned at me. "See, I got to."

He managed it very easily. That made me the sissy. Jeff opened the window on the fire escape and helped me in.

Ashley's apartment was a large-sized edition of his dressing room, as scrupulously clean and astonishingly neat, considering the amount of knickknacks he had amassed and assiduously arranged. Every square inch of flat surface was buried under tiny figurines in terra cotta and ivory, china animals, mostly cats, little snow scenes in crystal balls, cactus plants in hand-painted pots and an assortment of ashtrays and cigarette boxes that ran the gamut. The walls seemed almost to sag under the burden they upheld – framed photographs, white plaster masks, bits of tapestry, bracketed plants. Pieces of pale-green and yellow wallpaper peeped apologetically through the rare and far-between openings. There were two whatnots under the windows, the kind my grandmother kept in her front parlor, several small ja-panned tables and two overstuffed chairs. In a corner was a satin-wood desk with panels of painted medallions and floral scrolls and on top of it two burnt down candles whose melted wax formed fantastic cascades down their sides.

I stood there staring about me helplessly. I looked at Jeff; he was smiling and shaking his head. "The government should plow this room under."

"Find what you want and let's get out of here, Jeff. I'm nervous."

"As a cat?"

"Please, Jeff!" I went to the window and looked down Perry Street. Jeff started opening drawers. I thought I might as well cooperate. I opened a door; it was a closet kitchenette. I went into the bathroom, a tiny almost infinitesimal room, with Dubonnet and white monogrammed towels hung tidily over the tub. Between it and the lavatory was wedged a red bathroom scale.

In the medicine cabinet, nestling behind a bottle of Listerine, I found three white tablets, the size of aspirin. "Jeff!" I called. When he stuck his head in the door, I held out a tablet to him. "Look!"

"Yeah?"

"They're the same as I found in his dressing room!"

"I don't want them." He was examining some kind of electric vi-brating contraption with avid interest.

"Don't be stupid, Jeff, we'll have them analyzed. They may be mor-phine!"

Jeff went back into the living room, I followed him. We both stopped. There was the sound of steps on the stairs. They came briskly down the hall and halted before the door. I looked frantically at Jeff.

The door swung open and Ashley had closed it and slipped his keys into his pocket before he saw us. His expression changed from startled surprise to indignation, then to fury.

"Hello," Jeff said.

Ashley looked at me. "Snooping again!" His lips were compressed into a thin, prissy line. "This is unspeakable. I wish I hadn't caught you. I'm not up to a vile situation like this."

I couldn't talk. I would have given anything to have been in a concentration camp; anyplace someplace else.

"Ashley, I dragged Haila into this," Jeff said. "I'm the snooper and I'm sorry."

"Sorry! Don't be ridiculous!"

"I'm trying to solve a murder; that partly justifies my intrusion. You've been holding out on me; that completes the justification. And on top of that, I apologize. Do you forgive me and can we be friends and have a little chat?"

"How charming you are, Mr. Troy!" Philip sneered. "How did you get in here? Did that fool janitor ..."

"We didn't see any janitor. We crawled up through the plumbing." Jeff sat down on the arm of a chair and pulled a pack of cigarettes out of his pocket. Ashley opened the door.

"Now, if you don't mind, please leave." I started toward the door, but Jeff stopped me. Ashley glared at us; he was shaking. So was I. I wanted to run. But Jeff still hadn't moved from his chair.

"Ashley, where were you born? Was it London?"

Some of the rage left Ashley's face and caution took its place. "No, Portsmouth."

"Portsmouth? Hmm. Is that near Salt Lake City?"

"What are you driveling about?"

"About where you were born. And reared. Did you know a family named Young? The Brigham Youngs?"

"Please stop trying to be funny!"

"Or a family named Blanton? There was a daughter, Carol Blanton?"

"Oh, so that's it!"

"Yes," said Jeff. "So you better answer my questions. I'll be more open-minded than Peterson."

"I doubt that! But, yes, I was born in Salt Lake City. I adopted England as my native land for purely professional reasons. It was advantageous. ..."

"We know about that."

"You seem to know a great deal. But I left Salt Lake City when I was eighteen ... before Carol Blanton was born. And I've never been back since. Now get out of here! I won't stoop to talk to a pair of sneak thieves who pretend they're trying to solve a murder and ..."

I couldn't keep quiet any longer. I thrust the three white tablets I had found in the bathroom before Ashley's eyes.

"What about these? You're going to be very embarrassed, Mr. Ashley, if they turn out to be morphine! And what about your own sneaky tactics? Ducking us and pussyfooting around Radio City!"

"For the last time, get out of here!" Ashley's face was ugly. Instinctively, I stepped behind Jeff.

"If Mr. Ashley won't talk, Haila, I will. I know the answer to the mysterious mission at Radio City. And the tablets."

Ashley clenched his fists and started toward Jeff who glided around in back of me and spoke to Philip over my shoulder.

"The answer is strictly glandular. Fat! Obesity! That middle-aged spread." Philip wilted and looked as if he were about to burst into tears. "An actor must keep that schoolgirl figure. Those are reducing tablets. In Radio City, on the same floor as Vincent Parker, is the emporium of Madame Somebody, *Corsetière*. In the bathroom, note the scales, the reducing machine. In that closet is a girdle for every day of the week. No wonder our friend here raised a rumpus when you borrowed his tablets at the theater. You might have discovered what they were and ruined his glamour."

A small "Oh!" was all I could manage.

"It's nothing to be ashamed of, Ashley, even Irene Rich drinks grape juice. I've seen the ads."

"You son …" Ashley started to say.

"Uh-uh!" Jeff waggled a finger at him. Ashley turned his back and stamped to the window. I caught Jeff's eye and motioned toward the door. I wanted to get out of there.

"Ashley," Jeff said, "you shouldn't let your pride make suspicious people like Haila think you're a murderer."

He pivoted around to Jeff. His voice was loud with righteous anger. He was his old pompous self. "Now, are you satisfied? Now, will you leave before I have you thrown out by the police? I wouldn't touch you; you nauseate me!"

"We'll go in a second. Quietly," Jeff said. "As soon as you explain this." He held out a small slip of paper.

"What's that? Where did you find that?"

"In your desk."

Ashley whitened. "You've been in my desk? How contemptible of you!"

Jeff read from the paper: "I.O.U. five hundred dollars. Signed Carol Blanton. How do you account for that, Ashley?"

Ashley looked uncertain for a second, then gave a little deprecating laugh. He went to one of his porcelain boxes and got himself a cigarette.

"Oh, that," he said. "I must tell you about that."

"Yes, you must," Jeff said.

"Look here, I'm high-strung; you know that. This business has me all on edge. Finding somebody here startled me. Won't you sit? We'll have a glass of sherry." He went into the kitchenette. Jeff winked at me. Philip called, "It's really very bad wine, but I couldn't resist buying it because of the intriguing bottle." He came back with an intriguing bottle and three tiny wineglasses. He smiled at me. "Haila, some sherry?"

"No, thanks, Philip."

"Me, neither," Jeff said.

"I don't blame you. It's foul stuff." Jeff waved the I.O.U. at him. Philip chuckled. "Oh, yes! That silly I.O.U. It's worthless, of course. Just a joke. Carol and I played two-handed rummy several times during lunch hour while we were rehearsing. I invariably beat her. We played for five dollars a point … on paper, of course. Finally, we were playing for thousands of dollars a point. Poor Carol lost millions to me. And she would give me her I.O.U. It was a private joke between us, you see. Of course, I tore the slips up. I don't know how that one managed to be about. I … I know it sounds silly."

"It sounds awful silly," Jeff said. "I'm laughing."

Anger flamed anew in Philip's face. "Are you insinuating that I've been lying to you? That what I've said isn't the truth?"

"Exactly," Jeff said. "And stop sputtering. You see, I happen to know the truth."

CHAPTER FOURTEEN

My apartment had the look of an overstuffed florist shop when, shortly before five o'clock, Jeff and I returned to it. The living room was filled with roses – white roses, yellow roses, red roses. Everything that remotely resembled a vase had been used, even to a Mason jar that stood on the desk and bulged with long-stemmed Talismans. The butterfly table was spread with my Venetian cloth and my best silver sparkled in the light of two tall candles. At two of the places were corsages, each boasting an orchid, one brown, one purple. A cake, snowy white and pyramided, topped everything.

Carol came out of the kitchen wearing a soft woolly dress that I had bought early in the fall. It had a high neck and leg-of-mutton sleeves and was a sort of limpid blue that made her eyes seem a violet color and brought out shining golden lights in her hair. Pink spots of excitement glowed on her cheeks.

"Haila, may I wear this? Is it all right? I don't have anything for a party and this was hanging in your closet way in the back. I know you never wear it."

I hadn't worn it because it was the first Bergdorf number that I had ever owned and I had been saving it for my Sunday best, but there wasn't much to be done about it in view of Carol's pleading eyes and the tremulous hope in her voice. Surreptitiously, I shot a warning glance at Jeff. He had been with me when I bought it. I said: "Of course it's all right, darling. I'd forgotten I even had it. And it looks like a million dollars on you!"

"It should," Jeff said, *sotto voce*. "It cost damn near that."

I glared at him and changed the subject before there was any damage done. "Where's Steve, Carol?"

Carol frowned. "He left just a few minutes ago. He got a wire this morning from his mother. She's coming to town and he went to meet her train. He'll take her straight to his aunt's and come right back."

"I see."

Jeff said, sniffing noisily: "Is that food I smell in the kitchen? Or just more flowers?"

"It's food! Gallons of it, enough to feed an army. And more flowers, too. Steve got overenthusiastic."

"Maybe the guy's in love or something."

There was a knock at the door and Carol reached it in a hop and a skip. Clint Bowers stood there and we tried to not burst into a roar when we saw the tremendous bunch of roses he had brought. He took in the flower-laden room and he smiled as he put the roses in Carol's arms.

"I'm not staying," he said. "I just wanted to add my congratulations to your party."

Carol took his hand and pulled him into the room. "You've got to stay! I won't like my party if you don't!"

Clint demurred but among us we got him settled in a chair, his hat and coat tucked in a closet and his flowers in a milk bottle. If anybody needed a party, he did. Little gray lines had crept into his face in the past few days and when he smiled it only emphasized the troubled unhappy look in his eyes.

We sat around making conversation and hoping it was light until Carol excused herself and vanished into the kitchen. A moment later she was back, balancing a tray of long-stemmed glasses and a bottle of champagne that nestled in an ice-filled bucket.

"Steve said we weren't to wait for him. Jeff, will you do the honors?"

Jeff relieved her of her burden and with great ceremony popped the champagne cork. The wine gurgled into the glasses with a merry sound and we talked and made silly toasts and laughed a lot. Carol went around the room, switching on the lamps, and the place was flooded with a cheerful glow. As the champagne trickled warmly through us our little party grew cozy and almost gay.

"I ... I want to make an announcement," Carol said.

Her voice was suddenly so serious that we turned to her in surprise. But she was smiling timidly and her eyes were happy. She stood framed in the blackness of the big window, the lamplight playing softly on her hair, and she looked lovelier than I had ever seen her.

"I should wait until Steve comes, but I won't. I want you to know," she continued. "It's ... it's this. I've tried to do what I know I should, I've tried to be brave ... and well, I guess what I mean is noble. I've tried but I'm not good enough or strong enough and I can't go on any longer. I'm ... I'm going to marry Steve. Right away, as soon as we can be married. It's wrong of me and it's not fair to Steve. I wouldn't do it if I weren't such a coward, I wouldn't give in. But I am and I wanted you to know."

Even as she said it her eyes were begging us to refute her statement and I did. "Darling, it's wonderful! You're not being cowardly; you're doing what's right."

"Of course it's wonderful, Carol," Clint said. "We'll drink a toast to it! The line for refills forms at the right. Carol, you're first!"

She danced across the room toward him and held out her glass. She was only a step away from him when we heard the clicking sound at the window, and the glass on my little Gauguin hanging on the wall opposite went shattering to the carpet.

Jeff lunged at Carol, dragging her to the floor. Her head hit a table leg; she moaned and tried to rise. I started to her.

"Keep out of that window!" Jeff barked. "They might shoot again!"

I dropped down beside him. Clint Bowers was glued against the wall, frozen. The hall door burst open and Crowley appeared. When he saw us he plummeted to his knees.

"What happened?"

"They took a shot at Carol!" Jeff said. "It was fired from the hotel across the street. The Esquador." He crawled to Carol and bent over her. "She's all right. C'mon. You keep your neck down, Haila!" Crowley had already disappeared and Clint and Jeff followed him. I knelt beside Carol and tried to drag her to the couch. She was out and I couldn't budge her. There was nothing to do but wait for nature to take its course. What I needed was some champagne and a cigarette. Still on my all fours I obtained a supply and went back to squat beside Carol. The bullet hole in the window gaped down at me; I felt like a doughboy in No Man's Land.

It wasn't more than ten minutes before Jeff was back. "It's all right. You can stand up now."

"If only I can." Jeff gave me a hand up and I was surprised to find that I was trembling no more than a leaf.

Between us, Jeff holding her shoulders and I her feet, we lifted Carol and deposited her safely on the studio couch. She gulped once or twice and her eyelids fluttered. "I'm all right," she said and closed her eyes firmly as if she would rather not know just yet what had happened.

But I wanted to know. "What was it, Jeff? Who did it? Where did it come from?"

Jeff shrugged. "I don't know who did it. There are about twenty cops over there now tearing the place to pieces trying to find out. But they won't locate our gunman because he had plenty of time to clear out after the shot."

"Couldn't you even find out which room it was fired from?"

"We think so. It's a lavatory on the sixth floor, just opposite that window. Anyone could have got in and out of there without being noticed. The police are going through the register and interviewing everyone in the place but they know themselves they're wasting time."

"Where's Clint?"

"With the police. He's giving a play-by-play description from our side of the shot." He squinted suddenly at me. "Listen! You go to the nearest phone and call Amelia. Call Philip Ashley and Tommy Neilson. I'll take care of the others."

I was very dense. "Why? What'll I say to them?"

"Nothing. As soon as you know they're on the other end, hang up. And for crying out loud, beat it! It's probably too late now."

Light dawned on me as I rapped on the door of the apartment next to ours with one hand and pushed it open with the other. A tall sparse looking woman with iron-gray hair and a muddy complexion stood in the middle of the room, her hands working nervously in front of her.

I said, "May I use your phone? There's been an accident."

She nodded and pointed to a table in the corner near the window. "I thought something had happened ... the noise ..."

I said it was a shot through the window and found Philip Ashley's number in the book. I dialed it and let it ring four long times before I hung up. Then I found Eve North's number and called it.

"Hello."

I recognized Amelia's slow heavy voice and I clanked the receiver back on the hook.

"Your little roommate ... did they ... is she all right?"

I was running my finger down the B's to find the Bristol Hotel. I wished fervently that this tall gray woman would let me alone. She stood hovering over me and I lost my place and had to start over again. I found it at last and dialed the number.

"Good afternoon, Bristol Hotel," said a lilting female voice.

"Tom Neilson, please. Quick!"

There was a pause, then the voice came again over the wire, still lilting. "Sorry, Mr. Neilson has left word that he is not to be disturbed."

"He's got to be disturbed. I've got to talk to him."

"Sorry. Mr. Neilson has left word ..."

"Listen," I said, and my voice was definitely not lilting, "this is important. I'm calling for the police. You ring Tom Neilson's room and you ring it right away."

I heard the buzzes then, short impatient ones. I counted ten of them and I jiggled the receiver hook. "Will you have him paged, please?" I asked when the girl answered.

The gray woman touched me lightly on the shoulder. Her face was worried and she was biting her lip. "This Mr. Neilson you're calling. Is he a ... a suspect?"

"You bet your life he is," I said grimly, holding the receiver against my cheek.

"You mean it's possible that he might have tried to kill Miss Blanton?"

I nodded. I could hear a bellhop calling Mr. Neilson at the other end.

"And his first name is Tom ... Tommy?"

"Yes. Tommy Neilson. He was in our show."

She walked to the window and looked out into the street. "There's quite a crowd in front of the Esquador. Three police cars and I don't know how many policemen."

The operator at the Bristol was back. "Sorry, Mr. Neilson doesn't seem to be in the hotel just now. Is there any message?"

I hung up and started for the door.

"Wait a second! Please, just a second!" The woman was standing with her back to the window, grasping the sills with each hand, and the knuckles shone white through her bony fingers. I stopped. She glanced out into the street again, then back at me. Her lips tightened as she spoke. "I ... I think I have some evidence."

I looked at her sharply. "Evidence? You don't mean you saw who fired that shot?"

She shook her head. "No, no. Nothing like that. Nothing like that at all. Why, I was … I was in my kitchenette when I heard the shot, and when I ran to the window there was no one there. It's something else, something I … I overheard."

"Overheard? Where?"

"In your apartment. One night about two weeks ago. I was sitting in that big armchair over close by the wall reading. And the voices came out to me very distinctly. I had no intention of listening, absolutely none at all. I just happened to overhear, that's all." She blushed furiously as she spoke and I knew at once that she hadn't happened to overhear anything. The woman was a chronic eavesdropper. I thought of some of the rare and spicy tidbits she could have picked up in my apartment during the last year, and I felt myself reddening with her. For a moment we must have looked like a couple of Indian squaws. "Your little friend, Miss Blanton, was there. We've spoken to each other several times in the elevator and in the lobby and I recognized her voice immediately. The person she was talking to was a man whom she called Tommy. That's why I thought … when I heard you calling …"

"Yes. It was probably Tommy Neilson. He's been up several times."

"I don't believe that anyone else was there because they were quarreling."

"Quarreling? Tommy and Carol?"

"Oh, yes. Yes, quite violently. They raised their voices and talked very loud. That's why I happened to overhear them, you understand."

"Yes, of course."

"I couldn't hear all they said because they spoke so fast. You know how people do when they're angry. But I did hear one thing and it worried me even then. Not much, of course, for people say things they don't mean when they're angry and their tempers are aroused. But then, nothing had happened to Miss Blanton and I forgot about it, really." She stopped and knitted her bony fingers together, studying them intently. "I thought it wasn't any of my business because if I hadn't been sitting in that one chair I probably wouldn't have overheard. There's no reason why I should become involved in a thing like this simply because I happened to be sitting in that chair. But if this building is going to be filled with those strange-looking men who Jinx tells me are detectives and people are going to fire bullets into the window right next to mine, I suppose I'll have to make it my business."

"Yes, I understand." I thought that if she didn't get to the point I would do her some physical damage. "What was this one thing you heard?"

"I heard him say," she said slowly, " 'I will kill you first!' "

I gulped audibly. "You … you must be mistaken!"

She shook her iron-gray head. "No. Those are his exact words. 'I will kill you first,' he said. Of course," she added with a pathetic eagerness, "he probably was jesting. People say such foolish things when they're excited. I'm sure there's absolutely nothing in it."

I thought of Alice McDonald's story and then laughed at myself. Of course there was nothing in it. If Tommy Neilson had threatened Carol she would have told us. She would have been afraid of him, and she wasn't. Yet why on earth should this woman, who was obviously relieving her conscience and would give her right arm to have nothing to do with this mess, invent such a tale? I looked at her suspiciously. "Why haven't you said anything about this before? The papers have been full of the murder for two days now."

"Because I didn't want to get mixed up in any vile murder case," she said defiantly. "I'm a schoolteacher. I have my work to think about, my job to take into consideration."

"Well, thank you very much. I'll tell someone what you've just told me at once." I started for the door but she caught me before I quite made it.

"You … you don't have to tell the police, do you?"

"Naturally, I do. Why not?"

She fidgeted nervously. "They won't want to question me, will they? Detectives, I mean, and policemen. They won't be coming up here to my apartment?"

"They won't hurt you."

I left her looking not at all reassured and went back to my place. Jeff was sitting by the telephone scribbling something on a piece of paper and paying no attention to Carol who sat bolt upright on the couch and rubbed her chin with a tentative hand. Jeff tossed the pencil on the desk.

"Well?"

"Wait a minute." I walked over and sat down beside Carol. I came straight to the point. "Carol, did Tommy Neilson ever say that he would kill you? Or like to kill you, or anything like that?"

Her eyes met mine unwaveringly, but they were bewildered. She hadn't quite recovered from Jeff's left uppercut to her jaw. Jeff plopped down on the other side of her.

"What are you rattling about?"

I cocked my thumb over my shoulder in the direction of Miss Talmadge's apartment. "Over there is a maiden schoolteacher who is an inveterate eavesdropper and has been doing rather well lately. She heard a man and a girl quarreling here one night two weeks ago. The man said that he would kill her. The man was Tom Neilson. Carol was the girl." I heard Carol gasp but she said nothing. I went on. "This woman isn't any sensation hunter. She's a meek little soul who's been trying to get up enough courage to say this for the last two days. And I think that she's telling the truth." I had talked to Jeff but, out of the corner of my eye, I had watched Carol.

She sat very still and a strange little sound burst from her lips. She said slowly: "Yes, it is true. But he didn't mean it. He was talking the way ... the way you do when you're hurt and angry. He said it, but it didn't mean a thing. I swear to you he didn't even know what he was saying and I swear that Tommy never tried to kill me. I know he didn't."

"Why?" Jeff was looking at her intently.

"Because ... because he loves me."

"Suppose you start right out now, Carol, and clear this whole thing up for me."

Carol's hands were clasped tightly in her lap. She hesitated as though she couldn't find a way to begin. "It's awfully hard. It sounds so terrible and ... and damaging, and really it's silly and innocent. What Tommy said, I mean. You see, when we first started rehearsals Tommy was nice to me. He took me to lunch sometimes and to dinner and bought me cigarettes. I think that Haila asked him to ... to be kind to me." Over Carol's head I nodded at Jeff but didn't interrupt her. "He was swell and I liked him lots. He was always saying funny things and acting crazy and we had a good time together. And then all of a sudden there was Steve, and Steve and I loved each other and everything was so beautiful that I ... I just forgot about Tommy, I guess. And then I saw what had been happening to him and I hadn't even noticed. And I was scared and terribly unhappy."

"What had been happening, I take it, was that Tommy had fallen in love with you."

Carol nodded. "I couldn't help realize it, Jeff. I would have been a fool not to. I should have known it sooner except that I ... I wasn't paying much attention to anyone or anything but Steve. And then when I knew about Tommy at last I had to do something. He had been so sweet and I ... I just couldn't let things go on and hurt him even more. So I told him."

"About you and Steve?"

"Yes. He was terribly upset. He'd been drinking too and that made it so much worse. He talked like a dramatic little boy. He said he'd kill me, he said he'd kill Steve too. But he didn't mean it any more than if he were a kid speaking some kind of piece in school."

"Pretty progressive school," Jeff muttered.

"I almost had to shove him out. And then the next morning at rehearsal he came to me first thing. He said all the things that you'd have to say when you've been drunk and acted like an idiot. And he apologized all over the place."

"And wished you happiness?"

Carol smiled wryly. "No. He didn't go that far. But I asked him not to tell anyone about Steve and me and he said he wouldn't. And he kept his word too."

Jeff stood up. "You damn little dope! I guess they'll have to riddle you with bullets before you finally believe that the finger's on you. You've been so close to death three times that you could have heard it whizz by if you'd listened, but you still think no one wants to kill you. For God's sake, what do you think all this business is about? Do you think it's a practical joke?"

"It wasn't Tommy," she said stubbornly, almost crying.

"No, it wasn't Tommy. It wasn't anybody! It's all done with mirrors!" He was yelling at her, but she met his angry gaze and didn't flinch an eyelash. He turned and howled at me, "How about those phone calls?"

"Amelia was home. I recognized her voice. I didn't get anyone else."

"Neither did I. The thing was a fizzle except for eliminating Amelia. And that's a great stride in the right direction. I was sure that sniping out of a hotel window was Amelia's meat." He plopped down in a chair in disgust.

"Jeff, things are beginning to look a bit thick for Tommy. I mean besides his threatening Carol." I told him about Tommy and his message that he was not to be disturbed at the hotel. Jeff sat like a ramrod listening.

"And you're sure he wasn't there?"

"I know it. I let them page him all over the hotel. He wasn't in the building, there's no doubt of that."

"I guess we'll go and have a chat with Tom Neilson."

Carol sat up with a jerk. "Please, please don't go to Tommy. He'd hate it if he thought you knew about him."

Jeff said sarcastically, "We're not going to like it very much having a corpse around the apartment."

She had him by both arms, pleading with him. "Then don't tell Steve about it. Promise me that. He's got enough to worry about and this would upset him so. Please, Jeff!"

"I won't tell him. Stop shaking."

The door banged open and a fair-sized mob poured in and took over. Peterson was there, and two policemen in uniform and several others whom I remembered having seen at the theater the night Eve North was murdered. They began milling around, examining the fragments of my picture on the floor, digging in the wall for the buried bullet, photographing every conceivable thing in the room. My life from this point on promised to have very little to do with that thing called privacy. I sat close to Carol and held her hand while she answered the barrage of questions they fired at her.

We all heard the pounding of the steps in the hall before Steve Brown, breathless and white-faced, burst into the room. For a moment he didn't see Carol and his eyes searched the room in terror. Then Carol ran to him. He clasped her tight in his arms and neither spoke. They stood clinging to each other and there was a long, choking sob from Carol.

Jeff tapped me on the shoulder. "Come on, we've got some work to do."

I looked at Steve and Carol again. He had drawn her into the corner by the kitchen and wedged her there, standing over her like a bulldog. "If he guards her this assiduously from the police," I thought, "he ought to do all right by any stray murderers who happen around." I grabbed my wraps and, nodding to Jeff, followed him out.

The last thing I heard was Peterson's voice: "All right, Mr. Brown. I want to ask *you* a few questions."

CHAPTER FIFTEEN

TOM NEILSON glowered at us over the rim of a rye highball. "Who the hell cares why I wasn't in my room? The Bristol isn't a girls' dormitory. I don't have to sign out every time I decide to go someplace." He took a gulp that brought the Plimsoll line on his glass down about three inches.

For two hours Jeff and I had been tearing around Times Square and we had finally traced Tom to a bar on Forty-sixth Street where he was deeply engrossed in some solitary drinking. Now, as if finding him hadn't been enough to get a girl down, he was bent on being difficult.

Looking steadily at Tom, Jeff said: "Nobody gives a damn right now why you weren't in your room except Haila and me. But in an hour or so there will be about ten cops who are going to find out or else."

"Why?" Tom was belligerent.

Jeff gave it to him bluntly. "Because after you left word at your hotel desk that you were not to be disturbed someone took a shot at Carol from the sixth floor of the Esquador Hotel."

Tom's empty glass went down on the table with a resounding bang. "Was she ..."

Jeff said: "No. She's all right. They missed her."

Tom shook the ice around in his glass and drained it. "Carol leads a charmed life. She ought to go with a circus. Poisoned, stabbed and shot at, and still in the pink of condition." He beckoned the waiter and asked for another rye highball.

"Why did you leave word that you weren't to be disturbed when you had no intention of staying in your room?"

"I had every intention of staying in my room. I didn't want to be disturbed because I was going to take a nap."

Jeff smiled. "You're not going to tell us that you *were* in your room. That you were so sound asleep you didn't hear the phone."

"Oh, for God's sake! No, I didn't go to bed at all. Almost as soon as I got to my room Tony Eldridge came in. He told me that Max Shuman was sending a company of *Peter and Paul* to London. I stage managed the New York production and he thought I'd have a chance to get the job again. So I went out in a hurry. I didn't stop to call the operator and tell her. Why should I? And that's all there is to it."

"Where is Shuman's office?"

"On Fifty-third, just east of Madison."

"What time were you there?"

"I got there about five. Shuman was out. I talked to his secretary for a while and left about five-fifteen."

"Five-fifteen, huh?" Jeff rooted around in the little wicker basket and found me a potato chip. "And the shot came through the window at exactly five-thirty."

There was alarm in Tommy's voice when he spoke again. "Look, Jeff, I know what you're thinking! Shuman's office is only a couple of blocks from the Esquador. I could have got up there in time to take that shot at Carol!"

"What did you do, Tommy?"

"Well, I ..." He hesitated. "Damn it! This would happen to me. Well, I got here about six-thirty. On my way here I stopped at a bar on Broadway and had a couple of drinks." Jeff opened his mouth and Tommy said angrily, "No, I can't prove I was there! I didn't see anyone I knew. And the place was jammed; I don't think the bartender or anyone would remember me. What the hell are you trying to do to me, Jeff!"

"Nothing. I just wish you had an alibi for five-thirty this afternoon."

Tommy jumped to his feet, upsetting the glass the waiter had placed before him. "Do you mean to say I'm going to be mixed up in this thing because I was going around minding my own business? What the hell,

Jeff! Listen, I didn't take a shot at Carol. I didn't try to poison her and I didn't stab Eve North. I don't want to kill Carol! For God's sake, why should I?"

"You said you were going to," I said.

He sat as quickly as he had risen, but much more quietly. He looked from one to the other of us and his lips were very white. He said bitterly, "So she told you about that."

I rushed to Carol's defense. "No, she didn't tell us! She never breathed a word of it and wild horses probably couldn't have dragged it from her until we already knew. It happens that you were overheard. By a very helpful next door neighbor."

"What did Carol say?"

"Just that she saw you were falling in love with her and she was in love with Steve Brown. So she told you and you blew up and threatened her. And you needn't bother explaining that you were drunk and in a temper and didn't mean it because she's already done that for you."

"I'll make my own excuses," Tom said sullenly. He kept his eyes on the glass in front of him.

Jeff said, "But that's the way it was? You were drunk ..."

"I'd rather not talk about it. Let Carol do the talking."

"What about you and Alice McDonald, Tommy?"

"There's nothing about Alice McDonald and me except that we've known each other a long time. We're good friends."

"She knew about you and Carol, didn't she? And she didn't like it. It couldn't have been that she was jealous of Carol?"

"She didn't like it because ..." He snapped off. "It's none of your damn business why she didn't like it. But it wasn't because she was jealous. I tell you there isn't any of that sort of thing between us. I told her how I felt about Carol because that's the kind of friends Alice and I are."

"You still feel that way, don't you?"

"What?"

"You're still crazy about Carol Blanton?"

Tom scowled down at the table. "I guess so. Yeah. I suppose I am. But I'll get over it. I'll wake up some fine morning and bing! it'll be over. That's the way it happened and that's the way it'll go. I was sitting in Bowers' office when she walked in that first time." His voice softened. "That first time I saw her I knew Carol was for me. She started to read for Bowers and before she'd finished a page I was sure of it. I guess so much beauty and charm all rolled up together were too much for me. And talent. It wasn't a first reading she gave; it was a performance. That kid's going to be a star."

"If she lives," Jeff said.

Tommy's head came up with a jerk. "Yeah, if she lives ... she'll be a star. Well, there you have it. 'How T. Neilson fell in love ... and out again.' " His eyes dared us to smile.

Evidently Jeff had learned all he wanted to. He got up, chucking Tommy on the shoulder with his fist. "So long, Tom. And thanks. A lot."

Out on the sidewalk again, walking toward Seventh Avenue, I had trouble keeping up with Jeff.

"Where are we going?" I asked. He didn't answer. "Jeff, remember me? I'm the girl you're going to marry."

"Yeah, when I solve this more than slight case of murder."

He stopped, turned and started in the opposite direction, and ran plunk into Vincent Parker.

"New York!" exclaimed Vincent. "I can't take ten steps without meeting one or two of my best friends. In order to arrive any place promptly I gotta take a cab. What do the both of you know?"

"Nothing," Jeff said sincerely.

"You read my show, Haila?"

"Yes," I lied. I had fallen asleep on page three.

"Well, I ain't heard from Carol Blanton yet! Ain't she read it?" I shook my head. "Say, she ain't been murdered, has she?"

"Not yet."

"Swell! She'll be terrific in the part. Pack 'em in! Say, I ain't heard from Lee Gray either. I can't understand it. I been puttin' her name in the paper every day. You ain't contacted her, Jeff?"

Jeff's mind was wandering so I answered for him. "No, Vincent."

He said wistfully, "Carol Blanton and Lee Gray in the same show! I tell you people would flock to see them. But from miles! They'd come over from Jersey. Say, Jeff, if you should locate this here Lee Gray, you'll contact me immediately?"

"Huh? Oh, sure. You bet."

"Jeff, when I'm done a favor, Vincent Parker don't ever forget it. Sam Goldwyn done me a favor once and look at him today. Name somebody bigger than Sam!"

"Flimsy Fletcher," Jeff said.

"Who?"

"Fellow I went to school with. Weighed three hundred and ten when he was twelve."

Vincent was incredulous. "Yeah? How much does he weigh now?"

"The same. He's still twelve. So long, Vincent."

"Good-by, kids, keep in touch with me." Vincent looked at a passing cab, saw that it was occupied and hailed it at the top of his voice. Jeff dragged me on down the street.

"Haila, I'm leaving you here."

"Why?"

"You can't walk fast enough."

"Walk fast enough where?"

"Look. I'll meet you at your place in about an hour. Keep Carol there till then if you can." He stepped off the curb and started across Sixth Avenue. I watched him thread his way through the traffic tie-up and then, bunching my collar around my neck with one hand and holding tight to the brim of my felt hat with the other, I elbowed my way to Fifth Avenue and started up it.

It had been a two-faced day, warm and bright, with the smell of April in the air, and now, suddenly, it had pulled itself together with the coming of night and gone back to being November with a vengeance. The wind, swirling down the wide street, took sizable nips through my thin tweed coat and I lost no time making it to the sheltering canyon of Fifty-fourth Street.

There was a knot of men in front of my apartment building, two in uniforms of the city's finest, the others wearing the glum mask that is apparently a requisite for plainclothes men. I caught a glimpse of Peterson in deep conversation with the photographer whose equipment lay on the step at his feet. I said, "Hi, fellahs," as I walked past the men and went into the lobby where the boy who relieved Jinx on the day shift, a sad, morose-faced boy, took me up.

The apartment was in complete darkness and I reached for the switch and snapped on the ceiling lights. Then, quickly, I turned them off again and felt my way around in the blackness, pulling down the blinds. I had no desire to be a target for any guests of the Esquador Hotel. I locked and bolted the door and wriggled the knob experimentally, in spite of the two detectives stationed outside, and then lit the table lamp. Over the yellow shade I saw Carol watching me from the bedroom door. She had been crying and the powder she had smeared over her face in a gallant effort to hide the tearstains was streaked and pathetic. She must have seen all my precautionary measures for there was alarm in her eyes.

"Peeping Toms," I explained glibly, pointing to the drawn shades. I sat on the couch and lit a cigarette, resolving to do my darnedest to drive the thought of murder out of her mind for a little while at least. "Darling, I think it's swell about you and Steve. In fact, I ..."

"Oh, Haila, keep your fingers crossed! Steve's telling his mother about me ... about us, Steve and me."

"She'll say yes or I'll mow her down."

"Oh, if she doesn't I ... I don't know what I'll do. I won't be able to stand it! He should be back soon."

"If she says no, will that mean that Steve won't ..."

"Marry me? I wouldn't let him, I couldn't. I've caused Steve enough trouble, I ..." She moved restlessly about the room, stopping at last to curl up on the couch beside me. "Haila ..."

"What, Carol?"

"Haila, I'm leaving here. Tomorrow."

"Leaving here! Why?"

"I'm going to a hotel. I have some money now, my check for *Green Apples*, and if I need more Steve will let me have it. I won't like that, but I guess it's an emergency."

"I guess it is, but you're not leaving."

"I've got to, Haila. It'll just be for until Steve and I get married. If we do," she added and I could almost hear her breathe a silent prayer. "Oh, I know it's wrong of me, things being the way they are, but I wish we could get married tomorrow."

"Well, whenever the wedding is, you're staying here until it. I won't have you going to a hotel."

For a moment she didn't answer, then she said softly, "I'm afraid to stay here."

"But you're safer than in a hotel. Steve and Jeff and I ..."

"I don't mean that. I'm not afraid for myself. I'm afraid for you. Haila, when these things first began to happen I was so terrified and sort of numb about it all that I ... I was thoughtless and selfish. It never dawned on me how I was dragging you into this mess just by living here at your place. And you were so swell about it, I just ... well, I just took it for granted."

"Carol, don't be silly."

"And then, at first, everything was happening at the theater and I didn't think there was any danger here. Then today ... that shot. Haila, that bullet could have hit you! You might be dead now and all because I ... because of me."

"So that's why you're going?"

"I don't want to have happen to you," she said, her words scarcely audible, "what happened to Eve North. I'm all packed. I'll leave in the morning."

"Well, go in and unpack. You're not leaving here until you're Mrs. Stephen Brown. I won't have it. I'm in no danger, Carol! Why, that bullet didn't come within a mile of me. And there won't be any more bullets either." I put my arm around her shoulders. "Stop worrying,

Butch. We'll see this thing through somehow. Now let's have no more of this small talk. Let's discuss something really momentous such as, is there anything to eat in the house beside beans?"

There was a knock at the door and Steve was in the room. He didn't have to say a word, success glowed in his face. He took Carol in his arms but he was too excited to be affectionate; he had to talk. "We're going to be married! I'm going to be a husband! Look, look at me, I'm going to be a husband!"

"Oh, Steve!"

"You should have seen your mother-in-law's face when I told her, darling. She couldn't speak, she was speechless! Boy, I thought it was ... I thought her silence was foreboding, but I had just struck the old lady dumb. I knocked her for a loop! When I left she was going to bed!" Steve dropped into a chair and immediately jumped up. "I told her about you, about this, about everything, Carol. And Mother said" – his voice started to dance – "somebody should marry the poor little thing and take care of her!"

"But, Steve, that doesn't mean anything!" Carol's voice was tremulous.

"I showed her your picture and you're going home with me this weekend at Mother's command. It's in the bag. Mother never lets anyone in our house that ain't fit to marry."

"But she didn't say yes, Steve."

"She knows you're in the theater and she didn't say no! And when she sees you, darling, and when Dad sees you! Stop worrying." He kissed her. I turned my back and started to play he-loves-me-he-loves-me-not on an old cactus plant.

"Ouch!" I said. Carol and Steve laughed politely. I got it. Cupid didn't have to blow his whistle in my ear. I went into the kitchen and played with the pots and pans.

Jeff's greeting to Steve and Carol brought me back into the living room ten or fifteen minutes later at a gallop. He was already at the telephone. "Hello, has Peterson come in yet? This is Jeff Troy, he'll talk to me. It's important, something on the Colony case. ... Thanks, I'll hang on."

Steve and I fired excited questions at Jeff but he was connected with Peterson almost immediately. "Hello, this is Troy. I've been trying to get you every five minutes for the last half hour. ... Listen, Peterson, could you locate Greeley Morris and bring him up to Haila's apartment? ... I'm not asking you to run errands for me! This is important! I've got something I'll tell you when you get here with Morris. ... I'm not withholding evidence! When I tell you what I know, you'll want

Morris. I'm saving you time, that's all. ... He isn't at his hotel; I've just come from there. ... All right, I'll tell you! I know who Lee Gray is! I've found her!"

"Jeff!" I shouted.

"Please!" Jeff said. He turned back to the telephone. "You get Morris up here, Mr. Peterson, and I'll tell you." He hung up and took off his hat and coat.

"Well, Jeff?" I asked impatiently.

"Maybe I shouldn't tell you till Peterson gets here."

"Maybe you shouldn't, but you're going to!"

"Okay, relax."

Steve leaned forward in his chair, waiting. I glanced at Carol. She was staring at Jeff, her lips slightly parted, her hands clenched at her sides. None of us spoke. Jeff lit a cigarette with maddening care.

"Lee Gray is an actress and her name on the stage is Leila Gray. Ever hear of her, any of you? No? Well, she's not very well known. So far as I can find out she's only appeared in one play and then for only a couple of weeks. It was a tryout in England. In Manchester, to be exact. The play was *Green Apples*."

Steve said sharply, "*Green Apples!* But then ... then Greeley Morris would have known her. I understood ..."

"That Morris had never heard the name before. Yes, that is his story and he has stuck to it through everything."

"Why, Jeff?"

"That's one of the things I want Morris to tell us." Then Jeff went on musingly. "You know the funny thing about all this Lee Gray business is that the police were on the right track from the very beginning, only they didn't stay on it long enough. Their theory was that Lee Gray was someone in the *Green Apples* company, someone who had signed an assumed name to that note, thinking that Carol would understand it. It would have been difficult for an outsider to have got into the theater, up to Carol's dressing room and out again without being seen by anyone. But a very simple thing for a person in the company. They followed their theory for a little while. They checked that note with the handwriting of everybody in the cast, even the men's, although the writing was obviously feminine. But they missed checking one person ..."

"Who?" Carol breathed.

He looked at her quietly. "You."

Her hand went clutchingly to her throat. "I? But, Jeff, it was ... the note was ..."

Steve wheeled on Jeff, his face dark and stormy. "What are you talking about, Jeff? That note was sent to Carol. Why should they check her handwriting?"

"That's what we all thought. That's where we made our first mistake. Just because the note was found in her purse we assumed that she had been the recipient. We weren't bright enough to realize the truth. The truth was that Carol wrote the note herself and it was found before she had a chance to send it."

I laughed and the sound fell like a dull clatter in the tense silence of the room. "But, Jeff, it's silly, it's …"

"Look at Carol."

Her eyes were fastened on Jeff's face, held there as if hypnotized. Her lips parted and trembled, but there was no denial on them.

Jeff continued. "You wrote that note, didn't you, Carol?"

"Yes." It was hardly more than a whisper.

"And you left it in your purse where the police found it. I'm not positive to whom it was written but if I had three guesses, all of them would be Greeley Morris. Right?"

She nodded dully. "Yes. It was to Greeley Morris."

Steve said, "Carol!" and put his hand softly on her arm. She brushed it off with a gentle movement, her eyes still clinging to Jeff, and she didn't seem to know that it was Steve who spoke or Steve who touched her.

"And the thing you had to see him about, that thing which was so important, was to ask him not to tell anyone that you were Lee Gray."

She said, her voice a monotone, "Yes. How did you know, Jeff?"

"I guess I'm getting to be a detective. Haila told me that the reason you had such a tough time getting a start on the stage was because you were such a bad first reader, that you had to work into a part before you could do anything with it. Then yesterday Clint Bowers remarked about your wonderful first reading for him, that after he heard you Alice McDonald didn't have a chance for the part of Dina. I should have got it then. But I had to be re-cued and Tommy Neilson did it for me. He was in Bowers' office, he said, the first time you walked in, and that you didn't give a reading, you gave a performance. And it dawned on me at last that for being a bad first reader you were sure knocking them over right and left. I reached out and took a guess. Maybe you gave such a spectacular first reading because it wasn't a first reading at all. Maybe you knew that part in *Green Apples*. But how could you? The play was done in England. When Haila and I were visiting Morris at the Gotham I noticed that he had a half-dozen scrapbooks overflowing with clippings. I got in his room while he was out and …"

"How in the world did you get in his room, Jeff?" I asked.

"It was tough. Even after I convinced a chambermaid that I was a detective, I had to give her ten dollars and my fraternity pin with promises. We're engaged, but I think I can break it. She doesn't know my name. Besides I wouldn't marry a girl that didn't trust me. She watched me while I read Morris' scrapbook so I wouldn't swipe anything. Well, I found the London notices of *Green Apples*, no Carol Blanton. But the play was tried out in Manchester, and playing Dina was a girl named Leila Gray. I knew from the review who Leila Gray was. The critic described you pretty minutely, Carol. He raved about you."

Steve's fingers beat a nervous rhythm on my mantelpiece. He was watching Carol quietly, his face a stony question. She said, not looking in his direction: "I'll tell you about it if you want me to. There isn't any use hiding it now."

"No," Jeff said. "Maybe if you tell us everything we can help you."

"Carol Blanton's my real name. My mother's name was Leila Gray and I liked it. I took it when I went to London.

"Mother died when I was a baby, my father when I was sixteen. I was all alone. I found a job in a department store. I hated Salt Lake City, I hated the store and I hated everything about my life. I wanted to be an actress. And I saved my money, the little I earned. I finally saved four hundred dollars and then I won a dramatic prize that a woman's club gave. That was enough to go to London and enroll in the Royal Academy there. I'd dreamed about that for years. For the first time in my life I had what I wanted. There was nothing to remind me of that store. I had a little room, all mine, and new clothes and new work. A brand-new life in a brand-new country. Everything was wonderful, the way I'd planned it to be. It was while I was at the Academy that I met Greeley Morris."

She stopped and passed her hand wearily before her eyes. Steve had stopped his drumming and there was only the sound of our breathing in the room.

"He came to see our graduating exercises, along with a lot of other playwrights and producers and directors, all the really big people in the London theater. My performance had been good, he said; perhaps he could use me. He had a play now with a part that I might fit. He thought I had some talent, might someday make an actress of myself. I suppose he did like my acting, too. But that wasn't the reason he gave me the part of Dina in *Green Apples*.

"I worked for him. Oh, how hard I worked! He was nasty and sarcastic and sometimes I wanted to cry in front of everybody. But then I wouldn't. I was learning to be an actress. I had a part on the stage.

Everything was wonderful, too wonderful." She smiled bitterly. "Well, it was so far.

"Just before we opened in Manchester he started at me. Coming into my dressing room and pawing at me, following me home nights and everywhere I went. He wanted me to live with him and I ... I hated him. You don't know Greeley Morris. Oh, yes, you saw him in Clint Bowers' office, but you don't know him. You think I'm frightened now because someone's trying to kill me, but I was more frightened then. I locked my door at night, pushed the bureau in front of it. I carried sandwiches into my room and ate them there because I was afraid to go out. And at the theater, all those days and those nights, every minute of it was agony. He's ... oh, I can't describe him to you. I can't!"

Greeley Morris' dark, sardonic face rose before me. The thin, ugly smile. The cold, tweed-colored eyes. I didn't need Carol to describe him to me.

"It was the fourth night that we played Manchester that it happened. I was crazy with all those weeks of being afraid of Greeley Morris. I didn't know what I was doing any more. I walked onto the stage and stood there. I couldn't remember anything, my lines were gone. I could hear the prompter but I couldn't say the words. The audience was all laughing, some of them started to hoot. I ... I just walked off. They brought the curtain down, put in the understudy. And Greeley Morris was waiting for me in my dressing room."

She stopped, her eyes dark with the horror of remembering. For the first time she looked at us. "You're wondering why I didn't quit. I couldn't. It wouldn't have done me any good. I knew I couldn't hide from him if he wanted to find me. And I ... I needed the job. I'd spent more money than I should have. It was the first time I'd ever had any to spend and there were so many things I wanted. I had to have a job.

"A few nights later it happened again, I forgot my lines almost at the same place. This time I didn't go back to my dressing room. I walked straight out into the street, my costume on and my makeup on. I walked out into the street. I went home.

"The next day I started looking for a job. It wasn't any good. There wasn't a manager in London who would let me work for him. Morris had got there first. They knew I was unreliable; they knew I had memory lapses on stage. I had walked out of Greeley Morris' show.

"Once I nearly got a job, not a good one, but a job. A manager who had seen my performance in *Green Apples* and had liked me. I got as far as a week's rehearsals. That was all. Morris heard about it and I was fired.

"There was nothing for me in London then and so I came back. I changed my name to Carol Blanton again so that Morris couldn't find me, couldn't spoil my chances with the managers here if he still wanted to. And I was afraid he did.

"I pounded the pavements here for months. I did get a few chances to read for parts, but I read so badly. And I had had no experience. I couldn't tell them about *Green Apples*. I had to say, 'No. No experience at all.' Then one day I saw in the paper that Clint Bowers was going to do *Green Apples*. All of a sudden it came to me. There was a part I could do. Jeff, you saw what that critic said in Manchester. And Greeley Morris never came to America for any of his plays. He would never know if the girl who played Dina was Leila Gray. I was ... pretty desperate then. There was no money left, none at all. Well, it was worth the chance and I took it."

She studied her fingertips intently. "You know the rest. I got the job and the day we opened I heard that he was to be here.

"I didn't know what to do at first. And then I thought ... he was only to be here that one night and, if he shouldn't see me, if he should go on to Hollywood without knowing – I had to make Alice play that one night.

"I did it. I pretended my voice was gone, and then, when you had gone to the theater, Haila, then I remembered the pictures in front of the Colony, and I knew it wouldn't work. He couldn't help seeing that big picture of me plastered there, and he would know. It would be better if I played. Maybe he wouldn't say anything, maybe I could keep him from saying anything. You and Tommy came in when I was telephoning the theater to say that I'd be there. You didn't believe me, I could see that. But I ... I couldn't explain.

"I wrote the note when I was alone in my dressing room and after it was written I didn't know what to do with it. I kept asking myself if it was worthwhile to plead with him or if I should just keep still and take my chance. Even after the play I was still muddled up. I didn't know what to do. And then, suddenly, I was sick. The kind of sick when you think you're dying and nothing matters at all. I forgot about that note and Greeley Morris and my job, forgot about everything but getting home and into bed. That was all. The next thing I knew I was in Bellevue."

She sank on the couch and covered her face with her hands. After a moment Jeff said, "Did you think it was Greeley Morris who tried to kill you, Carol?"

"I ... I don't know. At first I did. When we met that morning in Bowers' office and he pretended not to know me, when he said that he had never heard of Lee Gray, then I thought he was the one. But the next night when Eve was murdered, he wasn't even in the theater. And then … then I knew it couldn't be he."

"Carol, why were you calling him at his hotel? When I answered the phone?"

"I nearly fainted when I recognized your voice."

"Where was Crowley when you called?"

"I had gone out for a walk and he was with me. And suddenly I had to talk to Morris. I had to find out what he was going to do. I didn't want him to tell the police about Lee Gray, the way he'd tell it, it would sound … If anyone told the police or Mr. Bowers or you, I wanted to do it."

"But if Crowley was with you …"

"I managed to lose him in the crowd and sneak into a corner drugstore without him seeing me. When I came out, he was running back and forth on Madison Avenue looking for me."

Jeff said ruefully: "If Crowley had only reported that he had lost track of you at that corner, and at that time, we would have known you were Lee Gray. Because I traced the call to that drugstore."

"He was so embarrassed at losing sight of me that I knew he'd never mention it to Peterson."

"The lug!"

Carol smiled faintly. "He didn't even know I had been in that drugstore; he couldn't have thought it would have mattered. I was only gone a minute. I knew the number and as soon as Jeff answered I hung up and ran out. I was afraid you had recognized my voice, Jeff."

"You only said one word. But if I had it would have saved you a lot of trouble and worry."

"Yes. Oh, I've almost told you all this … a thousand times. But I couldn't."

"Why, Carol?"

Her eyes found Steve's and there was a glistening of quick tears in them. "Steve. I didn't want Steve …"

He was beside her then, she was in his arms, sobbing into his shoulder. "It was such a nasty thing, all of it. So horrible, not like what I wanted for Steve and me. I was ashamed of it. And I was afraid of what Steve would do if I told him about Greeley …"

The white lines around Steve's mouth tightened like little bands, drawing it into a hard slit. "I'm going to be glad to see Mr. Morris."

"Steve!" Carol's face was ashen. "Steve, that's why I've been quiet! That's why I've kept all this inside me! I didn't want you and Morris to … Oh, Steve, you mustn't see him! Something will happen, Steve, something will happen if you do, and we'll … we'll lose each other,

Steve!" She turned to Jeff. She was crying. "Jeff, don't let Morris come here! You don't need to see him now. I've told you everything, I've explained it all to you! He doesn't have to come, does he?"

"Yes, Carol," Jeff said gently. "You see, we want Morris to explain a few things now."

"Then ... then make Steve go before he comes. Don't let him ... Oh, I'm afraid for Steve! He mustn't see Greeley Morris, he mustn't. ..."

We heard the elevator come to a groaning stop, quick footsteps in the hall outside, and then the impatient rapping at the door. Jeff turned the key in the lock. Peterson stepped to one side as the door opened, and Greeley Morris preceded him into the room.

CHAPTER SIXTEEN

IN a voice monotonous with strain and fatigue, and so low that at times Peterson had to lean forward to hear her, Carol retold her story almost word for word. Only once did he interrupt her. "London, huh? So that accounts for the blank between the time you left Salt Lake City and turned up here in New York. We were working on that now, Miss Blanton." He nodded curtly and she went on, occasionally glancing furtively at Greeley Morris as if she feared, despite Steve's reassuring nearness, he might rise and start toward her. But Morris hardly moved during the long recital except to light a fresh cigarette.

Peterson moved to the window when Carol had finished and stood looking down into the street, his hands clasped behind his back. At last he turned and, facing Morris, said abruptly, "So you knew Miss Blanton in London."

"I knew Miss Gray in London."

"When did you first know that Carol Blanton was to appear in your play over here?"

"When Bowers cabled me the names of the cast."

"When was that?"

"Just before the show went into rehearsal."

"So you knew," Peterson snapped, "that Miss Blanton was in New York and in your play."

Morris smiled. "Naturally. But I didn't know that Miss Blanton was Miss Gray."

"You have no way of proving that?"

"Of course not."

"But you recognized her as Lee Gray when you saw *Green Apples* on opening night?"

"Certainly."

"And yet you denied knowing Lee Gray. Why?"

"That's fairly obvious, isn't it? Miss Blanton had been poisoned on the very night of my arrival, unfortunately. The police, apparently, were searching for someone with a past connection to her. I saw no reason to offer the evidence of my connection with her by explaining Lee Gray and implicating myself. And since Miss Blanton seemed unanxious to do so ..."

"So. Very pretty. And the story Miss Blanton has just told ... was it ... has she been correct about your relationship with her in England?"

"Would you expect me to admit it if it were the truth?"

"Is it?"

"That I'm a degenerate, a maniac who scares little girls?"

"Why did Miss Blanton leave your show?"

Steve jumped up angrily. "Carol's told you why she left! Must you drag her through all that again? Isn't it bad enough that she has to stay here and ..."

Peterson interrupted him. "She doesn't have to stay here. She can leave now if she wants to."

"I'll stay," Carol said quietly. Her hand reached up to Steve, drawing him down beside her. "Steve, I've got to stay."

"All right, Morris. Why did Miss Blanton leave your show?"

"As it has already been pointed out, I drove her from it."

"By forcing your attentions on her?"

"Not at all. I fired her for incompetency. She had a nasty habit of standing on stage and not being able to say a line."

Steve said, "Yes, because she was so terrified of you that ..."

Morris' voice rose above Steve's. "No. Because she was drunk. On one occasion, the last, she wasn't even able to stand, she passed out on stage. We had to lower the curtain and have the understudy take over."

"That's a lie!" Steve said hoarsely.

Carol clutched at his shoulders with both hands. I could see that they were shaking. But her voice was steady.

"Yes, Steve, it's a lie. It's what he told the other managers in London about me. That's why they wouldn't give me a job, any of them. Don't listen to him, Steve."

Morris said calmly, "I told the other managers about you because I didn't want you to spoil their productions as you did mine."

"Go on, Mr. Morris, go on! Tell what you told them. Tell everything you said!"

"I'd rather not, really."

"No. You're afraid to. You're afraid in front of Steve, you know that he …"

Peterson said, "Take it easy, Miss Blanton."

She sank back on the couch trembling violently and Steve held her tight with one arm around her shoulders, his other hand clasping hers. Morris looked at the cigarette that he turned in his fingers as if it were the only important thing in the room.

"So you'd rather not talk any more about London, Mr. Morris?"

"No. I assure you it's as painful to me as it is to Miss Blanton and her young champion there."

"Nuts!" said Peterson. "Tell your story."

"Must I?"

"You're damn right. Miss Blanton was poisoned, as you pointed out, the night of your arrival. Your alibi for the night of Eve North's murder is phony and you have none for the time of the shooting today. And, most important, you've been withholding valuable evidence. If I were in your shoes, Morris, I'd talk. And loud!"

"Very well. It seems that my previous reticence has only implicated me in this mess when I had hoped for the opposite. So my story is this.

"I saw Miss Blanton, then Miss Gray, playing at the Royal Academy as she says, and I thought her a beautiful child giving a lovely performance. I cast her in *Green Apples*. When rehearsals started we were a happy group of people and, for a theatrical troupe, curiously lacking in backstage jealousies and petty intrigue. That cast was a playwright's dream, a contented, enthusiastic family.

"But in six short weeks that happy family was living in a cesspool. There wasn't a friendship left. My actors were behaving like a bunch of neurotics. My leading man and my leading lady hated each other, refused to speak off stage. The lovely young thing who had been playing Haila Rogers' part attempted suicide. Her engagement to the young stage manager had been mysteriously broken. My character man, a fine old chap, had suddenly become a dipsomaniac. That made two in my company, including Miss Blanton."

Jeff sidestepped in front of Steve as he started to rise. Carol sat rigidly, one hand covering her eyes.

Peterson growled, "Go on."

"The character man had been milked of every cent he had, and made a fool of, by my pretty ingenue. In those six weeks a brilliant young actress' career and love affair had been ruined by this ingenue's malignant slander. She had broken friendships, torn people apart with her lies and intrigue and ambition. That ingenue was Leila Gray."

There was a moment of white-hot silence before Carol, tears streaming down her cheeks, leaped to her feet.

"Now you see why I ran away, why I changed my name, why I've lived in terror of him! Now he's trying to wreck Steve's love for me, he's trying to break my life again!" She turned to Steve, her chin lifted bravely. "I knew he'd do this, Steve. That's why I wanted to send you away. Steve, darling, try to forget all this, forget how horrible he is and all his horrible lies. ..."

She fled into the bedroom. Steve stared after her, a bewildered, almost frightened look on his face.

"Steve," I said, "go to her. She needs you now. Don't stand there like that! Steve, why don't you go to her!"

Jeff said quietly: "Because what Morris said is true, Haila. All of it."

No one moved. Steve was still looking dazedly at the closed bedroom door and Greeley Morris watched him with anxiety. Peterson, the policeman, sat waiting.

I said, "No, Jeff."

"Yes. Don't you see that she's done the same thing to your company that she did in England? Only here someone tried to kill her for it, and that covered her up. Everyone was afraid to tell the truth about Carol for fear that it might throw suspicion for her attempted murder and Eve's death on them. Everyone but Alice McDonald. She knew what Carol was and she could speak. Carol hadn't given her a motive for murder. But when Alice told us you laughed at her. You didn't believe her."

"But you didn't either."

"It started me thinking."

Peterson said impatiently, "What has she done? And who did she do it to?"

"To Philip Ashley. She used the same technique on him that she practiced on that character man in England. In his room I found an I.O.U. for five hundred dollars. It was a silly game, he said, the I.O.U. was only a joke. But it wasn't a joke. It was real. And God knows how many more of them there were or why he was fool enough to have loaned her the money.

"Look at Tommy Neilson. She had him nuts about her, she took everything that Tommy had to offer and then she dropped him. She dropped him because she saw bigger game and that bigger game was Steve. With Steve there was wealth and position. No wonder she did everything in her power to keep the story of Lee Gray from coming out. That's why she was rushing the engagement and the wedding. She made him think that it was he who was doing the rushing. She talked about endangering his life, knowing that it would make Steve more anxious to marry her quickly and take care of her."

"But, Jeff," I said, "with me she was always ... she seemed such a child. I thought she was my friend. And she was, Jeff! She never did anything to me."

"Haila, she's been using you since the moment you met. She made as much money from *Green Apples* as you did, but she's borrowed from you, lived here, eaten your food, worn your clothes ..."

"But they were such little things! I didn't mind."

"... and she drank your liquor. Didn't the amount of liquor that little angel put away ever puzzle you, Haila? But she was watching her step pretty carefully. She never wanted Steve to see her drunk."

I forced myself to look at Steve. He was hunched down in a big chair, his face blank with shock. His eyes seemed strangely glazed. I turned away from him to Jeff.

"But I ... I can't believe all this! She couldn't have been so ... couldn't have been what you say and at the same time seemed ..."

Jeff said, "She was, Haila. She is a wonderful actress. Tonight when I announced that I had found Lee Gray the way she leaned forward and said, 'Who?' nearly made me think I was wrong. She told her fantastic story about Greeley Morris to Greeley Morris and never batted an eyelash. She lied to you about her voice the night the play opened, about everything. Think a little, Haila. It's true, isn't it?"

Steve stood up. Mechanically, he went to the table in the corner and picked up his hat. Without looking at any of us he moved to the door. We heard his heavy footsteps on the stairs outside. The door remained wide open.

Morris said suddenly: "I'd like to run along, Peterson. That boy. Perhaps I can ... he's too nice a kid to have had this happen to him."

"Go ahead, Morris."

My brain felt muddled, foggy. There was a sharp, biting ache at my temples. I walked to the bedroom door and stood looking at it. From behind me Jeff was saying, "All along I've known that there was some strange undercurrent, something I couldn't put my finger on, running through the whole company. And I knew that in some way it was connected with Carol. Everyone was too fond of her, too incredulous that a single hair of her pretty head should be in danger. There was something phony about it. I didn't know that it was because she was hated so passionately, and with such damn good cause, that everyone was leaning over backward for fear of being suspected of murder."

I turned at the sound of Peterson's voice. He stood in the doorway frowning.

"We've tried like hell to find a suspect," he said, "someone with a motive to kill Carol Blanton. I thought when we found Lee Gray we'd also get our suspect. Well, we found her. Before, we had no suspects. Now, as far as I can see, practically everyone in New York and England has a reason to kill her."

CHAPTER SEVENTEEN

The cars sped by below the window, even spaced and quiet, like models in an advertising display. Across the street, the doorman at the Esquador came out onto the sidewalk and blew his whistle. A cruising taxi rolled to a stop before him, picked up its passenger and rolled away. There was no sound in my apartment, and the night seemed to press down on the city outside and smother its noises to a low rumble.

It might have been an hour or just a few minutes ago that Steve had left the room. I wasn't aware of time or of people or of anything but the numb feeling that seeped through my body and the sharp ache in my head.

There was a little icy ridge around the frame of the window and I scratched it with my nail and it shredded and fell off. Behind me, pacing the floor, Jeff spoke musingly.

"You've learned that trick from Carol. That trick of draping yourself in the window. That's how she was sitting this afternoon before ..."

"Jeff, let's not talk. Not yet."

We lapsed into silence again and I closed my eyes. I tried to think things out, to think what I should say to Carol, how I would answer what she said to me. My mind closed on me and it was useless.

"Haila!"

Jeff's voice wasn't musing now. It was urgent and terribly excited. I swung around to face him, almost frightened.

"Haila, listen. This afternoon ... this afternoon at the party when that shot came through the window!"

"Yes?"

"Tell me everything that happened after we got here."

"But why?"

"Please!" His hands were working nervously together. "We got here a little after one. Think, Haila, try to remember. What did we do? What did we do exactly?"

"We talked to Carol for a few minutes," I said. My mind went struggling back mechanically over the afternoon. "And then Clint Bowers came with his flowers and Carol went into the kitchen. Is that what you mean?"

"Yes. Yes, go on."

"Then, in a moment, she came back with the bottle and some glasses. You opened the champagne and we drank."

"Where were we then, can you remember, Haila? Where were we sitting, you and I? And what was Carol doing and where was Clint Bowers?"

Suddenly the picture flashed before me, clearly, like a sharp bright etching. "You and I sat there on the couch, your feet were on the coffee table and I was busy knocking them off. Clint was in the big armchair in the far corner and the champagne was on the table right beside him. Carol was here where I am, in the window seat. I remember thinking how pretty the light looked in her hair."

"And then?" Jeff was a moving blur, pacing up and down before me.

"Carol told us she was going to marry Steve. She said it was wrong of her, it wasn't fair to Steve. But she was going to marry him anyway. I thought how brave and honest she was. And then we congratulated her and said it ... it was wonderful. And Clint spoke then, I think. He suggested that we have another drink. He said, 'Carol, you're first,' or something like that, and she went over to him. She had her glass in her hand. And when she got almost to him, the shot came."

Jeff stopped in front of me. "Are you sure, Haila? Is that it? Are you sure it happened just like that?"

"Yes."

"So am I." He walked aimlessly around the room, kicking up the corners of the rugs, smoothing them down again. He lit a cigarette, took one deep drag and smudged it out. He wheeled back at me. "Look, Haila. One more thing. I want you to think back again, hard. And pretty far. Do you remember the night *Green Apples* opened and I waited for you outside your dressing room? Eve North and Philip Ashley were fighting. Remember?"

"Yes, of course I remember."

"We could hear them through the walls. Tell me everything they said, everything you heard."

"Oh, Jeff, please! I'm a frazzle. I'm exhausted."

"I want you to reconstruct for me, that's all."

"My mind won't function any more. It won't. Reconstruct yourself."

"Haila, please ..."

"Oh, all right. Philip accused Eve of stealing a scene from him. He was mad because during his big speech Eve ..."

"When did that big speech come?"

"Listen; if I'm going to reconstruct, I'm going to reconstruct in my own way."

"Go ahead."

"I'm too tired to change my style."

"Okay."

"I've been through too much. I feel like crying."

"Wait just five minutes."

"I'm hysterical, Jeff."

"I know you are. Shall I hit you in the face?"

"Will it hurt?"

"I'll say. But it'll stop your hysteria."

"Can I slap you back?" I started to giggle, I couldn't help it. Jeff caught me on the cheek with his open palm. I rocked, then things went red.

When I pulled myself together Jeff was sitting on the floor groaning. I knelt beside him. "Jeff, what's wrong? Jeff, talk to me!"

"You louse! You hit me in the belly!"

"Oh, I'm so sorry!"

"Yeah." Jeff was up. He practiced breathing again.

"Shall I get you a cup of tea?"

"No, thanks. And let that be a lesson to you, Haila. Don't get hysterical around me. Now, where were we?"

"You were on the floor."

"C'mon, Eve and Philip. His big speech. Where is it in the play?"

"Almost at the end of the third act. Eve was supposed to be arranging flowers on the dining table while he talked. She said that there weren't any flowers on the table, that either Tommy or Phoebe Thompson was to blame for forgetting them. She said she had to do something while he droned along and Ashley said she needn't have rattled the complete set of silver, the glasses and the plates. Just upsetting the table would have been more effective. Ashley heavy sarcasm. There, that's it. That's what they were fighting about, and what difference does it make?"

"Were the flowers there?"

"No, I don't think so. I guess Eve was right."

Jeff stopped his pacing and with his back toward me looked silently at Carol's door. Over his shoulder I could see him waving out a match and splitting it with his thumb nail. When he turned he was puffing furiously at a half lit cigarette.

"That's just how it happened, isn't it, Haila? You're sure of that?"

"Of course."

He thumped his hand on my back. "Sweetheart, let's get married. I have just put the Colony Murder Case in the bag!"

I stared at him to see if this was a joke and I knew it wasn't. The eagerness in his voice and eyes was genuine. Before I could catch enough breath to speak he was sliding into his overcoat, moving toward the door. I rushed after him.

"Jeff, you know! You've found out who's been trying to kill Carol!"

He grinned at me. "Yes, I know."

"Was it Ashley? Is Philip Ashley the murderer after all?"

"I can't tell you yet."

"Tommy? Tommy ... Oh, Jeff, not Steve!"

"Don't try to guess, Haila."

"Jeff, you've got to tell me!"

His face went grave and both hands clamped my shoulders. "Don't ask me, Haila, I don't want you to know. It's ... dangerous. Believe me, Haila."

"But you ... then it's dangerous for you? Jeff, you've got to tell the police."

"Not yet."

I said furiously: "Oh, you don't know. You've no more idea than I have. How could you? Nothing's happened to show you."

"You just told me who the murderer is."

"I? I told you!"

He snatched his hat and gave me a preoccupied kiss on the cheek. I caught him as he reached the door.

"Jeff, where are you going?"

"Out and about, dear, out and about."

"What are you going to do?"

"I can't tell you that. But I'll tell you what I'm not going to do. Sleep. Not a wink. I'll call you in the morning. I'll keep in constant touch with you. G'night."

I stood before him in the doorway, blocking his exit. Suddenly, I couldn't bear his leaving, couldn't face the thought of a night in that place with no one but Carol. I felt my face go white, heard myself gulp as I spoke. "Jeff, don't leave me. Please, don't go."

He held my hand tight. "What is it, Haila?"

"Jeff, I'm frightened, really frightened. I'm afraid for you. I'm afraid for myself, to stay here along with ... with Carol. When I thought she was ... before I knew about her, I didn't mind. It seemed worthwhile then and I could be brave. But now, now I'm scared. I don't want to stay here with her. If someone tried now, tried tonight to ... to hurt her, I ..."

"Nobody's going to hurt Carol. Nobody's even going to try."

"But ..."

"Haila, I'll tell you this. Keep it under your hat for it isn't a good thing for you to know. God, we've been on the greatest goose chase that's ever been perpetrated. Look, nobody is going to kill Carol. Nobody ever tried to kill Carol. Have you got that? Her life's never been in danger, never for one minute."

"But, Jeff ..."

"It was that party this afternoon. God! If only I'd been awake. It's so simple. She stood in the window, Haila, she stood there for ten minutes. And then, after she moved away ... *after* she moved away, the shot came through. She draped herself in the window, a perfect target for the Esquador Hotel, and nothing happened. But after she moved away ... not till then, was the shot fired. Don't you see what it means, Haila? That bullet wasn't meant to kill Carol!"

"Wasn't meant to ..."

"That shot was fired through the window to keep us thinking that Carol was the intended victim."

"But if it wasn't Carol, then who was the murderer trying to kill?"

"Eve. Eve North was the victim all along. And the murderer made his mistake the first night, not the second. His mistake was when he poisoned Carol, not when he stabbed Eve."

"Eve North." I shook my head. It was too much for me.

"It was Eve who was supposed to have been killed. And she was! Carol's safe. And you're safe, so go to bed. I'll call you in the morning."

He left me in the doorway and I could hear him taking the steps three at a time. I glanced at the closed bedroom door and then at my watch. It was twenty minutes to three.

I got sheets and blankets out of the hall closet, stuffed one of the big sofa pillows into a case and made up my bed on the studio couch.

I didn't think I would disturb Carol.

CHAPTER EIGHTEEN

THE monotonous drumming of rain at the window awakened me and I sat up wondering why I felt glum and sour and hangoverish. Then I remembered. Carol was in my room and she and I had a few things to straighten out and there was no use putting it off longer. I went quietly to the bedroom and opened the door.

The room was empty and the bed had either been made or not slept in at all. There was a little gap between my row of dresses in the closet where Carol's clothes had hung and a vacant space on the shelf where I had stuck her suitcase. A sprinkling of powder and a few blond hairpins wedged into the cracks of the dresser drawer were all that remained of Carol's belongings. I breathed a sigh of relief and experienced my first kindly feelings toward her since Jeff had exploded his bombshell the night before. I was sincerely grateful for her quiet exodus, for I had dreaded the chat that was scheduled more than I cared to admit.

Well, that was that. And the next time I befriended a gal she would be a Golden Eaglet Scout or a certified Sunday School teacher.

I bathed and dressed and with a cup of strong black coffee at my elbow and the long neglected *Though Heavens Fall* on my lap, I calmly settled myself to wait for Jeff's call.

On page four I gave up. Every character was saying: "Carol was never meant to be killed. ... Nobody tried to kill Carol. ... It was Eve all along, Eve who was the victim. ... She sat in the window ten minutes ... a perfect target ... and then she moved away. ... Carol's safe ... a dipsomaniac ... a thief ... she blackmails people ... but no one tried to kill her. ..."

I shut *Though Heavens Fall* in disgust and flung it at the telephone. Twelve-thirty and Jeff hadn't called. Keep me informed, would he? Call me in the morning, keep in constant touch with me, was that what he had said?

I dialed his number and there was no answer. I called it every five minutes until one o'clock and then I decided to do some sleuthing on my own.

I called Steve Brown's hotel and the desk clerk said there was no answer. Tommy Neilson wasn't in his room. Philip Ashley told me in brief, unpleasant terms that he didn't give a damn about Mr. Jeff Troy's whereabouts. I dialed the Rehearsal Club number and succeeded in getting Alice McDonald away from an important script.

"This is Haila," I said. "Alice, have you seen anything of Jeff?"

"I've been locked up in my room all morning with an important script that ..."

"I know. Thanks. I thought maybe Jeff had called you. So long."

"Haila! Wait a second!"

"Yes?"

"Why would Jeff call me?"

"No special reason, I just thought maybe he had."

"Haila, I saw Carol Blanton walking down Fifty-third Street alone this morning. Isn't that ... dangerous?"

"No, it's all right. I mean … maybe you were mistaken, Alice. Good-by."

I hung up and for ten minutes paced the floor. I was wondering if I should call Greeley Morris and what would happen if I did when the phone shrilled in my ear. I jumped a mile before I picked it up.

"Hello, you big bum!"

"This is Alice. Jeff just called me, Haila. But he was in a hurry. I didn't have a chance to tell him about you."

"Where was he?"

"I don't know where he called from. But he's going to be at the theater at three. He asked me to get hold of Phoebe Thompson and Ashley and tell them to be there, too. I don't know what's happening, do you? He was very mysterious."

"Well, you know more than I do."

"Will you be there?"

"I haven't been invited."

"Don't be silly! Jeff seemed in a terrible rush. You're in this as much as anybody."

I replaced the phone and leaned back. Alice, Phoebe, Ashley and Jeff! Well, either Jeff was going to have the girls teach him and Steve to dance or something was going to happen. And he was going to let it happen without me. That's what he thought!

I changed into some old clothes, put on my plaid trench coat and started out. It was still raining in a steady downpour, but it wasn't a cold rain and it felt clean and soft on my face. I splashed over to Broadway. Before I got there the rain had turned to snow and the pavements were mush covered. The day darkened and the lights shone mistily through skyscraper office windows.

Through the great oval glass of the Maxwell place I thought I could smell the fragrance of the steaming coffee that was being served inside. At once I was hungry and cold and I stopped uncertainly to peer at my watch. Not quite two-thirty. There was plenty of time for a sandwich and a cup of coffee. Then, with a nice display of willpower, I turned my head and went on. It would be better to arrive at the theater a little early than a little late. I wanted to see Jeff's flush of pleased surprise when he got there and spied me.

Alice McDonald was standing at the entrance of the Colony stage alley. With her mannish black rubber slicker, an old felt hat pulled down over her eyes and overshoes on low-heeled brogans, she looked ready for a hurricane.

"Nice day, Alice, for you know what."

"I love it, the wind and the rain."

"Anyone here yet?"

"No, nobody. Let's go in."

"You bet."

"Oh, Nick's here. Asleep in his chair at the door as usual. We'll be careful not to waken the poor old man."

Together we sloshed down the alley, almost dark now, and through the stage door. Nick was at the low table just inside, his pipe in his mouth and his head bent over a sheaf of papers. He was sound asleep. There wasn't a movement from him as we slipped by and went out onto the stage.

Nothing had been changed since that tragic night when I had opened the door on stage right and found Eve North's dead body huddled behind it. Even the small hand props scattered about the room were as we had left them, the scarlet-tipped stubs of cigarettes that I had smoked still in the ashtrays. Half hidden by the blotter on the desk was the note that I had written while old Ben Kerry and I had played that last scene.

Except for a single shadeless rehearsal lamp that stood ludicrously in the center of that lovely set and filled it with a bleak white glare, it was all the same. It seemed strange to me, for no reason at all, that so much could have happened to all of us who played there while it remained serenely unchanged.

Alice's hand tightened on my arm and we walked over to the light. "Haila," she said softly, "has Jeff found out anything? Does he know ..."

"I haven't seen him since last night." I pulled my arm away from her. I didn't care for Alice when she got intense.

"He knows who the murderer is, doesn't he?"

"Jeff doesn't confide in me, the big goop."

"He knows; that's why he's having everyone meet here. He's told you who it is, hasn't he?"

"I said that ..."

"I know. You won't tell me. It's because you don't like me, Haila. You've never liked me; you're jealous of me – because I come from a family of great actors, because of my heritage!"

I turned my back on her and started for the door. I wasn't going to listen to a performance by a frustrated actress. I had taken three steps when she clutched my arm and swung me around.

Then suddenly, the light wavered, as if it had been a candle and I had blown on it, and went out. I wrenched myself free and reached out for the light. My hand met nothing but black emptiness.

"Hello! Anybody down there!"

"It's Haila, Clint, and Alice."

"As soon as I find my damn lighter ... here it is!" I saw the flare of his lighter like a miniature torch high above me. "I'm coming down."

"I'll be glad to see you."

I wondered where he had popped from and immediately remembered that a door opened from his offices onto the balcony. The flame disappeared as he started down the steps and was there again as he reached the orchestra. He groped his way down the center aisle, shielding the flickering lighter with his hands. He climbed up on the stage.

"I thought Alice was here."

"She is." But I couldn't find her. "Or was."

"Maybe she's afraid of the dark. She might have gone out."

"I think she's afraid of herself. What's wrong with the lights?"

"They're out in my office too. And the street lights are out. That happens sometimes during an afternoon storm. Every light in town burning at once, the strain is too great. Hey, Nick!" he shouted.

There was a startled grunt as Nick awakened in his cubicle and shuffled in. Clint sent him out for a flashlight, then said to me, "Where's Jeff?"

"He's due at three."

"I know, he called me this morning."

"Oh, are you invited to his party, too?"

"Come to think of it, I wasn't. He just asked for the use of the stage at three o'clock. God! This is a dismal place!"

"If Alice is in some corner making up for Hamlet's ghost I'll fold up. My nerves have been getting enough of a workout lately without Alice contributing."

"For the sake of your nerves let's wait out in the alley till Nick or the lights come back."

"In the snow? Not for Haila. I don't really mind the dark." I felt for the davenport that I knew was somewhere in the vicinity and sank down upon it. My eyes were accustoming themselves better to the darkness now, and I could distinguish the shapes of things vaguely. I slid over the couch and patted the cushions beside me. "Sit here, Clint."

He laughed. "No, thanks. It's going to be compromising enough for me to be found on a dark stage with you, let alone in any compromising position. Cigarette?"

I said, "Yes, please."

He came over slowly and handed me one, lit it for me. Then he moved across the stage to the big wing chair that stood before the French windows and I could see his face, slightly frowning, as he lit his own cigarette and sat down. My feet were wet and I slipped off my sopping shoes and curled my legs up under me. It was warm and comfortable and somehow cozy there in spite of the immensity of the place, or maybe because of it, and I inhaled deeply and nestled into the soft depths of the couch.

Clint's voice came across the stage. "What's this all about, Haila? Do you know? Jeff sounded pretty much in earnest this morning."

"He's getting hot, Clint, or thinks he is. He thinks he knows."

"Knows? Knows who ..."

"Yes. He knows who the murderer is."

There was a long pause and when Clint spoke again his voice was grave and quiet. "I hope to God he does. I want to get this whole mess over with. You know, Haila, that child's face is haunting me. A kid like Carol living with that thing over her head, a kid who never bothered anyone. God! I see those big frightened eyes every place I look. And her bravery makes it all the worse. If she'd break down ... if she'd ..."

I said, "Carol can take care of herself, Clint."

He didn't seem to hear me. "I tell myself that it's none of my doing, that all I did was give her a break that a thousand other girls would give their right hands for, a chance to be an actress. Yes, that's the way I doctor it up for myself. I gave the poor kid a break all right. A chance to be murdered, to live in fear and terror, a chance to spread herself all over the front pages in a gruesome murder case. If she should be ..."

The bitterness and self-reproach in his voice were beating at me. In the quick flame of his cigarette as he drew on it I could see his face, the sad tight lines around his mouth, the furrows between his eyes. I couldn't stand it.

"Clint," I said, "there's no reason for you to reproach yourself. Nothing's going to happen to Carol. Nothing was ever meant to happen to her. She ... It was Eve, Clint, who was supposed to be killed. The murderer meant to stab Eve, not Carol. The murderer meant to poison Eve."

I could hear him catch his breath. "Eve! No! God, no! Who would ..."

"Yes, Clint," I said gently.

His voice was shocked, almost breaking. "No, no. Not Eve. The poison ... Haila, the poison was put in Carol's glass. Not Eve's."

"Yes. Yes, I don't ..." I stopped.

If Eve was to be the victim, then the poison must have been placed in her glass. That much was certain. How had Jeff figured it out last night? Something about Philip Ashley and his fight with Eve. Did he mean Ashley was the murderer? It was something that Philip had said to Eve. "Why didn't you upset the table?" he had said. "You have the whole play to yourself and still you have to steal my one big scene, you have to rattle everything on the table ...

rattle everything on the table! Then if Eve had rattled the glasses ... if she had *changed* the glasses ...

"Clint," I said, "Clint, that poison *was* put in Eve's glass! And she changed the glasses herself! There were no flowers on the table for her to arrange and she ad libbed business with the glasses. And Carol got the one that was meant for her!"

"Yes," he said slowly. "Yes, that ..."

"But the next night there was no mistake. Oh, Clint, who could have wanted to murder Eve? Who could have hated Eve? You must know, Clint, you were her friend, the only one who really knew her. You've been so close to her and so loyal ... producing for her when she was no longer great, ruining yourself to keep her on Broadway, giving all you had through these years! Clint, you must have loved her very much or ..."

Then I suspected.

He didn't speak; there was no sound from behind the glow of his cigarette. Suddenly the theater wasn't any longer warm and cozy. It was an enormous cavern filled with cold dark danger. I wanted to get out. I stood up and the floor was hard and icy under my stockinged feet.

"Let's go out and wait for Jeff," I said.

"All right."

I didn't scream because I had pressed my hand tight over my lips, holding them closed before the sound got to them. The voice that had answered me had not been Clint Bowers' voice. But it was, it must have been, I told myself frantically. It had come from right behind that point of light. It was Clint Bowers' voice with all its pleasant friendly warmth gone. It was Clint Bowers' voice, harsh and cruel and with a deadly quiet.

It was then I knew.

The burning cigarette was there, unmoved, barring me from the stage door. I felt sick with the weak nauseous feeling that pervades you when you're coming out of ether. I couldn't run or fight or scream.

Then the light leaped toward me, the length of a step, and my head cleared and I snapped out of it.

Putting my cigarette behind me I crushed it between my thumb and forefinger. I crept forward toward the footlights, feeling for them with my toes, moving toward them by slow inches. Thank God for the rain and the snow that had soaked my shoes and had made me take them off. The lights couldn't have been more than three feet from the davenport where I had sat, but it was taking eternities for me to reach them.

Then the edge of their groove was beneath my toe and I stepped across the reflectors and lowered myself into the orchestra pit. Unless

I had moved far to one side, the center aisle should be almost in front of me. I reached out and swept my hand across the blackness and it touched one seat, another, and then no more.

I looked back. The cigarette was moving across the stage to the davenport where I had been, moving as stealthily as I had moved. I started up the aisle, feeling for the rows of seats, counting them as I passed. How many rows did the Colony have, how long would it take me to reach the back? The Music Box has fourteen rows. The Plymouth has nineteen. I thought hysterically, why doesn't Clint Bowers chase me through the Music Box? Then I'd know how far I had to go, I'd know when I had passed them all. Then I'd have a chance.

I could hear him behind me on the stage, moving about and bumping into things.

I could see the faint glimmer of daylight through some crack in the outside door. My hand tangled in the velvet portieres that hung behind the last row of seats and the brass rings above them clanged together and rattled. I stopped dead, holding onto the mass of velvet to keep myself from falling. He had heard the sound on stage. His voice came booming through the house.

"Haila, where are you!"

I made one last stab at keeping up this insane farce. "I'm going out the front door, Clint. Jeff will be coming by this way."

The voice was calm, laughing. "It's locked, Haila."

I didn't try to be quiet then, or to pretend I wasn't terrified. I felt wildly for the door. In my wet, sticky hand the knob was cold. I turned it and my hand slid aimlessly around while it stayed still. I put my coat over it and turned again. It was locked.

I ran from one door to another and they would not budge. I turned and with my back up close against the doors, I faced the stage. The light was coming down into the orchestra pit; now it was starting up the aisle.

Hugging the wall and sidestepping, I moved along the back of the theater, my eyes holding onto that small circle of light with an intensity that made them burn and water. I moved toward the side aisle. I was a step from it when the light turned too and crossed the row of seats toward the spot where I was going. He had seen me. Perhaps that tiny shaft of light that crept through the doors at my back had been enough to outline me for him.

I don't know if I dropped to the floor because the chairs offered a shield of protection from that advancing cigarette or if my legs had just refused to hold my body any longer. Through the chink between the seats I saw the light disappear and then appear again, like a revolving beacon, as Clint Bowers turned around. There was a faint shower of sparks as he smudged his cigarette against a chair. My beacon was gone. Now my ears would have to tell me where he was.

I crouched there for a second, then eased myself under the seats into the last row and lay there, my knees almost under my chin, my arms squeezed in around me, holding my breath to make myself smaller. I could hear him not four rows in front of me now, walking up the aisle. He would pass an arm's length from me. Or he wouldn't pass. He must hear my breath even though I held it, the loud roaring motor of my heart. If I lifted my head the fraction of an inch his outstretched fingers would be in my hair.

Oh, God, if I could only scream! If the muscles in my throat weren't frozen, if my tongue weren't glued to the roof of my mouth! And what if I did scream? What if my voice reached Alice wherever she was or a passerby in the alley outside? Bowers would get to me first. Why didn't the lights come on? Where was Nick? Or Jeff? Oh, God, where was Jeff?

And then I heard a rustle. It was faint and quite far, some place on the other side of the theater. I raised my head and my eyes fought the darkness for the fire door closest to me. I saw it there, only about six rows down. By crawling on my hands and knees, breathlessly, soundlessly, I could make it.

I squirmed down the side aisle, my hands scraping over the floor and feeling my way for me. I was even with the door when I first heard the noise. It came from the front of the house, somewhere near the stage. I backed into the row of seats and stopped and waited. It didn't come again. How could he be so quiet? How could he move about and not even dent that terrifying silence?

The fire door was in front of me, outlined by a thread of light. Only the length of one short aisle to go. Only a few feet. I could worm my way across the floor. I could throw myself against the door and be out in the alley with the daylight all around me and people passing in the street.

Crouching under the end seat, I stretched out my hand. It brushed against something soft. It was the cloth of his trouser leg that I felt. I saw his eyes, phosphorescent in the darkness, and they were wide and glazed.

A sharp stinging blow lashed the back of my neck and for a moment there was nothing. Then lights seemed to flash past my numbed brain. These, I thought dully, are the comets and shooting stars that you read about. But they weren't.

Bright, prosaic flashlights cut the darkness, piercing the great cavern, and above an uproar of voices I heard Jeff's, tense and biting, somewhere not far away.

CHAPTER NINETEEN

My head had almost stopped hurting, two ryes had helped considerably to numb the pain, but I still had the feeling of waking, cold and clammy, from some horrible nightmare, and knowing it was a nightmare and still not being able to throw off the dread and shock of it. I pressed my forehead against the cold plate glass that fronted the little Forty-fourth Street bar where Jeff had taken me and told me to wait for him. I dimly remembered seeing Clint Bowers surrounded by a group of men, one of whom was Peterson, and then Jeff led me away. And I vividly remembered having been cracked across the back of my neck. I had accepted the fact that Bowers had poisoned and murdered, but I wasn't able yet to believe that he had chased me all over a dark theater and then hit me across the back of my neck. He was too much a gentleman. Gentlemen may murder ladies, but they never strike one, that is, without killing her. And in my somewhat befuddled mind, Clint Bowers was still a gentleman.

By the time Jeff arrived I had filled the hollow place in the pit of my stomach with good rye, my headache was gone, and I was thirsting for knowledge. I cut him short when he started being solicitous. "I feel fine, better than I have for a week."

"Do you want another highball?"

"No, I want to hear about it. Where … where is he?"

"Where they always put producers who murder their leading ladies."

"Clint … Eve!" I shook my head. "Why, Jeff? Why and how and where and when?"

"I'm too tired to talk, Haila."

"Oh, you are, are you?"

"Yeah. I've just finished doing a masterly piece of deduction and detection that would have completely exhausted the brain of an Einstein. And, consequently, my brain is a bit tired."

"Jeff, tell me. Why did Clint kill Eve?"

"He didn't like her."

"Jeff," I pleaded.

"When I took on this case, little did I realize that it would be one of the most difficult, the most fantastic, but yet the simplest, the most prosaic of my entire career. ..."

"Look. I don't blame you for riding high, but a girl can stand only so much in one day."

"Forgive me, I'm so silly when I'm sober." He finished his drink with a complete lack of respect for the fine old brandy. He ordered another. "Last night with your own eyes you saw how I figured out that Carol's life was never attempted."

"Yes."

"Bowers arranged for that shot to be fired through the window to keep me and Peterson on the wrong track. He hired a gunman ..."

"Hired a gunman!" I interrupted. "How does one go about hiring a gunman?"

"There are ways and ways. You can advertise in the newspaper. Or you can happen to know an ex-bootlegger who has a brother who is out of work because of Mr. Dewey. You can get a gangster to knock off a friend for a grand. That's union rates. You can get a Gauguin knocked off a wall for chicken feed, especially when your employee is a great lover of Van Gogh."

"But, Jeff, that bullet might've hit one of us! Or Bowers himself!"

"Sure, it might have. But Bowers wasn't feeling sentimental about us or himself. And then, remember it was after dark, your room was brightly lighted and from the Esquador you could see into it quite clearly. The shot was fired when there was no one within range of that window. Bowers took care of that himself, if you remember. He called Carol away from it by proposing another drink."

"And did you know last night that all this was Bowers' work? That he was the murderer?"

"Sure. The minute I realized that Eve was the victim and not Carol, I knew who the murderer was. There had been so many strange undercurrents in Bowers' relationship with her. Undercurrents that I felt even while looking for Carol's murderer."

"For instance?"

"Remember when we were up in Bowers' apartment and saw all those beautifully bound copies of the plays he had produced before he started starring Eve?"

"They were practically all classics, or were after he did them."

"Yeah, and all of a sudden he starts producing drivel for Eve. He made money before, and he lost money with her. And he is generally conceded to be, even by Parker, one of the shrewdest businessmen on Broadway. Parker also gave him credit for being a great judge of talent, yet he kept doing plays for Eve when everyone knew that she was through, washed up, passé. Why would he do that, let her drag him down from being one of the most artistically and financially successful showmen in New York to just a notch above a tasteless shoestringer like Vincent Parker? Why, Haila?"

"Because he loved her?"

"Amelia convinced me that there were no men in Eve's life, no men at all, let alone Bowers. No, he didn't love her. And she didn't love him.

"The answer is that he produced plays for her because she made him do it. That much was obvious. But how did she make him? That's what I didn't know last night. The only thing. It took me the rest of the night to work up even a theory and all morning to do enough research to substantiate it."

"Research?"

Jeff grinned. "Sure, I'm scientific. Well, I knew there was blackmail going on in these parts, but blackmail for what? I looked for a clue in Bowers' life and couldn't find one. Then I looked in Eve's. Those burns of hers gave me an inkling. Nobody, apparently, knew about them but Bowers. And Amelia, of course. That was something. It proved to be the right something. In a nineteen seventeen newspaper I found the answer.

"That was the year of the theater fire in which Eve was burned. She was the company's leading lady, and the stage manager was a young man named Clinton Bowers. Well, Bowers just told Peterson a very gruesome little story about that fire.

"Seven people were killed in it, six of the audience and one member of the company ... the juvenile. His body was found in his dressing room. And they found the door to that dressing room locked ... from the outside. There was an inquest, of course, and the coroner's verdict was death by some person or persons unknown. There wasn't a scrap of evidence, there never was, and the case went unsolved. But it could have been solved. There was a witness. Eve North saw Clint Bowers lock that door."

"But, Jeff, why? Why did he do it?"

"He was rather reticent about the motive. It involved a woman who is still living. No one knew about that woman and Clint Bowers but the juvenile. He tried blackmail ... he worked on both of them, and when neither could meet his demands he threatened exposure. And he meant it. Bowers never thought of killing the boy to protect himself and the woman. He wasn't a murderer ... not in those days. He thought there was no way out.

"But then, between the acts that night, a fire broke out in the theater.

It was none of Bowers' doing. A short behind the switchboard caused it. No one person could actually be blamed. The flames swept through the draperies and scenery and in a moment the place was filled with overpowering smoke. Bowers slapped a wet cloth across his face and rushed to the dressing rooms. He found no one in any of them until he reached the top floor. And there he found his black-mailing friend groping hysterically for his door. In trying to save his wardrobe, apparently, he had waited a moment too long; the smoke had got him. Bowers took one step toward him and stopped. If, instead of leading him to safety, he shut the door and turned the key! The flames were gaining headway; the entire theater would surely be demolished. No one would ever know that the door had been locked. No one would have seen him do it. So Clint Bowers turned the key ... and rushed out of the theater.

"He was wrong on both points, of course. Eve North, trapped in her dressing room at the other end of the hall, had seen him turn the key before she slipped into unconsciousness, overcome by the smoke. Bowers hadn't seen her, hadn't heard her gasp for help. And consequently Eve was left to burn ... almost to death. The firemen got to her in time, but they didn't get to the juvenile until it was too late. And they did discover that the door had been locked.

"I don't know if Eve ever knew why Bowers had killed the boy. But that didn't matter. She didn't have to present the police with a motive to have Bowers hanged. She had plenty; she had been an eyewitness to the murder. But Eve never talked. Perhaps her own tragedy kept her quiet. Or perhaps, even then, she was saving her knowledge for a little nest egg."

Jeff stopped long enough to beckon the waiter. "I've got to have another drink; my throat's parched. That damn fire." He asked for another brandy and a large glass of water. "Now where was I?" he asked. "I wasn't listening to myself."

"Eve knew Bowers had killed a man and she kept quiet."

"When she got out of the hospital, despite her scarred back and arms that so few knew about, she took up her career again. She became famous and wealthy, the darling of the early twenties. Then she started slipping, her looks were going, her youth fading, and she wasn't a good enough actress. She was down, out."

"Poor Eve."

"Yeah, poor Eve, she had to resort to blackmail, a very esoteric type of blackmail, but blackmail. By then Bowers was the white-haired boy of the American theater. She simply said to him, 'You produce for me, darling; star me or else the whole world will know what young man locked another young man in his dressing room in the Detroit theater fire.' What could he do?

"He produced for her and starred her and ruined himself – financially and artistically. It must've torn him to pieces to do all those bedroom comedies and bad French translations after all the beautiful stuff he had been producing. It ripped him to shreds. The theater was his life. Some people let that happen to their lives. Why, Haila?"

"Go on, darling."

"Well, finally it got him. It was either Eve or he. Rather selfishly he decided it would be Eve. He just told us that he looked for a play for two years that would give him a chance to kill her. Finally he found *Green Apples*. It was perfect. It had a drinking scene exactly in the right place. But Phoebe Thompson forgot to put the flowers on the table. Eve, the trouper, rearranged the glasses instead of the flowers, and Carol, not Eve, got the poison.

"Bowers dropped the poison in Eve's glass just before the curtain went up on the third act. And what he must've gone through when Carol got it ... and when the play turned out to be a hit! He told us if Eve hadn't figured out that the poison was meant for her, he would have let her live, because *Green Apples* would've made enough money to put him back where he could produce other plays, too, the kind he wanted to do."

I suddenly remembered. "When you went in to talk to Eve between the acts the second night ..."

"Yeah, that was the first time Eve heard about the poisoning."

"And Clint was in the hall; he heard you and Eve; he realized then that ..."

Jeff nodded. "Right. When I asked her why she had been fussing around the table, she knew that she had changed the glasses, given Carol the poison that was meant for her. She knew then that Bowers was out to get rid of her."

"Why didn't she run? For her life!"

"I don't know," Jeff said. "The shock. She thought she was protected by the twenty people backstage. She couldn't imagine any way that Bowers could have her dead within thirty minutes. She couldn't believe that he would dare strike again so soon, or at the theater again.

"And when places were called, she took her place on stage as she had been doing for twenty-five years. Then Bowers watched for his chance. His first attack had been planned for months. This had to be one of the moment. That chance came at Eve's first exit in the second act – and everything worked into Bowers' hands. Eve, waiting there in the wings for her next entrance, leaned up against the scenery and the paint came off on her jacket. She whipped it off to look at it after she realized what she had done. Bowers watched her. They were alone on that side of the stage. He came up behind her quietly, held one hand over her mouth and stabbed her with the other. He wiped the knife clean of fingerprints on Eve's jacket and dropped it beside her body.

"It was then he had his inspiration – in the form of Carol's cape. He saw it on the banister where she had dropped it. Everybody was looking for Carol's murderer. He would keep it like that. He threw the cape over Eve, making it look as if she had been mistaken for Carol. It worked. And he was aided by the fact that nobody had an alibi backstage. Anyone could have done it. Then he tried to improve on his plan with the shot through the window. He couldn't stay quiet; he had to try and make himself safer."

"But, Jeff," I asked. "It sounds right but … but how were you going to *prove* it? It seems to me that it would all rest on whether Clint admitted or denied it."

"It did, my dear, it did." Jeff smiled sheepishly. "That was the trouble. There wasn't one single scrap of evidence or proof connected with the whole shebang. So I had to think up a way to force Clint's hand by showing him that I knew he had killed Eve North. Of course, my way wasn't nearly so effective, nor so dramatic, as yours."

"As mine? What do you mean?"

"You went to the theater, got yourself alone on a dark stage with him, dropped a nice juicy hint that you knew he was the murderer, then let him chase you around the theater and damn near kill you, so that I could bring friend Peterson and his boys in to make an easy, clean-cut arrest."

"Is *that* what I did? Boy! Am I the smarty-pants! But what were *you* going to do, Jeff? Let Clint chase you?"

"That idea never occurred to me. No, I had arranged a little social gathering. I asked Alice McDonald and Phoebe and Philip Ashley to come to the theater. Bowers had said he would be there. I was going to plunk him in the audience with Peterson beside him and a couple of New York's finest stationed at the doors and present a little playlet for him. I meant to show him how Eve had unconsciously switched the poison from her place to Carol's by doing that scene again. Philip Ashley was to play his part and Alice was to play Eve's. Then Alice was to impersonate Eve again, the next night, as she stood in the wings just before she was stabbed. Ashley was going to show how someone, sitting on that pile of furniture in back of the set where Bowers had been sitting by his own admission, could easily have slipped around to where

Eve was, stabbed her, and gone back to his place again without having been seen."

"But how could Clint have known that he wouldn't be seen?"

"He made sure of that. If the coast hadn't been clear he would have waited until it had been. He knew that sometime during that evening, shielded by the almost total darkness of backstage, his chance would come. And it did come. And he got an unexpected break to boot. Carol's wrap. That made him too cocky, though. He began cooperating with the police while they looked for Carol's murderer. He could afford to. They would never have found any connection between him and Carol because there wasn't any. It was because he was so sure of himself that I hoped my little charade with Ashley and Alice, and with Phoebe Thompson being my assistant, might shock him into giving himself away."

"Well, maybe it wouldn't have worked. But I've seen Bill Powell make it work in the movies, hundreds of times. Of course, as I said, your way was much surer."

"My way!" I suddenly had to laugh. "You know, I was scared to death when I found myself on that dark stage alone with Alice and I was so relieved when Bowers appeared and she sneaked out. Good old Alice! She would sneak out and leave me alone with a murderer."

"She didn't know. But the fact is she did a lot worse than that. She almost cooked your goose for good. If she hadn't buttonholed me and Peterson in the alley outside for five minutes, you would only have had to run around the theater a couple of times. And if she hadn't happened to mention that you were inside with Bowers for another minute, well, I guess there wouldn't have been any use mentioning it."

The shudder that zigzagged down my spine called for another healthy sip of my drink and I lost no time taking it.

"You see," Jeff went on, "you had frightened Alice."

"I frightened Alice! She scared the daylights out of me!"

"She thought from the way you talked that I had picked her as our murderer. Sure, the girl's wacky, but that's what she thought. She was scared stiff, and the first thing she wanted to do was explain to me why she left the theater opening night. In her mind that was our big point against her, since I had made so much of it."

"And did she explain it?"

"Sure. She left the theater to get her ring."

"A ring! Oh, Jeff!"

"You're laughing, huh? And that's exactly why she wouldn't tell us, especially you. She knew you'd laugh."

"But she gave up her big chance to play a part for a ring! It sounds awfully weird."

"She didn't know she was giving up her chance. And it seems this isn't just any old ring. It's been in her family for five generations and it had become a legend. The McDonald who was in possession of it never stepped on the stage without wearing it. And she couldn't break that family tradition. She hadn't known of course that she was going to play, so the ring was in her room, locked up. She knew she'd have time to get it and be back to the theater before the curtain. And she was. But when she did get back, Carol was there."

"But why didn't she tell Tommy why she was going?"

"She knew he wouldn't have let her go. She had to sneak out."

For a moment I let my mind drift back over those last five days. "Jeff, it's been horrible."

"Sure. Murder isn't a dancing thing. It isn't a waltz by Strauss. Murder is murder."

Jeff had been staring out the window when a moment later he said, "Haila, are you wondering what has happened to Carol, and what is going to happen to her?"

"Yes, I do think about her. And worry."

"Well, you needn't worry any more. Look."

At the curb a girl in a dark blue suit was standing beside a man. Her face was tilted up to his, one copper-colored curl escaping from the narrow brimmed hat she wore. There was a look of childlike wonder in her eyes as she listened to him talk. And Vincent Parker was loving it. We watched him call a cab and help her into it.

Jeff grinned. "Well, Parker found Lee Gray. And he'll have both Carol Blanton and Lee Gray in the same show. For the price of one salary! It'll be terrific! Pack 'em in! They'll flock clear from Jersey! Where is Jersey, Haila?"

I said, "Jeff, could we have another drink?"

"Why not? After all, I'm on my vacation."

"Jeff," I said, so suddenly it surprised me, "let's use the last week of your vacation for a honeymoon!"

"You mean get married?"

"It doesn't count unless you're married."

"Sure, I'll get married if you will! Why not? I said we would when I solved this case. And I did solve it. Despite what Peterson says. Sure we'll get married, just like people! I can afford it now on account of the reward. ..." He groaned.

"What's wrong, darling?"

"I caught the wrong guy!"

"You mean Clint didn't murder ..."

"No, I don't mean that. I mean he's the one who hired me! And I proved he committed the murder! I bit the hand that was going to feed us."

"We'll get married anyway."

"Okay, but we won't eat. Look, Haila, Bowers is a gentleman. Maybe he'll pay me. He's got to admit I did a good job."

"Clint Bowers isn't a gentleman! I used to think so but not any more! Oh, I could forgive him for murder. I could forgive him for that! But for striking a lady, especially when the lady was me …"

"You're all wrong, Haila, Bowers didn't touch you."

"Oh, he didn't!"

"No, he didn't lay a finger on you."

"He knocked me out!"

"No, Haila, what happened to you is something that I've been afraid would happen to you ever since you started being an actress."

"And what would that be?"

"You got hit on the head with a theater seat."

THE END

If you enjoyed Jeff and Haila in *Made Up To Kill*, ask for *The Frightened Stiff* (0-915230-75-5, $14.95) at the bookseller you purchased this book from. Look for future titles in this series. For more information on The Rue Morgue Press, please turn the page.

About the Rue Morgue Press

"Rue Morgue Press is the old-mystery lover's best friend, reprinting high quality books from the 1930s and '40s."
—*Ellery Queen's Mystery Magazine*

Since 1997, the Rue Morgue Press has reprinted scores of traditional mysteries, the kind of books that were the hallmark of the Golden Age of detective fiction. Authors reprinted or to be reprinted by the Rue Morgue include Dorothy Bowers, Joanna Cannan, Glyn Carr, Torrey Chanslor, Clyde B. Clason, Joan Coggin, Manning Coles, Lucy Cores, Frances Crane, Norbert Davis, Elizabeth Dean, Constance & Gwenyth Little, Marlys Millhiser, James Norman, Stuart Palmer, Craig Rice, Kelley Roos, Charlotte Murray Russell, Maureen Sarsfield, and Juanita Sheridan.

To suggest titles or to receive a catalog of Rue Morgue Press books write P.O. Box 4119, Boulder, CO 80306, telephone 800-699-6214, or check out our website, www.ruemorguepress.com, which lists complete descriptions of all of our titles, along with lengthy biographies of our writers.